games that boys play

Books by Todd Gregory

EVERY FRAT BOY WANTS IT

GAMES FRAT BOYS PLAY

Published by Kensington Publishing Corporation

games frat boys play

TODD GREGORY

KENSINGTON BOOKS
www.kensingtonbooks.com

KENSINGTON BOOKS are published by

Kensington Publishing Corp.
119 West 40th Street
New York, NY 10018

ISBN-13: 978-0-7582-4742-1
ISBN-10: 0-7582-4742-7

First Kensington Trade Paperback Printing: June 2011

10   9   8   7   6   5   4   3   2   1

Printed in the United States of America

games frat boys play

Prologue

*T*his, reflected police detective Joe Palladino, *is an aw-fully nice apartment complex for a college student to be living in. How the hell does he afford it?*

The Alhambra Apartments, he knew, started at a mere $1,500 per month for a studio, and went up—way up—from there. When they'd opened a few years earlier, his then boyfriend, Sean, had wanted to take a look at them. Joe had failed to see the point—there was no way they could afford the rents there, even with their combined incomes—but Sean had insisted, and it was easier to give in than have an argument. And yes, the place was gorgeous—you had to be let in by security, and there were fountains and tennis courts and swimming pools conveniently placed throughout the complex. Each building had a laundry facility, and near the clubhouse was an on-site dry cleaner. There was even a fully equipped workout facility with state-of-the-art equipment that put Joe's gym to shame. The apartments themselves were large, full of light, and luxurious—but after the tour, Sean had pouted all night long because they couldn't afford to live there, as though it were somehow Joe's fault. But everything had always been Joe's fault, which was why he'd dumped Sean shortly after that. There is, after all, only so much complaining that anyone can put up with. Sean wanted everything but didn't want to work for it—and Joe eventually tired of being compared to Sean's previous, much older boyfriend and being found wanting. Sean was young and handsome—and so thought everything should be handed to him. He didn't like having to work, and he didn't like that Joe's income wasn't enough for him to live a life of luxury and idleness while being supported.

"I don't know what you ever saw in him in the first place," his older sister Margie had sniffed in her patented condescending way after he'd broken up with Sean. "He has about as much depth as a dog dish."

He'd opened his mouth to answer her but had closed it again. There wasn't any point in arguing with her, because she was right. Sean had always wanted more than Joe could offer him. The three-bedroom house in the subdivision on the north side of town hadn't been enough for him. He'd always wanted the most expensive things—a car he couldn't possibly afford, the most expensive clothes and colognes and vacations. Joe had practically bankrupted himself trying to please Sean—but nothing was ever enough. And besides, Margie wouldn't understand even if he tried to explain how his heart had always swelled up whenever he looked at Sean, or that just touching Sean's skin had gotten him aroused. It had taken him a while to understand it all himself, but the truth was he'd really loved the way Sean looked and had hoped his love would change Sean somehow.

But, he reflected again, people change only if they want to. And you can't build a relationship on sex when you have nothing else in common.

It was a hard lesson to learn. And while he'd never admit it to anyone—least of all Margie—he still hoped Sean might come back home someday.

Sean was now with a surgeon about twenty years his senior and lived in a big house on Van Ness Avenue in the richer part of town. He'd run into Sean and his surgeon a few weeks earlier at a restaurant. Sean had put on a little weight and didn't look very happy. Joe couldn't help but feel a small sense of satisfaction at the obvious misery on Sean's face, which in turn made him feel small. *I shouldn't be happy that someone I once cared about isn't happy,* he'd thought at the time, and then shrugged it off. *If he seemed happy, that would have upset me, too. I couldn't give Sean the fabulous life he always wanted, and now he has it and it's turned out not to be what he wanted after all. Maybe he's just not meant to be happy. I certainly couldn't please him. I don't think Sean has ever known what he really wants, anyway.*

He shook his head as he waited for the gate to open for the car in front of him, and tried to shake it off. Sean had left two years ago and wasn't ever coming back. A memory of Sean's lean, naked body lying in bed waiting for him flashed through his mind, and in spite of himself he felt his cock stiffening inside his pants. He shifted in his seat and watched the car—a black Porsche—drive through the gate before easing his own foot up off the brake and drifting forward.

He flashed his badge to the security guard and waited for the electric gate to open again, pushing thoughts of Sean out of his head. *Two years,* he reminded himself. He hadn't been celibate, either, but he had yet to meet someone, either in a bar or online, that he wanted a second go-round with. Sex without love felt like a more complicated masturbation—fun at the moment but ultimately unsatisfying.

Get your head back on the case, he reminded himself. Not that it was much of a case. This was just a routine interview. He wasn't going to be making an arrest, unless the kid confessed. No one else had seen what happened, and there was really nothing to go on. His partner, Grace Rivera, was at the hospital waiting to talk to the kid who fell out of the window, and so he had headed over to this expensive apartment to talk to the only real witness to the incident. It was all just routine, nothing out of the ordinary, probably just a major waste of time.

But it beat hanging around the emergency room.

The gate finished opening, and he drove around the complex. The apartment he was looking for was, he knew, in one of the back buildings, having checked the Alhambra Web site before leaving the station. He drove past landscaped lawns and palm trees, splashing fountains and tennis courts deserted in the midafternoon heat. Even the sparkling blue swimming pools weren't in use, and the sun's reflection off the water was almost blinding. He found the building he was looking for and pulled into the parking area just behind it. He turned off the car and checked out the other cars in the lot. His Honda Civic looked out of place with the BMWs, Porsches, and Lexuses. There was even a black Hummer parked across two spaces in the far corner of the lot.

The unseasonably early heat wave that the entire San Joaquin Valley was suffering through blasted him in the face as he got out of the car. The temperature was to hit a high of 110, and Joe thought he could feel every degree of it. *If it's this hot in May, what is it going to be like in July and August?* It was so hot and dry, his sweat evaporated almost as soon as it appeared on his skin. He put some ChapStick on his lips, grabbed his bottle of water, and headed for the staircase. All the apartments opened into breezeways in the center of each building; the young man he was looking for lived on the second floor of Building L. When he reached the second-floor breezeway, a gust of hot wind coursed through, tinkling the chimes hanging outside some of the apartment doors.

He checked his notes again to verify the apartment number and knocked on L225.

Footsteps approached the door, and it swung open. "Yes?"

Joe caught his breath, glad he hadn't removed his mirrored sunglasses. He somehow managed to keep his face impassive. "Jordan Valentine?" he asked.

"It's Jordy. No one calls me Jordan," the young man replied. "May I help you?"

Joe pulled his badge out and flipped it open. "Detective Joe Palladino, Polk P.D. I need to ask you a few questions. May I come inside?"

"Sure." Jordy opened the door wider and stepped aside. "Come on in. Can I get you some water or tea or coffee or something?"

"I'm fine, thank you," Joe said, stepping into the air-conditioned cool of the apartment with relief. Jordy shut the door behind him. There was a hallway to the immediate left, and Joe remembered the layout of the two-bedroom apartments from his tour. That hallway led to the master bedroom, and as he walked farther inside he saw his memory hadn't failed him. There was a small kitchen to the left, with a bar opening into the large living room. The dining area was just off the living room. There was another door, just beyond the dining room table, that he knew led to the balcony. Another short hallway opened, that to the right off the living room. *Second bedroom and main bathroom*, he thought. "Do you live alone?"

"Yes," Jordy replied with a slight shrug. "I use the second bedroom as a study." He walked into the kitchen and started rooting around in the refrigerator.

"Ah, okay," Joe replied, wondering again where the money was coming from. *His parents must have money, and a lot of it.* The two-bedrooms went for twenty-five hundred when the complex opened; the rents might have even gone up since then.

"Have a seat, Detective." Jordy waved him into the living room. Joe walked on, looking around and taking it all in. The walls were painted cream, and the artwork on the walls looked to be originals—and expensive. The dining room set looked like mahogany. The living room set had also cost a fortune, and there was a gigantic flat-screen plasma television mounted on the wall opposite the couch. He sat down on the couch, sinking a few inches into its plush softness, and waited for Jordy to join him.

Jordy walked into the living room opening a plastic bottle of Coke. Joe removed his sunglasses and took another good look at him, and inwardly shook his head. *Can't let him see he's having an effect on me.*

Simply put, Jordy was one of the best-looking young men he'd ever seen in his life. Sean had been good looking, but Jordy Valentine had the kind of looks that stopped people in their tracks and made other guys just give up. He was tall, maybe an inch or two over six feet. Light brown curls with blond highlights cascaded around his face, framing it. The sunlight reflecting off the highlights created a halo effect. His olive skin was smooth and darkly tanned, and his grayish green eyes were almond shaped. Long, curly lashes set them off underneath the dark arch of his eyebrows. His lips were thick, pouty, and red over perfectly even, white teeth. He was wearing a pair of red CSU-Polk sweatpants, and his white tank top showed thick, well-defined muscles. His shoulders were broad, and the muscles in his back rippled beneath the tight white cotton as they tapered down into a narrow waist and a thick, round ass. He sat down in a wingback chair that probably cost more than Joe made in a month and curled his legs up underneath him. His stomach was completely flat, even when sitting down. "I suppose this is about Chad York," Jordy said, recapping his Coke and placing it on a brass coaster on the table next to his chair. He sighed. "I probably should have stayed at the house, right?" He turned his head and gazed out the window. It faced the parking lot and the swimming pool just beyond it. There was still no one at the pool in the oppressive heat. "I just didn't want to deal with it." He shrugged. "If it makes me look bad, I don't care."

Interesting. Joe simply nodded. "Would you say the two of you are friends?" He kept his voice neutral.

"Friends?" There was a hint of amusement in his voice. Jordy ran his left hand through his curls. "No, I wouldn't say we are friends." He laughed softly. "Do you know what a *frenemy* is?"

Joe shook his head. "No, I can't say that I do." He'd been out of college for over thirteen years, and the world had changed a lot since then.

"It's someone who's both your friend and your enemy at the same time," Jordy explained. "That would probably be a more accurate description of how we feel about each other. Does that make sense?"

Joe didn't respond for a moment, thinking. "You mean he was someone you knew, you moved in the same crowd, you were friends of a sort, but if you failed at something he'd enjoy it? And vice versa?" *I've got some of those in my life,* he thought, smiling inwardly.

"You nailed it." Jordy's voice was cold. "It's worse than that, actually. A frenemy always undermines you, roots against you, and not only wants you to fail but will actively try to make you fail. A frenemy will sleep with your boyfriend and pretend to be sorry later, but he really isn't."

He looked down and swallowed. "He is okay, isn't he?" he asked in a very small voice.

"He hasn't regained consciousness yet." Joe pulled out his little notepad and flipped through the pages of notes from the fraternity brothers he'd talked to, keeping his eyes down. *He's gay, this gorgeous guy is gay,* he thought to himself, trying to maintain his professional distance. His cock began to stir again inside his pants. He swallowed and cleared his throat. "You were there when he fell." It wasn't a question.

Jordy nodded. "Yes, I was."

Professional—stay professional. He's a witness and a possible suspect. Forget about fucking him, forget about what he looks like under those sweats. Joe looked straight into those gray-green eyes and decided to go for a shock. "Would it surprise you to hear that some of your fraternity brothers think you pushed him?"

The reaction wasn't what Joe was expecting.

Jordy stared back at him, his gaze never faltering for a moment. He opened his mouth, closed it again, and then a smile began to play at the corner. He bit his lower lip, and then gave in to the impulse he was fighting and started laughing.

It was a nice laugh, deep and hearty and full of mirth.

"No," Jordy finally managed to get out, struggling to catch his breath and put a serious look on his face. "It doesn't surprise me at all. But it's not true. I didn't push Chad. Chad fell." His eyes glittered. "Beta Kappa is a fraternity of frenemies, Detective—a real viper's nest." He shook his head, curls bouncing. "The biggest mistake of my life was pledging that place." He turned and looked back out the window. He laughed again.

"You think this is funny?" Joe fixed his sternest "I am the law" stare on Jordy. *Damn, he's good looking,* Joe thought to himself again, careful to keep his face impassive and stern. *I've never seen him in any of the bars. But maybe he doesn't go to bars. He might not be old enough.* He swallowed and tried to get his thoughts under control. *He's good looking, but he also might be a criminal. Don't forget that.*

He closed his eyes for a moment and visualized his sergeant naked. That always worked.

Jordy stopped laughing, forcing a serious expression onto his face. "Actually, I do. I suppose that seems heartless to you." He watched Joe's face for a reaction. Getting none, he went on. "I wasn't laughing about Chad falling. I was laughing because some of my so-called *brothers* are a bunch of mean-spirited assholes always ready to believe the worst." He rolled his eyes. "I was laughing at the hypocrisy, Detective. I spent an entire semester getting the ideals and mission and all this other high-minded bullshit about integrity and brotherhood shoved down my throat, and the worst part is, I believed it. I believed every word of it, and it was all just a bunch of bullshit. My so-called brothers don't have the first fucking clue as to what brotherhood is, or what the fraternity supposedly stands for. Were you in a fraternity, Detective?"

"I'm asking the questions here," Joe snapped. In spite of himself, he remembered his own days at CSU-Polk. No, he hadn't joined a fraternity. He'd worked two jobs to put himself through school, and when he wasn't working he was studying in his roach-trap, run-down, crummy apartment. He hadn't lived in a luxury apartment complex or joined a fraternity. He'd hated the Greeks who'd come into the restaurant where he worked, so condescending with their money and privilege, the sorority girls all stuck-up bitches, the guys all condescending assholes. He pushed those memories out of his head. *Stay objective. Don't let your per-*

sonal prejudices color your investigation. "So, you're saying you didn't, in fact, push Chad York out the window of his room?"

Jordy's face darkened for a moment. "I'll bet it was Bobby Dunlap who told you I pushed him, right? And after Bobby said it, the others joined in." He shook his head. "Look, Detective, I'm sorry Chad fell and I hope he's okay. But the notion I pushed him is, well, preposterous." He shrugged. "I don't want Chad dead. We aren't friends, we've had some issues, but I didn't want to kill him or anything. I didn't push him out the window." He chewed on a thumbnail. "No matter what my *brothers* might say, I didn't push Chad out that window."

"I'd like to believe you, Jordy." Joe raised his eyebrows. "I really would. But what I don't understand—and maybe you can clear this up for me—is why didn't you stick around after he fell?" Joe spread his arms and smiled, keeping his eyes on Jordy's face, watching for a reaction of any kind. "I mean, if I'm talking to someone and they fall out of a second-story window, I'd yell for help and then bust my ass getting down to him to make sure he was okay, to see if he needed an ambulance or some help. But you didn't do that, Jordy. You didn't shout, you didn't go check on him, you didn't do anything. All you did was walk out of the fraternity house, get into your car, and drive away." Joe leaned back against the sofa cushions and folded his arms. "That's the part I don't get, Jordy. Can you explain that to me?" This was the heart of it. No one had seen anything. There had been Beta Kappa brothers in the yard below the window, but they had been sitting at a picnic table drinking beer (and probably smoking pot, given how red their eyes were and how disoriented they'd been) and saw nothing. The upstairs hallway of the fraternity had been empty. The only two people who really knew what happened were Chad York and Jordy Valentine. But several brothers had seen Jordy run out to his car and leave without checking to see if Chad was okay.

And Jordy was right. Bobby Dunlap *had* been very quick to insinuate that Chad's fall might not have been an accident.

"Jordy hates Chad and everyone knows it. They hate each other, and you can't be neutral. It's pretty much ripped the house apart. You have to choose sides. And really, what was Jordy doing up there in his room anyway? So Jordy is up there in someone's room that he hates and that person just happens to fall out the window and Jordy doesn't call for help or stick around to see if Chad is okay or if he needed help or anything. He just took off."

Bobby Dunlap was a square, squat young man of about twenty with dirty hair and a soft body. He'd been wearing a white T-shirt with food stains on it over a pair of long shorts. His feet had been bare, and there was dirt under his toenails. He smelled bad, a vague combination of sour sweat and urine and armpits and stale beer that slightly turned Joe's stomach. And Bobby's voice was breathless and low, his face becoming more animated as his insinuations became more squalid. Bobby reminded Joe of a kid from his own school days, a kid he didn't like, who liked to talk about everyone else, always in that same mean-spirited conspiratorial tone.

Jordy was right—he'd been on the verge of dismissing everything Bobby had said when some of the other brothers came forward and began hesitantly confirming the gossip. One of them—he couldn't remember his name, just that he was a strawberry blond with freckles and cute in an Opie Taylor kind of way—said, "They were always fucking with each other, trying to steal each other's boyfriends, posting nude pictures of each other online. It was terrible the way they kept going at each other, and that made it hard on all of us here at the house. I mean, we're *supposed* to be brothers."

Joe had fought down his own contempt for the Greek system—which had obviously become a lot more gay friendly than when he'd been in college. *Wasn't it the Beta Kappas,* he wondered, *who'd burned the Lesbian-Gay Student Organization's booth in the Quad?*

Things at CSU-Polk had certainly changed in thirteen years.

"I didn't see any point in sticking around." Jordy shrugged. "He fell. I heard shouts from the courtyard, so I figured someone would call 911, and there were guys out there to help him out." He looked out the window. "I just wanted to get out of there. I didn't push him. Chad was sitting in the window. He lost his balance and fell. One minute he was there, the next minute he was gone."

"So, you just stopped by to have a chat with Chad? What about?"

"Chad called and wanted me to come by." Jordy's face was impassive. "He wanted to talk, maybe cease hostilities." He smiled faintly. "I mean, I was getting sick of the whole situation between us, and I went because I thought it would be nice to get everything settled between us once and for all." He shrugged. "It kind of didn't work out that way."

"Some of your fraternity brothers heard the two of you arguing." Joe kept watching Jordy's face, trying to read it, but without much luck. It was unsettling. Joe was usually good at reading faces, able to tell if someone was lying to him. He was almost always right. But he couldn't get a read on Jordy. *Maybe because he's so good looking you can't be impar-*

tial? You can't think clearly? You can't get beyond being attracted to him?

Joe cleared his throat, never looking away from Jordy's eyes. "What were the two of you arguing about?"

Jordy rubbed his eyes. "It's not important, and it doesn't have anything to do with him falling. It was an accident."

"A lot of people heard you yelling at each other." Joe watched him, evaluating his body language. *There's something he's not telling me, something he doesn't want to talk about. I don't think he's lying about not pushing Chad York out the window, but there's something more to this story and he doesn't want to tell me about it.*

Jordy got up and walked over to the window. "It's a long story."

"I've got plenty of time."

"It doesn't matter. I didn't push him. He fell," Jordy insisted. He sighed. "I'm so sorry I came here. It was a mistake. Everything has been a mistake." He laughed again, but it had a bitter ring to it. "That's where it all really began, Detective."

"Why don't you start at the beginning?" Joe asked, keeping his voice quiet, sympathetic, and encouraging. "I find that usually helps, you know. Just start at the beginning, and tell me everything."

"I got into Harvard, you know." Jordy turned his back to Joe and looked out the window. Even in the shapeless sweatpants, Joe could see the curve of his muscular ass. He laughed again and reached up to close the blinds. His tank top rode up, revealing two deep dimples just where the curve of his buttocks began. His waist was small, and his tanned skin was completely smooth. He lowered the blinds and turned around, tugging the shirt down as he did so— but not before Joe caught a glimpse of the defined muscles of Jordy's abdomen. The sweatpants had also ridden down a bit in the front, showing the waistband of a pair of 2(x)ist underwear.

Joe struggled to keep his mind on the interview at hand. "Harvard?"

Jordy sat back down in the chair. "Yeah. But I had this great idea—which seems incredibly stupid to me now—that it would be better for me to come here for a couple years before I went there." He paused, then offered as explanation, "I went to a boarding school in Switzerland, St. Bernard of Clairvaux—and I didn't really have the slightest idea of what American kids my own age were like. I didn't have any friends there, you know. I thought—I thought if I came to school here for a couple years . . ." He yawned and stretched, every muscle in his arms and shoulders flexing. "I should have just gone to Harvard. But I thought it would be fun to be a 'normal' student at a 'normal' university for a while first."

"Really?" *Focus, Joe, focus on the task at hand. Forget he's the best looking guy you've ever met. Forget that sexy body and that hot ass under the sweatpants. Do your goddamned job.* He swallowed. "A boarding school. I don't think I've ever met anyone who went to a boarding school."

Jordy nodded. "St. Bernard was a great school. Mom and Dad sent me there when I was ten. It is one of the best schools in the world—and you can't get in just because you can afford the tuition. You have to be smart, too." He smiled. "And I am very, very smart. I love to learn. I have an insatiable curiosity." His eyes got a faraway look in them. "My parents weren't exactly thrilled with the idea of me coming here, which kind of made me want to come here all the more." His expression darkened. "If I knew then what I know now . . ." He shook his head. "But you don't care about any of that, do you?"

Joe shrugged. *How rich is this kid?* And in spite of himself, he thought, *God help this kid if Sean ever meets him. Gorgeous AND rich? Sean would grab on to him like a leech and never let go.*

"I'm an only child," Jordy went on. "My parents travel a lot, and I always joined them on vacations." He cracked a smile. "I've been on every continent. I've been to Antarctica *twice*—we spent Christmas there last year. Talk about a white Christmas—it doesn't get much whiter anywhere than Antarctica."

"What does your father do?" Joe knew the interview was getting off-topic, but he was curious. *Would you be this curious about him if he weren't this incredibly beautiful young man?* a mocking voice whispered in his brain, but he ignored it.

"You don't know? No one told you?" Jordy barked out a bitter laugh. "There's a surprise. It's why they gave me a bid to join Beta Kappa to begin with—because of who my father is." His eyes flashed with anger. "My dad developed a computer program called EZ Accounting. Have you heard of it?"

Joe nodded. Who hadn't heard of EZ Accounting? He had it on his home computer and used it to pay his bills and balance his checkbook. Their commercials were all over television. "Your dad invented that?"

Jordy nodded. "He did it when he was in his twenties, right out of MIT. He made a couple of hundred million dollars, and the money just keeps rolling in." He flashed that heart-melting smile again. "Mom has a master's in English Literature and another one in Art History. She went to Harvard. I got perfect scores on all of my college entry tests." He blushed a little bit. "Like I told you, I am really smart. My GPA at CSUP is 4.0, and I haven't really had to crack a book yet." His voice was a little smug. "I can see why my parents didn't want me to go to school here, even for a couple of years. The classes here are really easy."

"You are smart," Joe agreed.

"So, I applied for admission to CSU-Polk, and I got in." Jordy waved a hand. "Like there was ever any doubt about it. I was so excited . . . we all came up for orientation, and Mom and Dad got me this apartment. Hayley, my mom's interior designer, came up and did all the decorating right before I moved in. She did a good job, huh?"

"It's a lovely apartment," Joe replied.

"You're really polite." Jordy tilted his head and scrutinized Joe's face. "I mean, you're sitting there listening to me prattle on and on about all of this when all you really want to know is whether I pushed Chad out that window."

"Did you?"

Jordy shook his head vigorously. "No, I didn't." He made a face. "Oh, don't get me wrong, I wanted Chad to suffer. But I don't believe in violence of any sort. I wasn't raised that way. And I did make him suffer. . . ." His voice trailed off.

"Why don't you start at the beginning?" *Now*, Joe thought, *now we're onto something*. He pulled a digital recorder out of his jacket pocket. "Do you mind if I tape this?"

"No, go ahead," Jordy replied. "I'm not worried. I haven't committed any crimes."

Joe gave him what he hoped was a friendly, reassuring smile. "Just start at the beginning. Don't leave anything out."

"Okay." Jordy took a deep breath. "It all started last August, when I moved into this place. Mom and Dad came up with me, to help me get settled. . . ."

Chapter 1

No one looking at my parents would ever guess they're worth over seven hundred million dollars, give or take.

"You're absolutely sure about this?" my father asked, helping himself to some more breadsticks from the basket in the middle of the table. He squinted at me through his horn-rimmed glasses. "I mean, it's not too late to change your mind. I could make a few calls—"

My mother smacked his hand, giving me a warm smile. "Terry, we've been over this a thousand times." She rolled her eyes at me. "He wants to have a *normal* college experience before he goes to Harvard." She emphasized *normal*, making me smile a little to myself. She'd been against my decision much more vehemently than Dad in the beginning, but once she came around she was firmly on my side.

We were sitting in a booth in the Olive Garden on Shaw Avenue, about five blocks from the campus of California State University–Polk. The place was largely deserted, which was probably the norm for three in the afternoon. Our waitress, a pretty young girl whose name tag read COLLEEN, refilled our iced tea glasses. She had no idea she was about to get the biggest tip of her serving career—Dad always tipped several hundred dollars, no matter where he ate. He'd worked his way through MIT as a waiter and never forgot what it was like to bust your ass for a few bucks. I smiled at her, and she smiled back.

Dad certainly didn't look like he was capable of tipping that much. He was wearing a red CSU-Polk T-shirt over a pair of worn-looking jeans. He was balding, and he had pale pink skin that turned tomato red with any exposure to the sun. They'd just spent a week in the Bahamas and were about to head off for Tanzania to check on a health clinic they were funding. Dad was chubby and always had a kind of distracted air, like he wasn't really paying attention to what was going on around him because he was lost in thought.

He certainly didn't look like someone who could buy the place with a single phone call.

Likewise, Mom didn't go in for expensive clothes or jewelry. She didn't wear a lot of makeup and was letting her dark brown hair go gray. She wore it really short, and she was dressed just like Dad. Her face was freckled from walking on the beach, and the only jewelry she wore was her wedding ring—a plain gold band. They looked like a nice middle-class couple—an accountant and his wife, maybe, who loved nothing more than spending an evening reading a good book with the television on for background noise.

No one would ever guess that they were so rich they couldn't spend all their money if they tried. And they did try. They gave a lot of it away—but no matter how much they gave away, more came rolling in. They'd both grown up dirt poor and never forgot where they came from. They always tried to give back as a thanks to the universe for their great good fortune.

"Normal," my dad mused, absently munching on a bread-

stick. "Normal is highly overrated." He waved his breadstick before taking another bite. "If we were normal—"

"I want to have a normal college experience before I go
to Harvard in a few years," I said. It was pointless rehashing
the argument. I'd won the debate and was enrolled at California State University–Polk—and he wasn't going to talk
me out of it. "You've always said, Dad, how growing up normal really prepared you for life, and you both want me to be
normal."

"But that's just it, Jordy. You *aren't* normal, son." Dad finished the breadstick and reached for another one. Mom
smacked his hand and he goggled at her ruefully. She raised
a warning eyebrow and he meekly put his hands back in his
lap, giving the bread basket a longing look. "You have a genius IQ, you speak four languages fluently, and you've
never been in school with"—he paused for a moment, trying to find the right word—"*regular* people your own age."
He shrugged. "It can be rough. I just don't want you to be
hurt, son."

"I know, Dad." I grabbed the breadstick he'd been trying
to get. "But I want to know what it's like." I took a bite and
sighed. The Olive Garden's breadsticks were awesome. "I
mean, I want to *experience* it. Besides, I think it will make for
an interesting anthropological study—the difference between a place like St. Bernard and a campus like Polk
State—the relationships between students, students and
the faculties, and so forth. It will make for a very interesting
paper."

He sighed. "But for the paper to be authentic scholasti-
cally, you have to be removed emotionally from the people
you come into contact with. You can't be friends with them,
son. You have to remain objective." He frowned. "I just
worry, son." He looked at Mom, who just patted his hand.

"I'll be fine," I insisted.

Dad made his money before I was born, so even though I'd heard the stories about what life had been like for them when they were poor, it was something I'd never experienced. I'd had tutors until I was ten, when I was old enough to go to St. Bernard of Clairvaux, a private boarding school in the Swiss Alps.

I'd both loved and hated St. Bernard.

I loved that St. Bernard was an excellent place to learn, and the teachers pushed us to work hard. I have an excellent memory, and if I read something I never forget it. I rarely had to study for exams, and usually spent the time my schoolmates spent cramming and memorizing doing extra reading. I loved reading and learning. While my classmates were off skiing or skating or whatever outdoor activity caught their fancy, I was in my room reading.

I hated that my classmates, without exception, were the children of nobility or royalty. There was always a title somewhere in their family. And they were all snobs. Even though my parents probably had enough money to buy and sell theirs, the fact my parents couldn't trace their descent back to Charlemagne or Saladin or some Roman emperor made me beneath their notice, but not beneath their contempt. I had a single room almost the entire eight years I was there, because no one would room with me. I wasn't sure, but maybe they thought rooming with me would somehow make my common-ness rub off on them or something. They mocked me to my face, and who knows what horrible things they said about me behind my back. It hurt, and I hated them and hated being there. Every day was a struggle not to cry in front of them, but every night after lights out in the solitude of my room, I would cry until I fell asleep. There were times when I wished I would die so the cruelty would stop. And I counted the days until the Christmas break, when I could tell my parents face to face I wanted to go somewhere else.

I met them in Cairo that year, determined I wasn't ever going back to St. Bernard. They met me at the airport, and when the time finally came when we were in our suite and I was going to tell them, my father preempted me. "We're so proud of you," my father said, his voice breaking. "The dean called me to tell me what an excellent student you are."

I gulped.

"One of the best things about having all this money," my mother said as she opened the blinds, exposing an amazing view of the pyramids in the distance, "is being able to make sure you get the best education in the world."

"I know some of the other kids probably aren't very friendly," Dad went on. "Some of them are class snobs, right?" I nodded. "That makes absolutely no sense. As if being born into a certain family means you're better than someone else born into a different one. It's who you are, how smart you are, and what you can accomplish that really matters, am I right?"

"Yes, Dad."

"So just ignore them." He patted me on the leg. "Just focus on your education, and making the most of this opportunity."

"Okay."

So, I never told them the hell that St. Bernard was for me. I didn't have a single friend in the eight years I was there. It was incredibly lonely, but I lost myself in the world of books—and the Internet. The Internet was a godsend. I could talk to kids back in the United States to alleviate my loneliness, and I kept as low a profile as I could around the

school. But it wasn't the real world—it wasn't even remotely close. I envied the kids I talked to online—the ones
who went to public schools and lived real lives. I wanted to
have real friends. I wanted to go over to someone's home
after school and study with them. I wanted to go bowling
and ride a bicycle.

I wanted a normal life.

And even though I was accepted into Harvard when I
was fourteen—Dad was right about that St. Bernard pedi-
gree—I decided I wanted to go to a state school for two
years first. Maybe Harvard wouldn't be as snobbish as
St. Bernard, but I wanted to experience something more
normal first. And the more I thought about it, the more I
liked the idea. How could it possibly hurt me to go to another university, not as famous or expensive, for the first
two years? How could it hurt for me to go to school with
kids who didn't spend their summers in palaces or on
yachts or on islands in Greece?

It wouldn't, I finally decided, and made up my mind
once and for all.

And it *would* make a good paper.

I'd started doing research my junior year, and went
through many Web sites and catalogues before I settled finally on CSU-Polk. The university wasn't even one of the
better universities in California—Stanford, Berkeley, USC,
and UCLA—but it was adequate. It didn't draw a lot of rich
kids—its student base was primarily middle-class kids who
often had to work at least part time. It seemed perfect, and
was centrally located—almost equally distant from San
Francisco as it was from Los Angeles. And Polk itself was a
charming little city of a couple hundred thousand people in
the middle of the San Joaquin Valley. A little on the conservative side, it is best known for raisins and grape production. It came down to CSUP, Kansas State, and the University

of Tennessee—but I finally decided Kansas and Tennessee were probably a little bit too conservative. My decision made, I filled out the application and waited to hear back. I was pretty certain I'd be accepted—I'd already been accepted into Harvard, after all—and sure enough, after about a month the enrollment package arrived.

And the struggle with my parents had begun. Mom was against it in the beginning, and Dad was on my side. Ironically, after Mom was convinced, Dad began to have misgivings, and the two of us had to work on him.

But it had all worked out as I'd known it would, and here we were, sitting in an Olive Garden in Polk, a week before school started.

"Besides—" I finished eating the breadstick, then smothered a grin as Dad watched me mournfully. He really loved Olive Garden's breadsticks. "You agreed it's a good learning experience for me. And we agreed—two years here and I'll make up my mind on my major, and then Harvard." That was what Dad was most worried about—my indecision regarding my major. And while the money didn't really matter, he was impressed that I didn't want to waste money at Harvard trying to figure out my major. He thought it showed a responsibility toward money he really liked.

I didn't really know what I wanted to be when I grew up, but I knew I wanted to work in a field I found rewarding. Even after Dad sold his software company, he and Mom kept busy operating a charity foundation, traveling all over the world building health centers and schools. Some of my schoolmates at St. Bernard were aimless—despite the excellent education they were getting, they were really just counting the days until they were old enough to access their trust funds. Dad and Mom were always afraid I would turn out that way.

"Well, if you change your mind..." Dad's voice trailed

off as Colleen brought the bill. He slid a credit card into the tray and she took it away. He glanced at his watch. "Look at the time! We've got to get to the airport, Mandy." Colleen brought the tray back, Dad signed the receipt, and slid five hundred-dollar bills into the little leather folder. As we walked out the front door, I heard a rather loud "OH!" from behind me. I looked back over my shoulder at Colleen, whose face had gone white. Her mouth was making a perfect "O" as she stared at the five hundred-dollar bills in her hand. I laughed to myself.

If I ever ate there without my parents, Colleen was going to be incredibly disappointed in her tip.

I hugged and kissed them in the parking lot and then waved as they drove their rental car out into the traffic on Shaw Avenue.

I got into my own car and started it, waiting for the air conditioning to cool it down before heading to my apartment.

I *was* nervous. I had been alternating between excitement and full-out terror ever since I'd arrived in Polk the day before. I would never let them know, of course—they'd just worry, and I figured they were already plenty worried on their own without any assistance from me. What if I couldn't hack it in this environment? What if I couldn't make any friends? What if the kids at St. Bernard were right and I was some kind of freak? I wasn't worried about the academic side of things—I'd already preordered my textbooks, and none of them looked challenging.

But socially?

I reassured myself from time to time that it couldn't be that hard to acclimate. If I didn't fit in and make any friends to begin with, I would treat it like a scientific experiment. I would observe behavior, see what worked with kids who had lots of friends and what didn't, and then adapt accordingly. It couldn't be that hard. I was very smart—but I had to be careful not to seem too smart. I had started doing research online—leading social workers' and therapists' studies on group dynamics, power structures, and so forth, in my peer group. Some of the behaviors they deconstructed seemed a bit far-fetched to me. There was one in particular that I thought was kind of a stretch. A clinical psychologist named Dr. Mark Drake had done a study of a group of male college students who had, at the instigation of a "group leader," behaved in some pretty horrible ways—drinking, date and gang rapes, and so on. Dr. Drake had concluded that the need for the group leader's approval had convinced the weaker members of the group to do things they ordinarily, under normal circumstances, would never have done.

It seemed incredibly stupid to me, and *weak* was not a strong enough word to describe the followers who had allowed one person to have so much power over them—and could be so easily influenced into doing things they *knew* were wrong. I found it incredibly hard to believe, and I finally decided that Dr. Drake's conclusions had to have been faulty.

Psychology, after all, was hardly an exact science.

And even if Dr. Drake's conclusions were accurate, this activity had occurred at a small, elite college in the Northeast where all the students came from privilege; it surely wasn't much of a reach to conclude that this conduct had been the result of ennui.

Surely the students at CSUP wouldn't be like that. From all the research I'd done on the school, the majority of the student body came from the middle class. And I found it hard to believe that kids from a middle-class background would act as poorly as spoiled kids whose parents gave them everything on a silver platter. Some of the students at St. Bernard had fallen into that same category—and I'd avoided them at all costs.

But I was also incredibly excited. I had my own apartment—my own *place*—for the first time in my life, and I was starting a new adventure, a whole new beginning. I was going to be me for the first time. At St. Bernard, everyone knew who my dad was—we all knew who we all were—but I didn't want to be known as Terry Valentine's son. I wanted to be just Jordy Valentine, another student among the seventeen thousand or so at CSU-Polk. I wanted people to like me for me.

And there was another reason I hadn't shared with my parents.

It wasn't like they'd care one way or the other that I was gay. Of course they would be supportive—they always were. But while I knew at some point I would have to have a conversation with them about it, the whole thought of talking to my parents about my sex life made me squirm. I was a virgin, and I wanted to get that out of the way before I went to Harvard. I'd watched a lot of pornography I'd found on the Internet, and I couldn't wait to give it a try. Maybe, if I was really lucky, I'd fall in love.

Mom and Dad were not homophobic. Dad's assistant Lars was gay—and I knew Dad had written a check for several hundred thousand dollars to fight the passage of that horrible Proposition 8 ballot initiative he said was an insult to the U.S. Constitution. But knowing I was gay would just make them worry even more than they already were. The San Joaquin Valley was pretty conservative, and so was Polk. But the university had a reputation as one of the most progressive campuses in the state, and in California that was saying a lot. Polk also had a pretty strong and vibrant gay community. The Greek system was one of the few in the country that welcomed gays and lesbians with open arms. I figured it was better to get my feet wet as a young gay man in a smaller city with a strong community rather than jumping into San Francisco or West Hollywood or New York with both feet. No, these two years in Polk were going to be all about me finding myself before I left for Harvard.

So I was a little nervous but a lot excited.

I pulled into the driveway for the Alhambra Apartments and swiped my entry card at the guard gate. I'd wanted to live in the dorms, but this was a battle I let my parents win. The Alhambra was a gorgeous luxury complex with heavy security—way out of the price range of the average student—and I'd allowed them to get me an apartment there as a compromise. The security would make them feel better, and it was a really nice place. I'd picked out the furniture I wanted, and Lars took care of getting the apartment set up for me. He'd even stocked the kitchen with groceries. I drove around to the building I was going to call home for the next two years and pulled into a parking spot underneath a palm tree. I sat there in the car for a few moments, taking deep breaths. Opposite the building was a swimming pool. When I got out of the car I saw a guy climbing out of the pool, and I caught my breath.

He was tall, and once he was out of the pool he shook his head. Drops of water flew in all directions. He was deeply tanned, and his skin was smooth other than a slight patch of hair in the center of his impressively developed chest. His entire body was defined and sculpted muscle. His waist was very narrow, and the cuts between his six-pack were deep. Two deep grooves ran from his upper pelvic bones down toward the top of his low-rise, white bikini. The white Lycra clung to a long, thick penis that reached from the center of the bikini almost all the way to his right thigh. Underneath was a thick set of balls. I gasped a bit, unable to tear my eyes away from this godlike apparition. He turned around, and my own cock began to stir inside my pants. The bikini exposed the top of his crack, and his ass was firm, compact, and round. I watched, enthralled, as he ran his towel over his skin, wiping away drops of water. Every muscle in his body flexed when he moved, his broad back rippling as he bent one way and then the other. Finally, he finished and stretched out on a lounge chair, placing a pair of sunglasses over his eyes.

No one at St. Bernard came even remotely close to that level of perfection.

The spell broken, I couldn't help but grin. If this was the kind of view I was going to get, I was going to like it here just fine.

I locked up the car, walked around to the staircase, and climbed up to the second floor. I was just putting my key into the lock when the door across from mine opened. "Hey, neighbor!" a voice said from behind me.

I turned and smiled. "Hi. I'm Jordy."

He stuck out his right hand and grinned at me. "Blair Blanchard." His robe fell open, revealing a navy blue bikini. I caught my breath. Blair was a little shorter than me, and the broad smile lit up a handsome face, creating dimples in his tanned cheeks. His hair was bluish black and curly, cropped a little short, and his bluish green eyes were set on either side of a sculpted nose. His lips were thick and his body lean, definition lines cut into every muscle. A trail of curly black hairs ran down from his navel to the waistband of the bikini. The bulge inside the blue Lycra was impressive, but nothing like the guy at the pool's—but then, that guy was practically a freak of nature.

This apartment complex was apparently full of gorgeous guys who wore tiny bikinis.

Oh, I was *definitely* going to like it here.

"Nice to meet you." I shook his hand. His grip was strong, and I noticed the veins bulging in his forearms.

"Welcome to Polk and the Alhambra." He let go of my hand and scrutinized my face. "You're here for college?"

I nodded and opened my door. "Yeah. Can I get you a drink or something?"

"No, I'm not thirsty, but thanks." He grinned at me. "But I do want to see the inside of your apartment." He winked. "Jeff and I saw the furniture being delivered yesterday. You have excellent taste."

"Jeff?"

"My boyfriend."

My heart sank. *Of course he has a boyfriend,* I told myself as I beckoned him to follow me inside. *Gorgeous guys like him are undoubtedly all taken.* "Does he live with you?" I asked as I went into the kitchen and opened a can of Coke.

Blair walked into the living room and whistled. "This is really nice." He plopped down on the couch. He looked at the painting hanging over the wide-screen TV and whistled again. "Is that a Lindsey Smolensky?" He looked at me, his head cocked to one side and his eyes narrowed just a fraction. "Those are worth a fortune. My dad has a few at his place in Palm Springs."

"Just a print," I lied, cursing at myself. So much for just being another college student! I made a mental note to have the painting shipped back home.

"Oh, come on, now, don't bullshit a bullshitter." He crossed his legs, exposing the bulge in his blue bikini. I tried not to stare. "For one thing, this place ain't cheap, Jordy. Neither is any of this furniture." He gave me a wink. "Don't worry—there aren't many students living here, and

any student you might have over wouldn't know the difference between that painting and something you bought at a
gas station." He narrowed his eyes. "I gather you don't
want anyone to know you have money?" He grinned. "Hey,
it's okay, really. I know the feeling. My parents are Steve
Blanchard and Nicole Blair."

It was my turn to goggle at him. "Seriously?" They were
two of the biggest film stars in the world. Even at St.
Bernard, where the faculty disdained popular culture, I'd
heard of them. I'd never seen any of their films, but it was
almost impossible to go on the Internet and not run across a
photo of one or the other. I could actually see the resem-
blance to both of them in his face.

He threw his head back and laughed. "Yes, seriously. So I
know where you're coming from, right? You don't want people to like you because you have money, right? You want
them to like you for you."

I nodded.

He shrugged. "Cute. Me, I don't care why people like me
as long as they like me." He made a gesture with his hand.
"Then again, only someone with the most pedestrian of tastes
wouldn't like me." He grinned, blinking his eyes rapidly.

I laughed. There'd been no one like Blair at St. Bernard.

Blair got up and walked over to the door to my balcony.
He unlocked it and pulled it open. "Ah, you're lucky—
you've got a pool view." I was just about to say something
about the gorgeous hunk at the pool when Blair screamed,
"JEFF! JEFF!"

I walked out on the balcony just as the hunk in the white
bikini got up from the lounge chair and looked, shielding
his eyes.

"NEW NEIGHBOR!" Blair shouted, gesturing at me
with his arms, and then waved for him to come over.

"That's your boyfriend?" I managed to stutter out as I watched the god in the white bikini gather up his stuff and start shuffling toward us across the parking lot.

"Tongue back in your mouth, young one." Blair shook his head at me. "Yes, that's my boyfriend, Jeff Morgan, he of the godlike body that stops traffic, makes pussies drip, and gets gay men hard with just one glimpse of his physical perfection." He blew me a raspberry. "I suppose you're wondering what a schlub like me is doing with such a perfect specimen."

"Actually, no," I replied. "You're just as sexy as he is."

Blair blinked at me a few times, and his face softened into a smile. "I do believe you're serious, bless your heart." He reached over and touched the side of my face gently. He sighed. "I know, it's not like I'm some kind of a troll or something, but I've gotten used to not being noticed whenever Jeff's around."

"I don't understand." I was confused. Blair was one of the best-looking guys I'd ever seen, and his body was sexy. Sure, Jeff was incredible, but so was Blair.

"You really don't, do you?" Blair smiled a little sadly. "You'll learn fast enough, I'm afraid. I'll go let him in."

I walked back inside the apartment just as the front door opened and a divine creature walked in. His towel was draped around his tanned shoulders, and I couldn't do anything but stare. "I'm Jeff," he said, offering me his right hand.

I shook it and opened my mouth to say something, but nothing came out. He was gorgeous, without a doubt, but I *knew* him from somewhere. An image from the Internet flashed through my mind. "Oh, my God, you're Colt Madison," I blurted out before I could stop myself. My knees felt weak.

How many times had I beaten off to his pictures online?

Jeff blushed under his tan, and Blair laughed. "I told you, Jeff, you could have been a huge porn star." Blair turned to me. "He does just one video shoot and you wouldn't believe the fan mail. Every gay porn producer wants him to come back to work. Jeff, this is Jordy."

"I told you, I don't want to do that anymore." He turned to me and flashed a smile that made my knees start to buckle. "Thanks, though, Jordy."

"But you dance in the gay bars . . ."

"I don't have to fuck anyone, either." Jeff cut him off. "It's different, Blair, and you know it." He put his big hand on my shoulder. "I'm a go-go boy, Jordy. I hope you won't think badly of me. I only did that one shoot—I did several different scenes in one weekend, and they used them in several different movies." He sighed. "It gives the impression that I did a lot of movies. I've regretted doing it ever since—it doesn't seem like I'll ever live that down, either."

"Think badly of you?" I gulped. "I think it's *cool.*"

"Tongue back in your mouth, child," Blair commanded. "I take it you've never met a porn star before?"

"I'm not a porn star!" Jeff insisted.

"Darling, I'm teasing you," Blair said patiently. "Now, Jordy, are you a freshman?"

I knew it was rude to stare at Jeff, but I couldn't take my eyes off him. I nodded.

"Perhaps you should rush our fraternity," Blair went on when he realized I wasn't going to say anything else.

That got my attention away from Jeff. "A fraternity?"

"Beta Kappa, the best house on campus," Jeff said. "That's where we met."

I swallowed. "Is Beta Kappa gay friendly?"

Blair laughed. "We wouldn't have asked you to rush if it weren't, Jordy."

"How did you know—"

"Outside of the fact you recognized Jeff from his venture into the gay porn industry?"

"Oh."

"You'll love Beta Kappa," Jeff went on. "It's a great house, and the brothers are all really cool. Why don't you come over for dinner and we'll tell you more about it?" He sniffed his armpits and frowned. "I really need to get in the shower."

"Six o'clock," Blair directed as they walked out my front door.

I opened my mouth to say I'd just eaten but shut it. It wouldn't kill me to eat again, so I nodded.

The door shut behind them, and I plopped down on the couch.

A fraternity.

A gay-friendly fraternity at that.

I smiled. I wanted the college experience, and what better way to get that than to join a fraternity?

I took another swig from my Coke and leaned back on the couch.

Jeff and Blair were so nice, and sexy. I closed my eyes and imagined the two of them in bed together, their naked bodies covered in sweat as—

My hand crept down to my crotch. I'd been hard from the moment Jeff had walked into my apartment. I undid my shorts and slid them down, wrapping my hand around my cock.

What would it be like to kiss Jeff? Or Blair?

I summoned up the memory of a scene from one of the movies of Jeff's I'd downloaded. My hand started moving up and down on my cock as I imagined that beautiful body on top of me, his lips pressing against mine, that huge cock rubbing against mine as he pushed my legs apart and began trying to push it inside of me.

I came almost immediately, my entire body going rigid with the orgasm.

I laughed out loud.

I was definitely going to love it here.

Chapter 2

I swallowed and steeled my nerve, resisting the urge to get out my cell phone.

You wanted to do this on your own, I reminded myself. *You can't call Jeff and Blair now and beg them to take you to Beta Kappa. They'll think you're an idiot.*

It was the first night of Rush, and I was standing at the end of Fraternity Row. Ten fraternity houses facing each other across a pedestrian mall stood in front of me. Guys were strolling along the sidewalks, a steady stream going in and out of each house. *You can do this. This isn't St. Bernard, this is somewhere you're going to fit in and have lots of friends. This is why you came to school here. Jeff and Blair have thoroughly prepped you on what to say, how to act. You can do this without their help.*

I took a deep breath and started walking. Beta Kappa was at the end of Fraternity Row, right across the mall from the Sigma Chi house.

The first week of school had been remarkably easy. None of my classes seemed particularly challenging, as I'd suspected. According to Jeff and Blair, pledge semester would be rough and time-consuming; not having a conflict with studying would make it much easier on me. My main fear with my classes was actually being bored; I'd found myself nodding off a few times in my eight a.m. Comp class. My Biology class was so basic as to be laughable, and my History of Western Civilization class looked to be equally easy. I'd already gotten a good start on my term paper for it. I didn't think I would have a problem with Algebra—I'd gone much further at St. Bernard in math—and Intro to Sociology looked simple.

I'd bought some new clothes and gotten a haircut. My new clothes fit well, but I hadn't been able to style my hair the way it looked when I'd left the salon. I finally gave up and didn't bother with the gel, combing it flat and parted on the side. I thought it looked okay.

Blair and Jeff had offered to take me to Beta Kappa and introduce me to the brothers, but I'd said no. They thought I was crazy, and said so in no uncertain terms.

"I want to get a bid on my own," I'd insisted. "You guys have done enough for me already." As I walked now up the mall toward the house, my stomach began to knot up. *Stay calm, it's just a fraternity house, and it IS Rush. They're going to be nice and friendly because they want people to join. This isn't St. Bernard. These guys aren't princes and nobility and the sons of billionaires. These are just normal, typical guys, and they aren't going to look down their noses at you.* It was important to me to get a bid on my own, without any more help from Jeff and Blair. The "Rush boot camp" they'd put me through had already given me a leg up on the other guys rushing. At my insistence, Jeff and Blair had even agreed to not show up for the first night of Rush. I was on my own, and as I walked past the other houses I started to relax. *You're getting yourself all worked up for absolutely no reason. Just because you didn't fit in at St. Bernard doesn't mean you aren't going to fit in at Beta Kappa. You're smart, you're funny, and you have a lot to offer, just like Blair and Jeff said. Just be yourself and don't be nervous,* I said to myself over and over as I drew closer and closer to the end of the mall.

And before I knew it, I was standing in front of Beta Kappa.

I swallowed nervously again.

Just go up the walk and inside, I told myself. *There's no reason to be nervous.*

Yet in spite of myself, I flashed back to being ten years old and arriving at St. Bernard. I remembered my roommate, a French kid named Guy deMontespan, looking at me as though I were something he'd stepped in. *"I am descended from Louis XIV, the glorious Sun King,"* he'd said, his lip curling into a sneer, *"and they put me in a room with some nobody American?"*

It was the last time Guy spoke to me. He'd complained and gotten switched to another room. I wound up with a single room because no one else wanted to be my roommate. And I'd stayed in a single room for eight long, lonely years.

That's the past, Jordy. No one here knows you were the most unpopular student at St. Bernard. No one here is going to judge you because you don't have royal blood or because you can't trace your ancestry back to the Crusades. This is the United States and things like that don't matter here. Here you're judged on your merits, and that's what the brothers will do. You're an A student. You speak four languages.

And my parents were stinking rich.

I put that thought out of my head. Mom and Dad always drilled into me the importance of standing on my own. So what if I was a failure at making friends at St. Bernard? This was a whole new world. No one here knew I'd been lonely and picked on there. I was making a fresh start.

Maybe I should have come with Blair and Jeff. Why am I so

stupid? They already know everyone. They could have introduced me around, and it wouldn't be like I'm a total stranger.

I shook my head and forced the negativity out. I squared my shoulders, bit my lip, and took a deep breath. The front door of the house was wide open, and I could see a table set up just inside for registering. The house wasn't like the others on the mall—the others looked like plantation houses with wide verandas and columns. The Beta Kappa house was more modern looking. To the right of the entryway the house was about a story and a half high; the wall facing the mall was all glass but hidden behind curtains. To the left it was two stories high. That was the dormitory side—two floors of rooms to house the brothers.

A group of guys brushed past me and headed up the walk to the front door. *This is it,* I told myself, and followed them. Just inside the door I could see the entryway into the larger room, and over it was a sign reading WELCOME PROSPECTIVES TO CASINO NIGHT! I could see a couple of blackjack tables set up, and the dealers were relatively attractive young girls. The group of guys who'd passed me had stepped to the side, filling out application forms while a guy seated behind the table was making name tags for them. I took a deep breath and walked up to the table.

The guy making name tags was good looking, wearing a tight red polo shirt over a pair of jeans. His dark hair was gelled so it stood up in the center of his head, and he had a light dusting of pimples on his face. His ears stuck out a bit, and he had a gap between his front two teeth. His own name tag read BRANDON BENSON, RUSH COMMITTEE. He looked up at me and gave me a strained smile. "Hi." He slid a stapled form and a pen toward me. "Your name?"

"Jordy Valentine," I replied. He started making out a name tag for me.

"You need to fill out the application," he said without looking up. He was having trouble fitting VALENTINE on the tag, having to squish TINE onto the end. He handed me the name tag as I filled out the form. It was relatively simple, actually, but I hesitated when I got to the part about my parents' annual income. I didn't have a problem with writing 4.0 as my high school grade average (which was what my grades at St. Bernard translated to), and I didn't have a problem with listing my address at the Alhambra, but my parents' annual income? I laughed to myself. Truth be told, I actually didn't know what their annual income was. I hesitated, and said, "Um, Brandon?"

He looked up.

"I don't know what my parents' annual income is."

He rolled his eyes. "Then estimate. It's not rocket science." He gave me a strange look.

"Okay," I replied, scratching my head. *Okay, be conservative. If Dad and Mom have assets of about seven hundred million and earn a basic 6% interest per quarter, that would be forty-two million per quarter, which would be about a hundred twenty-five million per year.* Pleased with myself, I wrote that amount in the blank and was about to continue filling out the form— the next section was *Hobbies and Interests*—but paused as I noticed someone else walking up to the back side of the table. I glanced up at him and did a double take.

Gorgeous was probably not a strong-enough word. There had been a lot of good-looking boys at St. Bernard, I'd done my share of looking at men on Internet porn sites, and both Jeff and Blair were handsome enough to be underwear models. But this guy was in a completely different class than anyone I'd seen before. He was tall, a few inches over six feet, and he had thick blond hair parted in the center and hanging down almost to his chin on either side. Like

Brandon, he was wearing a tight red polo shirt that hugged a strong chest and biceps. His bare arms were lined with veins under his darkly tanned skin. His eyes were wide and blue, his hair bleached white blond by the sun. His shoulders were broad and his waist narrow, his stomach completely flat. He didn't look like he had an ounce of fat anywhere on his body. His teeth were strong and white, and he had deep dimples in both cheeks. He didn't acknowledge me at all—all of his attention was on Brandon. His name tag read CHAD YORK, RUSH CHAIRMAN.

"What a bunch of losers we're getting," he said, slipping into the chair next to Brandon. "I'm starting to think we might be better off not bidding anyone this semester, the way this is going."

"Tell me about it," Brandon muttered as I slid the application back to him.

Chad chose that moment to notice me. He looked me over from head to toe in a slow-moving glance that made me shift uncomfortably from one foot to the other. One of his dark blond eyebrows went up, and the corner of his mouth also went up. He stood up and stuck his hand out at me. "Chad York, Rush chairman. Welcome to Beta Kappa." It sounded canned and insincere.

"Jordy Valentine." I shook his hand and gave him a smile.

"You have spinach in your teeth." His smile didn't falter, but his eyes widened.

Mortified, I closed my mouth.

"The bathroom's just down the hall." He gestured over his shoulder. "You probably want to do something about that." He turned back to Brandon, made a face, and they both laughed.

I wished a hole would open in the ground and swallow me whole.

"Seriously, go do something about that." Chad didn't look at me, just waved his hand in dismissal.

My face felt like it was on fire as I stumbled past the table and down the hall. *Nice going, way to make a great first impression, why oh why didn't I check my mouth before I left the apartment, would it have killed me to brush my teeth again, you just made a complete ass out of yourself in front of one of the hottest guys you've ever seen, thank God Blair and Jeff aren't here.* I reached the saloon doors that led to the communal first-floor bathroom and shoved my way inside. Standing in front of a mirror, I bared my teeth. Sure enough, there was some spinach lodged between the canine and the front tooth. I grabbed a paper towel with my shaking hands and removed it, taking some deep breaths, fighting the urge to leave and forget all about Beta Kappa. I turned on the cold water tap and splashed some water on my face. I looked at myself in the mirror and could see tears filling my eyes. *This is going to be no different than St. Bernard, you were so stupid for thinking you could get a fresh start, it wasn't the guys at St. Bernard, it was YOU, you're never going to have any friends and you sure don't belong here, you might as well just slip out and head home, no one would notice you were gone anyway . . .*

"Hi," a voice said from behind me. "You rushing?"

I jumped.

"Sorry, didn't mean to scare you," the voice said.

I turned and found myself looking at a guy about my height. He was heavier than me, and his shirt was a little too small for him. His stomach strained against the front of it. His arms were thin, and his skin was very pale. His mousy brown hair looked a little greasy, and angry red pimples were scattered over his face. He was wearing a pair of tortoiseshell glasses that had slid partway down his nose. His teeth weren't straight, and his lips were narrow and thin. His name tag read ROGER DEVLIN. His face was expressionless. "Yes," I replied. "Yes, I am."

"I'm Roger, one of the brothers here." He shook my hand. His hand was soft, warm, and a little moist. "Nice to meet you, Jordy." He narrowed his eyes and examined my face. "Are you okay?" he asked, crossing his arms.

"Uh-huh." I nodded. "Just a little overwhelmed, I guess. I've never been to anything like this before. . . ."

A sardonic smile crept across his face. "And let me guess, you met our estimable Rush chairman, Chad." He barked out a laugh, shaking his head. "Charming, isn't he?"

"He seemed nice," I said cautiously, remembering Blair's advice—"*Never criticize a brother, even if one of them invites you to. Don't criticize the house under any circumstance, even if you think the paint is hideous and the carpet an abomination. All it takes is one brother to blackball you and keep you out. No matter how tempted you are, no matter how friendly a brother might seem, remember they are evaluating you and deciding if they want to let you in. Even as a pledge you don't criticize a brother to another brother. Once you're an active, you can do or say whatever you want, but until you're initiated you can be bounced at any time. Don't forget.*" "I didn't get much of a chance to talk to him. But he did seem nice."

"Then you've got pretty low standards," Roger replied, still smiling. "He didn't even give you the time of day, did he."

What? "I didn't ask," I replied, confused. "I have a watch." I held up my arm to show him. "See?"

He gave me a funny look, and got a look at my watch. His eyes widened and he whistled. "Dude, that's a TAG Heuer." He threw back his head and started laughing. "I'll just bet Chad didn't see that—if he did you sure as hell wouldn't have been able to ditch his ass."

"What does my watch have to do with anything?" I was puzzled. I looked at it. It was just a watch. I'd gotten it for my last birthday.

"Oh, Jordy." His smile broadened. He was actually kind of cute when he smiled for real. "Your parents have money, don't they?" He pointed at the watch. "That watch cost enough money to pay for a year's tuition, books, and lodging here at Polk State." He cocked his head and examined me from head to foot the same way Chad had—but it was different. I didn't feel like I was under a microscope. He shook his head. "I don't get it. Your clothes are nice, nothing too expensive, but they are definitely new. But you're wearing a watch worth about ten grand."

"I don't really care about clothes," I replied. "I mean, I guess I do. But I'm used to wearing a uniform. I—" I let my voice trail off. I heard Blair saying, *"Don't offer too much information, and don't talk about yourself too much. If someone asks you a question about yourself, answer it but be brief. You don't want them to think you're self-absorbed."* Instead, I added, "I have a lot to learn, I guess." I looked down at my pale blue pullover and the new jeans. I'd thought they were perfectly fine—Blair had picked them out for me.

Maybe Blair picked them out on purpose, so people would—

I dismissed that thought. Blair and Jeff had been nothing but nice to me. They weren't the kind of people to play mean jokes.

Or were they?

"Obviously." He seemed absolutely delighted. "In fact, I'd pay good money to see Chad's face when he reads your application." He was practically dancing in place. "He probably treated you like you were something he stepped in, didn't he?"

"He didn't seem particularly interested in me, if that's

what you mean," I replied. "But he's probably meeting so many guys—"

"Yeah, you're right, that's probably it." Roger smothered another grin. "Look, take some advice, okay? Chad York can't be trusted. We were pledges together, and I know Chad pretty well. Believe me, once he reads your application, he's going to be sweet as sugar to you." He started laughing again. He stopped when he saw my face. "Sorry." He wiped at his eyes. "I'm not laughing at you. I'm laughing at Chad." His face darkened. "I told everyone making him Rush chairman was a mistake."

"But why would reading my application make a difference?" I was confused, trying to remember my answers to the questions. "I don't understand."

"Never mind." He waved his hand. "I never said a word. Want me to show you around?" His eyes glinted. "Being a Beta Kappa is like having fifty best friends," he said in a singsong voice as he held the saloon doors open. "Joining Beta Kappa is going to be the smartest decision you'll make in your entire college career."

"Okay." I was really confused but decided to let it go. *I'll figure it out later,* I told myself as I followed Roger out of the bathroom.

The tour didn't take very long. Beta Kappa was a nice house, and I liked that it was homey rather than palatial like the other houses on the mall. Roger kept up a steady stream of chatter as he showed me around. The building was in the shape of an L, with the long side being the two-story dormitory where the bedrooms were. The rooms were small, and it was amazing that two guys could share such a small place—all the rooms were about the size of the spare bedroom in my apartment—but there was a welcoming feel to the place that I liked. Roger never gave me a chance to say anything—he'd ask me if I had any questions, but before I could answer he'd start talking about something else. He introduced me to other brothers we encountered—also leading a prospective around—but other than "nice to meet you" I didn't get a chance to talk to any of them. They all seemed really polite and genuinely interested in me. I felt my own confidence starting to come back. *So who cares if you had spinach in your teeth when you met the Rush chairman? You're making a good impression on the other brothers. And Chad probably wasn't being mean—you were just being oversensitive. He was doing you a favor—and what WOULD be the polite way to tell someone "you have food in your teeth"?*

I felt a lot better when the tour ended. Roger led me back into the big room, which he said doubled as their dining room and the party room. They'd done a good job setting up Casino Night. In addition to blackjack tables, there were a couple of roulette tables, and a crowd had gathered around a table where a pretty Asian girl was playing craps. "I'll go get you some chips so you can play. Wait for me here." Roger gave me another smile and wandered off. I stood by myself, taking it all in. Everyone looked like they were having a good time, and Blair and Jeff had been right. I liked Beta Kappa, and I wanted to join. I felt like I belonged, despite the rough start.

I leaned back against the wall, watching the Asian girl as she continued her hot streak, the crowd around the craps table cheering her every toss of the dice, when Chad York suddenly loomed up in front of me. "There you are!" he said, his face wreathed in a huge smile, his eyes open wide.

I inhaled sharply. He was so damned handsome that it almost hurt to look at him. "Here I am." I smiled back at him.

"I've been looking for you everywhere," he went on. "I wanted to apologize if I seemed rude when you got here."

He put his right hand on my shoulder and looked into my eyes. "I'ts just that I'm in charge, and I'm under a lot of pressure—the whole success of this semester's Rush is my responsibility."

My knees felt weak as I stared back into his impossibly blue eyes. "It's okay." His hand felt hot on my shoulder—like an electrical current was flowing through it into my body and down into my groin. "I would imagine that would be a lot of pressure." I shifted a little bit. His cologne smelled fresh and clean.

I wanted to kiss him. I wanted to put my hands on his thick chest. I wanted him to push me up against the wall—

"That's very kind of you, and understanding. Thank you. I'd hate for you to get the wrong impression of Beta Kappa because of me." He waved a hand around the room. "So what do you think of Beta Kappa? Has anyone taken you on a tour?"

"I like it. I like it a lot," I replied. "Roger showed me—"

"Oh, I'm so glad. We're really the best house on campus." He went on in that vein for a while, but I wasn't really listening. I was watching his face, the way his chest muscles rippled under his shirt, how his arms flexed with every movement. He was gorgeous, a Greek god come down from Olympus to mix with mere mortals. I wondered what his stomach looked like. I wondered if he had golden hairs on his chest. I wondered what it would be like to kiss his lips. He finished his spiel. "Would you like something to drink?"

"Um—"

"Will you excuse me for a moment?" He gave me a pleading look, and when I nodded, he said, "I'll be right back with a Coke for you, I promise." He walked over to another group of guys and separated one of them from the rest. He put his arm around the guy's shoulders and led him away.

I couldn't stop staring at his ass.

His jeans were tight and hugged his round butt like a rubber glove. It was big and hard and perfectly round.

"Earth to Jordy," a voice said behind me.

Startled, I caught my breath and smiled at Roger. "Sorry."

"He does have a phenomenal ass, doesn't he?" Roger looked over to where Chad was standing with his back to us, talking to some other guys I didn't recognize. "Unfortunately, it's attached to the rest of him." He handed me a stack of chips. "I was right, wasn't I? Butter wouldn't melt in his mouth, right?"

"That doesn't make sense." I frowned. "Body heat and saliva would break down butter in anyone's mouth. It wouldn't be possible."

"It's an expression." Roger frowned at me. "It means—well, hell, I don't know what it means. You're right, it's dumb." Roger laughed and clapped me on the back. "Come on, Jordy, let's play some blackjack."

To be honest, I've never understood the appeal of blackjack. It's so incredibly simple. All one has to do to be successful is simply keep track of the tens and the face cards and bet accordingly. It's really all about the law of averages and calculating odds. Out of fifty-two cards, there are sixteen with a face value of ten, and of course the four aces. You have a one in three chance, basically, of getting a ten from the dealer every time you take a card. All you really have to do is count the cards. I started counting and calculating, accumulating a rather large pile of chips, when Chad came up behind me and said, "Wow, you're doing well."

"It's easy," I replied. "All you have to do is—"

"Yes, yes." His smile never faltered. "Would you mind coming with me for a moment?"

I grabbed my pile of chips and walked with him out of the party room.

"So," he said as we walked down the hallway. "Your application said you went to St. Bernard of Clairvaux Academy? Where exactly is that?"

"A little town called Inhofen." When he got a puzzled look, I smiled. "No one really knows where Inhofen is. It's a little village about twenty miles from Gstaad."

"Shtod?" He looked confused.

"Switzerland," I replied. "It's in Switzerland. Most people have never heard of Inhofen. I mean, it's no wonder, all that's really there is the school. The skiing isn't very good there, so no one ever goes there. It's not one of the big tourist destinations in the country."

"Okay," he said, a strange look on his face. When we reached the staircase to the second floor, he knocked on a door to the right of it. He opened the door. "Go on in."

I walked in. A muscular guy in his early twenties was sitting behind a desk. In a chair next to him sat another guy about the same age. The guy behind the desk gave me a dazzling smile. *Is everyone in this house drop-dead gorgeous?* I wondered.

"Hi, Jordy," the guy behind the desk said, rising and offering me his hand. I shook it. "I'm Chris Moore, president of Beta Kappa." He was about six feet four inches tall, with dark blond hair and a muscular body. His eyes were gray, and his smile was warm.

"I'm Eric Matthews, the pledge marshal." The other guy offered me his hand. Eric was a little shorter than Chris, with dark hair and brown eyes. I shook his hand. His biceps bulged as we shook hands. "Have a seat, Jordy."

I sat down in an uncomfortable, hard plastic chair.

"I was looking at your application," Chad said, closing

the door behind him. "Your parents have an income of one hundred twenty-five million per year?"

"I really don't know," I replied, getting a little nervous. "I just estimated. I'm sorry. I didn't know I was going to be asked, so . . ."

"Estimated?" Chad's voice was low. "You just estimated?"

"Well, I know their net worth is about seven hundred million, give or take," I went on. "So, I just figured if their money was in a basic savings account at 6% interest per quarter, that's what their annual income would be." I shrugged. "We never really talk about money much, honestly."

"How did your parents," Eric asked, "make their money?"

"Did they inherit it?" This was from Chris.

"Oh, no." I laughed. "My dad was a software designer and started his own company when he got out of college. He invented EZ Accounting . . ."

"Oh, my God." Eric gasped. "Is your father Terry Valentine?"

I nodded, looking from face to face. "Yes. Is that a problem?" I swallowed. *Maybe Beta Kappa is no different from St. Bernard after all. They don't want me because of who my father is—but why?* My heart sank. I closed my eyes and wished I were a million miles away.

They exchanged glances.

"Well, we'd like to offer you a bid to pledge Beta Kappa," Chris said, smiling. "Would you like to accept? You don't have to accept right now—"

"Oh, yes, I accept!" My heart felt like it was going to explode in my chest. *They want me!* "I can't think of anything I would rather do than be a Beta Kappa!"

Eric cleared his throat. "Are you sure you don't want to check out any of the other houses first? We don't want you to think we pressured you into joining us without giving the other houses a chance."

In my head, I heard Blair saying, *"If someone asks you if you've checked out the other houses, even if you haven't and don't want to, tell them yes. Don't seem too eager to join Beta Kappa. We're also required by Interfraternity Council rules to encourage prospectives to look at other houses."*

But they'd already offered me a bid.

I took a deep breath and forced Blair's voice out of my head. "I really like it here," I said. "The moment I walked into the house I felt like I belonged here. I'll be the best pledge you've ever had. I'll be the best brother you've ever had. I really, really want to pledge Beta Kappa. I mean, I'm an A student, and I can help brothers study and tutor and . . ." My voice trailed off.

Idiot! I yelled at myself inside my head. *Blair said not to seem too eager. You've blown it. They're going to change their minds and ask you to leave.*

"In that case," Chris said slowly, pushing a small piece of cardboard across the desk to me. I glanced down at it.

> The brothers of Beta Kappa fraternity
> would like to cordially invite you
> to accept a bid to pledge our house.

Underneath those words were the signatures of Chris as president, Eric as pledge marshal, and Chad as Rush chairman.

There was a blank for me to sign my name.

I took the pen Eric was offering me and signed.

"Welcome to Beta Kappa, pledge," Chris said with a big grin.

I smiled back at him. "Thank you." I fought back the tears I knew would be inappropriate.

I remembered Guy deMontespan and his friends sneering at me.

I remembered all those meals eaten at a table by myself those eight long years at St. Bernard.

I remembered all the slights, the veiled and not-so-veiled insults, the teasing, and the pranks.

Finally, I had fit in somewhere.

Things were going to be different from now on.

Chapter 3

"You know, I wanted you from the first moment I saw you," Chad said, pulling his Beta Kappa T-shirt over his head, "even with the spinach in your teeth."

I gulped. I was sitting on the bed in Chad's room at the house. His body was even more phenomenal than I'd imagined. His skin was darkly tanned, and there wasn't a single hair on his torso. His pec muscles were highly developed and firm, with a deep cleavage running down the center. His nipples were purple, the size of half dollars, and erect. His abdominal muscles were chiseled with shallow crevices between them, just above the flat plane where two deep lines descended from the top of his pelvic bones to the waistband of his underwear, which was just visible above the top of his faded, low-rise jeans. "Do you like my body?" he purred as he walked toward me, running his right hand up and down his abs while his left hand tweaked and pulled at his right nipple. I could see his thick, hard cock outlined through the jeans. Near where the tip was, a small wet spot was forming on the denim. He tossed his head, and his thick, white blond hair bounced around before falling back perfectly into place. He paused just in front of me, so close that I could lick his abs without having to move at all.

"Your body is—is perfect," I was barely able to whisper. I tried to focus on breathing, because I was afraid I might hyperventilate. My cock was getting hard, and I wanted him so badly it was all I could do not to reach out and yank his pants down. I could see the outline of his hard-on through his jeans. It was just centimeters from my face. Tentatively I reached out and brushed my trembling fingers against it.

Chad's entire body shuddered, and he threw his head back, emitting a low moan. He pulled harder on his nipple. He turned his back to me. His perfect ass was right there in front of me, and he slid his jeans down. His tight white underwear stretched across the two round cheeks.

I reached up and touched it. It was solid and hard.

"Yes," he whispered. "Do you like my ass? Do you want to fuck me?"

I licked my lips. I tried to answer, but no sound came out. I was having trouble breathing. I'd never been this turned on in my life. I leaned forward and pressed my lips against the right cheek. Through the white cotton it felt hot and solid. His entire body trembled as I moved my lips to the other cheek and kissed it as well.

"Do it," he whispered.

My hands shook as I reached up and slowly slid the underwear down. My cock strained against my jeans; my balls were aching. His ass was white, a stark contrast to the tanned skin just above. He had two deep dimples in the small of his back just above where the curve of his ass began. The milky white skin was perfectly smooth and hairless. I kept sliding the underwear down until it was at his ankles, and he gracefully stepped out of them and kicked them to the side. He bent forward at the waist, and I pushed his cheeks apart, revealing the pink flesh inside.

I stuck my tongue into the hole there.

He growled as I tried to remember how it was done in all

the porn I'd watched on the Web. I started licking and lapping. The taste was nothing like I'd expected. There was a sweet tang to his hole. It tasted sublime, and I wanted to get my tongue as far inside of him as I could. I started moving my lips and suckling, moving my tongue in and out and around as he moaned. "Yes, yes, that's it, oh, God, that's incredible, yes, don't stop, oh, God, that's so good."

I dropped my right hand to the fly of my pants and undid them, touching my own cock as I worked his ass with my mouth.

"I want to fuck you," I said finally, pulling my head back and taking in the firm muscles of his back, the incredible beauty of his form. He was like a statue I'd seen of Apollo in the national museum in Athens. I'd never thought such physical perfection was possible in a human, despite the gorgeous studs who starred in porn movies and posed for underwear ads. Chad was so beautiful, he was perfection, he was everything—

And I woke up as my cock erupted.

I sat up in bed, rubbing my eyes, trying to catch my breath.

The digital clock on my nightstand read 4:45. It was dark outside, and as I shook my head I realized it was just a dream.

And not just any dream—my underwear was soaked. I'd had a wet dream.

I swung my legs out of the bed and pulled my underwear off, carrying it to the washer in the laundry room and tossing it inside.

I hadn't had a wet dream in years.

I walked into the bathroom and turned the spigot on.

This isn't good, I told myself as I stared at myself in the mirror. When the water was hot, I soaked a washcloth and cleaned myself up. *I hate being a virgin.*

I was probably the only virgin on campus. Just like St. Bernard.

You're fooling yourself if you think Chad is going to be interested in you, a voice mocked me inside my head. It sounded like Guy deMontespan. *Take a good look at yourself in that mirror. You're dumpy and you're ugly. Chad is beautiful. Beautiful guys are only interested in other beautiful guys, and you are far from that. You aren't even remotely close. All you are to him is just another pledge he won't notice, he won't pay any attention to. You know you don't have a chance with him—he doesn't even know you exist, and even if he did, he'd never want you. Not now, not tomorrow, not ever in a million years. You know it. Guys like Chad go for other guys like Chad—you know, like Blair and Jeff? When have you ever seen a guy like that with a guy like you?*

Never, that's when.

"Shut up," I said out loud. "You don't know what you're talking about."

I walked back into the bedroom and put on another pair of underwear. I sat down on the bed. The voice was probably right, much as I hated to admit it.

I was just fooling myself.

We'd had our first pledge meeting the night before. I had been the first to arrive, and Pledge Marshal Eric had directed me to a room he called the Chapter Room. It was just off the foyer, and as I sat down on a couch I looked around. The walls were covered with photographs and paddles. Eric had left me alone in the Chapter Room. I could hear the television in the main room—some of the brothers were watching an NFL game. As my other pledge brothers had started arriving, it soon became painfully apparent that I was the ugliest guy in our pledge class. Well, maybe *ugliest* was too harsh, but I was certainly the least attractive out of all of them. There had been ten of them, and every last one of them looked like he'd been an athlete or a jock in high school. Even the ones who seemed to be out of shape had big, muscular arms. I'd sat there, nodding when someone said hello, wondering what I'd been thinking, joining a fraternity. I wouldn't have anything in common with any of these guys. They weren't going to like me. I'd been crazy to think so.

I'd kept watching, hoping someone would sit down next to me and start talking. No one did. Some of them seemed to already know each other and were joking and laughing. No one acknowledged me other than with a nod. No one said hello, no one introduced themselves to me, nothing. I remembered seeing them at Rush, but for the life of me couldn't remember their names.

This was going to be a complete and utter disaster.

You can always depledge, that horrible voice had whispered inside my head, but I ignored it.

Relax already, I told myself. *Give them a chance.*

I guess I'd been expecting too much from my pledge brothers. This was our first meeting of many to come, and we were all going to get to know each other. All the brothers had made a point of talking about the bond between pledge brothers—but bonds weren't formed instantly; they had to be forged over a semester of working toward a common goal, and our common goal was initiation into Beta Kappa as full brothers.

That was the most important thing. That was what I had to remember.

I'd never wanted anything in my life as much as I wanted to be a brother.

The night I'd accepted my bid, all the brothers had been really cool and welcoming to me. It was wonderful being hugged, clapped on the back, and having my hand shaken over and over. I had been very careful not to say or do anything stupid in front of any of them. I finally felt like I belonged somewhere. I had gone back to the blackjack table and kept winning. I met so many brothers I couldn't keep their names straight—which was unusual, considering my total recall. I figured it was the excitement, the rush of being accepted and welcomed somewhere. It was an amazing, amazing feeling—one I hoped would never end. I was determined. I was going to be the best pledge ever in the history of Beta Kappa, not just at CSU-Polk, but Beta Kappas everywhere. The brothers would never regret their decision to offer me a bid.

I was going to make them all proud.

When Casino Night had ended, I'd said good-bye and headed straight home. I'd floated up the stairs to the second floor of my building on a cloud and started pounding on Jeff and Blair's door. "All right already, calm down already!" Blair had said as he opened the door. All he had on was a pair of white briefs, but I was so excited I didn't try to sneak a peek the way I usually did. Blair and Jeff had absolutely no shyness about their bodies, and at first I was disconcerted, but I was so used to seeing them almost naked at that point that I didn't get hard.

"They gave me a bid!" I'd said, practically bouncing up and down with excitement.

Blair's face had lit up and he'd thrown his arms around me. "Hurray! Jeff, did you hear that? They gave Jordy a bid!" He'd pulled me inside their apartment. "We were just about to spark up a joint—care to join us?"

"I don't smoke," I'd reminded him. He was always offering me pot, and I always turned it down. It killed brain cells.

"This is a banner day!" Jeff had come out of the bedroom, wearing only red underwear. "Did you tell him, Blair?"

"I got the lead in the theater department's production of *Sweeney Todd*," Blair had said with a big grin. "Oy, the rehearsal schedule is going to be brutal."

"But that's great!" I'd replied, watching him light the joint and take a deep hit before passing it over to Jeff.

"It's going to take up almost all of my time," Blair had replied. "But if you ever need me, you can text me." He exhaled. "Good thing we went alum, huh, Jeff?"

"Alum?"

"We're alumni," Jeff had explained. "At the house. You can do that after six semesters as a full active. We don't have to attend things anymore if we don't want to."

"Oh." I'd felt a little disappointed. "So you won't be around the house much, either, Jeff?"

"I'm not a genius like you," Jeff had replied sadly. "I've got eighteen units this semester, and I need to get a 4.0 to get my GPA up—this semester and next." He sighed. "Between studying and dancing at Fusions, I'm not going to have a spare moment." He had patted Blair on the leg. "So, Blair getting the lead is kind of a godsend. I don't have to worry I'm ignoring him."

"Well, if you need any help studying . . ."

"You just need to focus on making sure you make the most out of your pledge semester," Blair had interrupted me. "That's the most important thing—and you can always reach us if you need to."

The rest of Rush Week had been really nice. Chad was friendly but occupied with everything that was going on, and I found myself watching him whenever I thought no one would notice. I couldn't get over how good looking he was. He was always dressed nice, and the clothes flattered his physique. Roger told me Chad was one of the gay brothers, and his two best friends in the house, Brandon Benson and Rees Davidson, were also gay.

Brandon and Rees were also really good looking. Not as good looking as Chad—no one was, except maybe Jeff Morgan, and he was taken—but still. Rees was really tall, about six three, and was about 220 pounds of solid muscle. He'd played football in high school and still seemed like a jock. He always wore tank tops and sweatpants or basketball shorts. I didn't understand why all three of them were single. Roger had said that despite their closeness, none of them had ever hooked up together as far as he knew. The major difference between Chad and his two best friends, though, was obvious as soon as either Rees or Brandon opened their mouths.

Rees was dumb as a post, and Brandon not much smarter.

"Chad's the brains in that outfit," Roger had said bitterly. He'd been in their pledge class, and I got the distinct impression Roger really didn't like any of them. "Not that it would take very much, if you know what I mean."

Roger didn't seem to fit into Beta Kappa. During Rush Week, none of the other brothers said anything negative about any of the others. They gave the impression the house was just one big happy family. Roger was the sole exception. Roger seemed determined, in fact, to say something negative about everyone else in the house. It confused me. If Roger disliked so many of the brothers, why had he bothered to pledge and go through initiation?

I liked Roger, though. He was actually kind of funny. And I liked that he spoke his mind. There was something almost refreshingly honest about him. And from all the reading I'd done, the notion that all the brothers were close was a little hard to believe.

Surely, some of them didn't like one another.

I sighed and sat there on my bed for a moment, debating on whether to go back to bed and sleep some more. My first class wasn't until nine. But I was wide awake, and so I went into the kitchen and started the coffee.

The pledge meeting had actually turned out to be a lot of fun. I had studied the faces of my pledge brothers. They were an interesting assortment of guys. I had been just about to say something when the door opened and our pledge marshal, Eric Matthews, walked in. He slammed the door shut behind him, startling everyone, and silence fell on the room.

"Welcome to Beta Kappa!" he had said with a broad smile. He wasn't wearing a shirt, and I couldn't help but stare at his chiseled torso. A patch of dark hair sat in the deep cleavage between his pecs, and a line of black hair ran down his flat stomach from his navel and disappeared inside his gray fleece sweatpants. From the way his bulge moved around inside the sweatpants, he didn't appear to be wearing underwear. I made myself look away and locked eyes with one of the pledge brothers whose name I couldn't remember. He was cute, with blue eyes and dishwater blond hair. He grinned in an *oh, you caught me looking* kind of way and winked at me. I grinned back.

Eric sat down on the floor. "All right, guys. You are about to embark on a journey that's going to change your life—for the better. Your pledge semester is all about learning about the house, learning what Beta Kappa stands for, and getting to know all the brothers. But before we go any further, I want to make something very clear: While Beta Kappa has to be a priority for you, if there is ever a conflict between your pledge responsibilities and school, school wins every time. Our motto is *alma mater first, and Beta Kappa for alma mater.* You are here to get an education, okay?"

Everyone had murmured assent.

"So, first things first." He grinned. "I know some of you already know each other, and you met during Rush, but we're going to go around the room. Say your name, what year you are in school, your hometown, and your major. I'll start. Eric Matthews, senior, San Diego, California, and my major is business administration." He turned to the pledge I'd made eye contact with. "Okay, you're next."

"Jon Preston, freshman, Madison, Wisconsin, and I'm pre-med," the cute boy said. He was tapping his right foot on the floor.

I was next. I cleared my throat. "Um, I'm Jordy Valentine, freshman, undecided major, and I'm not really sure what my hometown would be," I said, feeling kind of silly.

Eric frowned. "How can you not know where you're from?"

I felt my face color as everyone in the room stared at me. *Great, your first pledge meeting and you've already made a total ass out of yourself.* "Well, my parents' main home is outside of Seattle, but I haven't lived there since I was ten," I had said, struggling to keep my voice from cracking. I could hear my heart beating, and resisted the urge to flee.

"Their *main* home?" Eric had looked confused. "Well, where have you lived since then?"

"Inhofen, Switzerland." I bit my lip.

"Seriously?" This had come from a guy on the other side of the room, and I forced myself to look at him. To my surprise, he was actually looking at me in awe rather than contempt. *"Switzerland?"*

I nodded. "I attended a boarding school starting at ten. Mom and Dad are hardly ever in Seattle. They travel a lot. They have several other homes as well." I shrugged. "So I don't know what my *hometown* would be. I'm sorry, I know that probably seems dumb—"

"No, it doesn't," Eric replied. He smiled. "Why don't you just call Seattle home? That would be easiest."

"Okay." I smiled back at him. "I'm Jordy Valentine, a freshman from Seattle, and I am undecided."

"Great." Eric beamed back at me.

The guy sitting to my right said, "My name is Mark Dunne, I'm from Merced, California, I'm a sophomore, and my major is graphic design." He gave me a reassuring smile. He had brown hair and was kind of slender, almost too skinny. His shirt and shorts were too big for him, and his legs were covered with thick black hair.

I made a mental note. As each one of my pledge brothers went through the litany, I'd memorized their information.

The guy who'd been so awed about my sojourn in Switzerland was Gary Musson, a junior from Madera, majoring in broadcast journalism. He had thick brown hair, blue eyes, a round face covered with pimples, broad shoulders that tapered down to a narrow waist, and a deep voice.

Kevin Dorton was a good-looking blond from Santa Barbara, a freshman majoring in advertising. He had deep dimples in his gold-tanned cheeks, and thick arm muscles. Like Gary, he had a narrow waist, and his tanned legs were muscular and smooth.

Next to him had been Ryan McNair. Ryan was really tall, with hair so dark it was almost black, with a light tan and green eyes. He was also really slender, like Mark Dunne. He was wearing a white polo shirt and a pair of blue checked madras shorts. He'd kicked off his sandals and was draped loosely over a folding chair. He was a freshman from Santa Rosa, majoring in public policy.

"Public policy?" Eric smiled at him. "You want to work in politics?"

Ryan blushed beneath his freckles. "I want to be a presidential adviser someday."

"I'm Jacob Hinton," said a tall, good-looking boy with olive skin and curly brown hair. Out of all of us, he was probably the best-looking pledge. He had strong cheekbones and a pointed chin, thick red lips, and the greenest eyes I'd ever seen. His shoulders were wide, and he was wearing a red T-shirt over a pair of khaki shorts that reached his knees. He had thick, muscular calves, and his voice sounded almost musical. He also had the longest lashes I'd ever seen on a man. "I'm a sophomore from Lake Tahoe, and I'm majoring in physical education." He flashed a smile at all of us that made my heart flutter a little bit. "Yes, I'm going to be a gym teacher." He laughed. "I want a job where I can always wear sweats."

Everyone laughed, and I thought, *He could give Chad a run for his money in the hot department.*

"I'm Marc Schiphol," a stocky blond guy with blue eyes said after we stopped laughing. He, too, had big biceps, but he was thickly built with a bit of a belly. "I'm from Ann Arbor, Michigan, a junior, and I am majoring in exercise physiology."

"How do you spell that last name?" someone asked.

"It's Dutch," I had replied without thinking. "It's the name of the airport in Amsterdam. S-C-H-I-P-H-O-L, right?"

Marc had stared at me, his mouth open. "Nobody ever gets that right. How did you know?"

I felt my face flushing. Everyone was staring at me again. *Learn how to keep your stupid mouth shut,* I had scolded myself. *Nobody likes a know-it-all.* "Like I said, it's the name of the airport in Amsterdam. I've flown through there a couple of times."

"Wow," Marc said, shaking his head. "You're pretty smart."

I didn't say anything. I sat in silence as my last two pledge brothers introduced themselves. Cal Ford was a freshman from Kearney, Nebraska, majoring in English literature. He was a redhead with more freckles than I'd ever seen before on anyone, but his eyes had a mischievous twinkle I found really appealing. The other was Phil Shea, who was also really tall and lean, with thick lips and dark eyes. He was from San Mateo and was majoring in music.

Once the introductions were complete, Eric had grinned and said, "Okay, the first thing you all are going to need to know is that information about your pledge brothers. As pledges, you are a unit. If one pledge messes up, you all have messed up. Tomorrow night, you are going to get your pledge manuals. Your pledge manuals are broken down into lessons you have to learn each week. Every Monday night, before the brothers have their meeting, we have a formal dinner. Everyone is expected to dress up for dinner—that means you have to wear dress pants, dress shoes, a nice shirt, and a tie. You need to be here tomorrow night at five-thirty. The junior actives—last semester's pledges and the newest brothers—will show you how to serve dinner. It is the pledges' responsibility to serve the brothers dinner each Monday, as a gesture of respect to the brotherhood. Does anyone have a class conflict with Monday nights?" He'd looked around the room, and no one said anything. "Good. So remember, you have to be here tomorrow night by five-thirty. Do not be late—if anyone is late, everyone is considered late. Is that clear?"

We all had murmured assent.

"While the brothers are having our meeting, the pledges

have a meeting of their own upstairs in the library. The brothers' meeting is secret and is for brothers only. You are not to leave the library and come downstairs until I come upstairs and get you. This is a good time for you to go over your lessons, help each other to make sure you know the lessons—remember, if any one of you doesn't know the lesson, none of you do—as well as talk about pledge business." He'd smiled. "Tomorrow night's lesson is you need to know the information you just learned about each other— name, year, hometown, and major. You will be quizzed about this after the brothers' meeting. Also, tomorrow night you will be electing officers—a president, a vice president, a secretary, and a treasurer. Each pledge class has two responsibilities as a class—you have to make a pledge class paddle"—he gestured around the room—"and hanging on the walls in here are paddles from past pledge classes, to give you an idea of what you're going to need to do. Also, each pledge class has to provide a gift to the brotherhood as a gesture of appreciation for being invited to join the brotherhood. The last pledge class donated new ceiling fans for the master room. You have until the end of the semester to finish your paddle and provide the gift. Does anyone have any questions?" When no one responded, he'd started passing out sheets of paper. "On this paper are the names of the executive officers of the house, their majors, their pledge classes, and their hometowns. You need to know these for next week's lesson, and you also need to identify these brothers." He smiled. "No one had better get the information about *me* wrong. I also included my cell number on here. If you ever have any questions, or are ever unable to make Monday night meeting or *any* event at the house, *you need to let me know as soon as possible.* I cannot stress enough how important this is. If you do not show up and I don't know about it, you can be dropped. The brotherhood takes attendance very seriously. I would also recommend you hang out awhile after this meeting and write down your pledge brothers' information, since you will be responsible for knowing it tomorrow night. Does anyone have any questions?" When no one responded, he'd smiled again. "Okay, then I will leave you to it." He stood up and walked over to the door. "Welcome to Beta Kappa, pledges."

The door shut behind him.

We sat in silence for a moment, and then Jon Preston had said, "Did you seriously go to a boarding school in Switzerland, Jordy?" His eyes were wide open, and he sounded awed.

"Yes." I shrugged. "It's not really a big deal."

"That's so cool." This had been from Jacob Hinton. "I've never even been outside of California. What was it like?"

"Do you speak Swiss?" Marc Schiphol had added.

I smothered a grin. "There's no such language. They speak German, French, or Italian. Most Swiss speak all three, and a lot of them have some English, too."

"Do you?" Ryan McNair had asked. "Speak all three, I mean?"

I nodded, biting my lower lip.

"Cool!" Jon had replied. "I was an exchange student in Marseilles for a year. I'm fluent." He added in French, *"Ça te dérangera si on se parle en français de temps en temps. Je suis inquiet que je perdrai mon aisance."* (Would you mind speaking French with me sometimes? I'm worried I'll lose my fluency.)

"Je serai ravi," I'd answered in the same tongue. *"Nous pouvons parler des camarades devant eux sans qu'ils sachent."* (I would be delighted. We can talk about the brothers in front of their faces and they won't know what we're saying.)

"C'est dommage que le reste de la classe ne parle pas français!"
(Too bad the rest of the class doesn't speak French!)

We'd sat around for another half hour, getting one another's information and talking, getting to know our fellow pledge brothers.

It was a great feeling. No one made me feel like an outsider—on the contrary, they were all welcoming, friendly, and nice.

I'd always wondered how it would feel to belong somewhere.

It was better than I could have imagined.

After the meeting had broken up, I was walking out to my car when I ran into Chad in the parking lot. He and two other brothers—Brandon and Rees—were getting out of a red Camaro. "Hi!" I said.

Brandon and Rees had ignored me. They were carrying twelve-packs of beer and just walked on into the house.

But Chad had waited. He smiled. "Your first pledge meeting, Jody?"

"Jordy," I'd corrected him. "My name's Jordy."

"Oh, sorry." He shrugged. "I'm terrible with names. Anyway, welcome to Beta Kappa. I look forward to getting to know you."

"Yeah, me too."

"See you tomorrow." He had waved his hand and taken off.

I'd just stood there in the parking lot, watching him walk away. I couldn't stop myself from staring at his ass. It was phenomenal. And when I got back to my apartment, I'd undressed and lain in my bed, jacking off while I'd imagined what he looked like naked.

And now I'd had a wet dream.

I sighed and poured myself a cup of coffee. I got the assignment out of my backpack. I didn't need to go over my pledge brothers' information; I'd committed that to memory when they'd introduced themselves in the chapter room. But I needed to know the exec board's, and there was no time like the present, since I couldn't sleep.

But as I went over the information, my mind kept wandering back to my dream, and I kept fantasizing about Chad.

I was falling in love.

Chapter 4

"**O**kay, pledges," Eric Matthews said from somewhere behind me. "Your big brother is standing behind you with your family beer. He is about to put it into your hands. Once he does, you need to finish it as quickly as you can. When you are done, turn it upside down on top of your head. When you are *all* finished, then and only then will I tell you to remove your blindfolds and turn around and meet your big brother. Do you understand?"

"SIR, YES SIR!" we roared back in unison.

"I can't *heeeeeeeeeeeeeeeeeeeeeeeeaaaaaaaaaaaaarrrrrrrrrrrr* you!" he shouted back at us.

We shouted our response again, and I hoped Brother Eric wouldn't make us yell again. My voice was growing hoarse, and my throat was beginning to hurt a little bit. I tried swallowing, but my mouth was completely dry.

The so-called sir sandwich was something we'd gotten used to in the weeks since Rush had ended. It was used when a brother addressed us as a group or as an individual—and only when we were inside the house. The university considered this to be *hazing*, and so it was forbidden when any outsider—including little sisters—were around. I didn't think it was that big of a deal, personally—the idea was to teach us to respect the brothers who'd already gone through and survived the pledging experience. Other requirements were kind of fun. Every time we saw a brother for the first time that day, we had to shake his hand and say, "How's your day going, Brother Eric?" It was another gesture of respect, and it also was helping us learn their names. Every assignment we were given as a class seemed designed to subsume the individual into the pledge group, bonding us together as a unit that eventually would be incorporated into the unit of the brotherhood.

I'd done some research on it—it was the same thing soldiers were required to do, and it had infiltrated the fraternity system after World War II when returning soldiers went to college on the GI Bill.

Pledging had gotten tougher since the halcyon days of Rush, when the brothers had been trying to get us to join. Now that we had pledge pins on our lapels, things had changed a bit—the gloves had come off. It actually wasn't that bad. Some of my pledge brothers complained about it in our meetings up in the house library while the brothers had their own meeting—but it was always the guys struggling to learn their lessons every week. Going up on the hearth after the brothers' meeting and being forced to recite our lessons in front of the whole house in the dim light was a bit unnerving. We weren't allowed to make eye contact with any of the brothers—we weren't even allowed to look at them when we were marched into the Great Room. We had to stand on the ledge around the fireplace, about two feet off the floor. The brotherhood all sat on couches or the floor in complete silence. We had to hold our heads up and look straight ahead at the far wall. The first time we went up there I was absolutely terrified and almost slipped as I stepped up onto the hearth. But when Eric called on me to identify the pledge standing to my left, his hometown, and major, I spoke clearly and my voice didn't shake. I always knew the required lessons, and so Eric rarely called on me anymore. Whenever he did, I was able to recite it clearly without stumbling and was always rewarded with finger snaps of approval from the brothers. I was determined to be the best pledge ever in the history of Beta Kappa—and it didn't hurt that I had an excellent memory and learned quickly. I could say the Greek alphabet backward and forward, I knew the Creed of Beta Kappa, and I could recite without pause the Badge of Beta Kappa.

I was having a great time. My pledge brothers all seemed to like me and had elected me vice president of our class. We'd already had a car wash to raise money for the gift we had to buy the house, and I had a few other fund-raisers planned. My talents for organization definitely were coming in handy. I'd also finished all of my required brother interviews, and my little black book—which had to be signed by all of the brothers after we completed an assignment they gave us individually—was almost completed. I loved being a pledge, I loved everything about Beta Kappa—and even though sometimes being a pledge was a little rocky, I was happy I'd accepted the bid. The vast majority of the brothers were cool.

Finally, I belonged somewhere.

Mom and Dad still weren't completely on board with my joining a fraternity. "If it affects your grades, you're out of there," Dad had warned me just that afternoon on the phone. "I'm not sure this is such a good idea, but your mother and I are going to trust your judgment. You aren't drinking, are you?"

"No," I'd replied. It wasn't strictly true—sometimes at

parties I allowed myself a cup or two of beer from the keg, but that was it. I didn't get a buzz or get drunk. At first, my pledge brothers were a little put off by my not drinking—as were the brothers—but soon they saw the advantage of always having a designated driver around. Seeing the brothers drunk made me wonder why anyone would ever want to get so wasted—some didn't know their limits and kept drinking until they threw up or passed out or both. I couldn't quite grasp how this could be fun. The only time I ever threw up was when I was sick, and I thought it was unpleasant. I also didn't much care for the taste of beer, which was what the brothers usually had available. I also didn't see the appeal of not being able to think clearly, stumbling around, or slurring my words when I spoke.

I was definitely in the minority on that score.

I was just wondering how I was going to get out of drinking the family beer when someone reached around me and put a cold bottle in my hands. Even with the blindfold I could tell it wasn't the normal-sized beer bottle—it was the quart size. My heart sank. I wasn't going to be able to drink it all; I'd fail. Panic gripped me. Maybe I could just spill most of it?

Don't be such a wimp. Just drink the stupid thing. It's not going to kill you, and obviously the point of the evening is to get drunk.

"DRINK!" Eric screamed from behind us, and the room erupted from silence into a cacophony of shouting voices. My heart started pounding. I took a deep breath. *Just do it, Jordy.* Several people were shouting at me, and I could sense how close they were standing to me. I raised the bottle up to my lips and started drinking. The beer foamed and sloshed as I tried to swallow it down, but it was hard. With the bottle tilted up, my mouth would fill with beer and I couldn't swallow it fast enough to keep up with it. Beer poured down the sides of my face, running down my neck and soaking my shirt. I tried to breathe through my nose as I kept drinking, but most of it was winding up *on* me rather than *in* me. The noise didn't let up. The brothers screaming at me kept it up. I heard some cheers from around me as some of my pledge brothers managed to finish their beers. I kept trying to down the damned stuff, and gagged. More beer foamed and spilled down the side of my face. In my ear a voice whispered, "Don't worry about it, Jordy, just turn it upside down on top of your head. Let it spill on you. No one cares."

With a sigh of relief I took the bottle away from my mouth and swallowed another mouthful. My eyes were watering and my nostrils were burning. I gulped in air as I turned the bottle upside down on top of my head. More beer soaked my hair and cascaded down the back of my neck, and I leaned forward against the wall, still trying to get enough air. I felt dizzy, and the beer was churning inside my stomach. A hand patted me on the back. "Nice job, Jordy," someone said. I couldn't place the voice.

Eric blew a whistle and my head was spinning. I felt like I was going to throw up. I fought the urge and kept gulping air.

"Let's have a round of applause for our pledges!" Eric yelled, and the brothers cheered. "Nice job, pledges," Eric went on as the cheer died down. "This is an important night, pledges. You are about to find out who your big brother is. Your big brother is your mentor, your best friend in the brotherhood. He is there to help you, to guide you, to teach you in the ways of the brotherhood. He had a big brother, who had a big brother, who had a big brother, a family that traces all the way back to the original founders of Beta Kappa, links in a chain of brotherhood that join us all together."

I bit my lower lip and dared to hope.

At our last pledge meeting we had to write down the names of three brothers we wanted for our big brothers. I didn't hesitate for a moment before scribbling *Chad York* down as my first choice.

I couldn't stop thinking about him. He was always polite to me—not overly friendly but not cold, either—and I'd enjoyed my interview with him. He was a sophomore from Woodbridge up in the Sierra Nevada Mountains, near Yosemite National Park. He was majoring in advertising and art history, and he hoped to work for a museum when he graduated—preferably one in San Francisco. He had several younger brothers and sisters, had played basketball and run track in high school, and had gone through Rush with several guys he'd gone to high school with. "They all wound up at Sigma Alpha Epsilon," he said with a slight smile, "but SAE was a bunch of homophobic assholes, so I wound up here at Beta Kappa. Best decision I ever made in my life."

I wanted him. And maybe it was the wrong reason to choose a big brother, but I hoped it would bring us together.

The last two choices didn't matter to me, so I wrote in *Roger Devlin* as my second choice and *Eric Matthews* as my third.

Silence descended as I started breathing normally again. I still felt nauseated, but I was excited. This was it. My heart was pounding in my ears.

"Remove your blindfolds, pledges," Eric ordered.

I reached up and pulled the soaked rag off my head, blinking in the light.

"Turn around and face your big brother."

I bit my lower lip to keep a big, stupid grin off my face, and turned around.

Roger stood there, a huge delighted grin on his face. "Hey," he said, taking the empty bottle from me.

Disappointment surged through me. *Chad didn't want me.* I wanted to run out of the room and hide somewhere. *You insensitive asshole, it's not Roger's fault and he's obviously really happy—don't spoil this for him.* I forced a smile on my face. "Cool," I managed to say as my stomach lurched and tried rejecting the beer I'd swallowed. "Thanks for taking me, Roger."

"Why wouldn't I?" Roger pulled me into a big hug. Over his shoulder, I could see Chad hugging Jacob, a huge smile on his face. I forced myself to look away.

Of course he picked the best-looking pledge as his little brother, a horrible voice whispered in my head. *Did you really think you had a chance? He doesn't even know you exist. You're not good enough for him. He'd never want someone like you in a million years—he doesn't even want you as a little brother.*

I squeezed Roger back, blinking my eyes so I wouldn't cry. I took a few deep breaths.

"Are you okay? You look a little green," Roger said, stepping back a bit.

"I think I'm—going—to be *sick.*" I pushed my way past Roger and ran out of the room and down the hallway, all the while trying to keep the frothy, foamy beer down as it fought its way up into my throat. As I ran I was vaguely aware that brothers were following me, chanting something that sounded like *Puke! Puke! Puke!*

I pushed through the saloon doors of the first-floor bathroom and made it into one of the stalls as a stream of foamy beer erupted out of my mouth and my nose. It splashed against the back wall of the stall, and I bent over the toilet as it kept coming up. It didn't seem possible. *I hadn't swallowed that much, had I?* I thought I'd spilled most of it, but somehow more just kept coming up, and every time I thought I was finished my stomach lurched and even more foamy liquid came streaming up. As I heaved, tears running down my face, I could hear the brothers still chanting *Puke! Puke! Puke!* behind me.

Finally, I was finished. I stood there, my hands on my knees, catching my breath as the brothers cheered behind me. I wiped my face and turned to face the brothers. They were grinning at me.

"One pledge down, nine more to go!" someone shouted, and the brothers all ran out of the bathroom—except for Roger.

He smiled ruefully at me. "Don't be embarrassed, Jordy." He shrugged. "You don't drink, so you shouldn't have had to try to chug a quart of beer. But it's tradition." He held up his hands in a "what can you do" gesture that didn't make me feel any better. "But you don't have to drink any more, if that helps. The whole point of the night is to make all the pledges puke—and since you already have . . ." His voice trailed off.

"I'm a shitty pledge," I said. My head was still spinning, and I felt woozy. If this was what being drunk felt like, I was never going to drink again. I tried walking out of the stall but slipped and staggered and grabbed on to Roger to stop from falling.

"Come to my room and I'll give you some sweats to wear, get you out of those wet clothes." Roger smiled at me. "I'm so glad you picked me as your big brother. I couldn't believe it when Eric told me. I thought for sure—" He stopped talking and shook his head. "Never mind, come on."

I followed him out of the bathroom, holding on to the wall for support as we headed down the hallway to his room. Everything seemed tilted, and the floor felt like it was moving.

I didn't choose you. I chose Chad. But he didn't want me.

Tears welled up in my eyes as I followed Roger. He unlocked his door and held it open for me. I wiped the tears away and smiled bravely at him. "I still don't feel so good."

"You're just a little drunk." He smiled. "Fortunately you puked up most of the beer, so you won't get any drunker." He tossed me a towel, and I started rubbing at my head. He started rummaging around in his closet and tossed me a pair of red sweatpants and a CSU-Polk sweatshirt. I took my wet clothes off, folded them, and pulled the sweats on. I sat down in his desk chair.

Why didn't Chad want me? What was wrong with me?

You don't look like Jacob, the insidious voice mocked me again. *Why choose a Honda when you can have a Bentley?*

"Are you okay?" Roger asked again.

I was about to say something about Chad when I looked at him. He was so happy I was his little brother, I knew I could never, ever tell him I'd picked Chad first. I just nodded instead and forced a smile onto my face. "I was worried you might not want me," I said, hating myself for lying.

He laughed. "Are you kidding me? I couldn't believe it when Eric asked me if I wanted to take you. I was so sure I'd never get a little brother. I mean, it's not like I'm the most popular guy in the house. And I got the coolest pledge out of the whole class." He gave me a delighted smile, and I couldn't help noticing how much better he looked. His entire face lit up when he smiled—and it was so much better than the perpetual scowl he usually wore.

My disappointment started fading. So what if the big brother I'd wanted hadn't wanted me? Was it a good idea to pick a big brother I was attracted to in hopes of getting to date him? No, it wasn't—that was a *stupid* reason to pick someone. I remembered what Eric said about the role of a big brother. Roger filled that role far better, and he *had* been my second choice.

It wasn't like I'd been pawned off on someone I hadn't picked.

But I'd been so sure Chad would take me.

You were sure, the voice mocked, *you were hoping, and convinced yourself Chad would take you. Why would he?*

I shook my head.

"I'm hardly the coolest pledge," I said, watching as Roger pulled a box out from under his bed and expertly started rolling a joint.

"Yeah, you are." Roger licked it to seal it before lighting it. "You're not like the others—you're not like the rest of the brothers here, either. You're different."

"I don't want to be different," I said, watching as he inhaled. "I want to be like everyone else."

He laughed. "I meant different in a good way. Jeez, Jordy." He took another hit. "You don't want to be a lemming, do you? Different is good, man, really good. It makes you stand out, makes you get noticed. People who are like everyone else never get anywhere in the world, they just blend in. Who wants to blend in? I sure don't." He shrugged. "Do you know what usually passes for intelligent conversation around here? 'Dude, I fucked the Delta Zeta with the huge tits.' " He shook his head and took another hit. "You, on the other hand, have a brain. You think." He held out the joint to me.

I looked at it dubiously. "I don't know if I should. Marijuana affects your memory and kills brain cells."

Roger grinned. "You see what I mean? No one else around here would even think twice about smoking a joint." He winked at me. "Just this once. For me, okay? To celebrate? Come on, Jordy, live a little. Just this one time won't hurt you."

Never give in to peer pressure, I heard my father say. *Never,*

ever do something to fit in. You're your own person, and you know the difference between right and wrong. And anyone who tries to get you to do something you don't want to do isn't your friend in the first place.

On the other hand, it was just this once. Roger was right—getting stoned once was hardly going to kill me.

I reached over and took the joint from Roger. I looked at the thin line of white smoke curling up from the red ember. "So, what do I do?" I asked.

"Well, you suck on the end, and then hold the smoke in until you can't anymore." Roger grinned. "Just know you're going to cough really hard the first time."

"Wow. That sounds just great." I rolled my eyes. "I can see the appeal." He laughed, and I took a deep breath and raised the joint to my lips. I did as he said, sucking on the end. I wasn't able to hold the smoke for very long. I started coughing almost immediately. My lungs felt like I'd inhaled fire. My eyes were tearing and I couldn't stop coughing. He handed me a bottle of water from the minifridge. I managed to choke out a "thank you" as I twisted the cap off and gulped water down.

I put the bottle down on the desk and wiped at my eyes. "That was *awful*," I said, and was about to add, "I'll never do that again" when a strange mellow feeling began creeping through my brain. Goose pimples rose on my arms, and I could feel every single hair follicle on my body tingling. It was a weird feeling—but at the same time it was nice. The nausea in my stomach was gone—a definite plus—and there was this really pleasant euphoric sensation creeping over me. I started to resist it, but closed my eyes. *Don't fight it, just go with it. That's the whole point of smoking, to feel like this.* I relaxed and went with it.

I couldn't help myself. I started giggling.

Roger took the joint back from me and took another hit. He grinned at me as he stubbed it out in an ashtray. "I think that's enough for you, my young Padawan."

"Padawan?" I made a face. "What does that mean?"

Roger stared at me. "You've never seen any of the *Star Wars* movies?"

"Oh, yes." I nodded and smiled at him. "A Padawan is of course a Jedi Knight in training." I giggled. Why did everything seem so funny? "Of course I've seen the films. They are an integral part of modern American pop culture." I nodded. "My senior year I spent a lot of time watching popular films online. *Titanic, The Matrix*—" My voice trailed off. I couldn't think of the names of any of the other movies I'd watched. I tried to concentrate and summon the titles, but they wouldn't come. "That's weird. I can't think of any of the others." I shrugged. "But the *Star Wars* mythology was a classic rendering of the struggle between fascism and democracy, broken down into a simplistic message of good versus evil for easier absorption by the audience."

Roger threw his head back and laughed. "See what I mean, Jordy? You aren't *like* anyone else! Anyone else would just say they were cool. But not you." He shook his head.

"That's bad, isn't it?"

"No, Jordy, it's *great*. Don't ever change, okay? Don't let them turn you into a Beta Kappa clone." He rubbed his eyes. "I don't know what it was like for you at your Swiss school—"

"St. Bernard."

"—but I can tell it wasn't a good experience for you."

"I *liked* St. Bernard," I insisted. The mellow feeling was actually quite delightful. "I got an excellent education there. I was challenged and stimulated intellectually."

"I'm not talking about your education," he replied. "Did you have friends there? Were you popular?"

"I—" I stopped. I'd never told anyone what it had really been like there. Maybe it was the pot, but I could tell Roger was actually interested—he really wanted to know. "It was awful." My eyes welled up with tears. "I didn't have any friends. The only people who treated me like a human being were the teachers. The other students were terrible. They looked down on me because I was an American. They looked down on me because I wasn't of royal or noble blood. They picked on me. They made fun of me. Then they got bored and just ignored me, which was lonely but it was better. But I showed them all. I was smarter than all of them. I got better grades. The teachers thought I was the best student in the history of the school. I made up my mind I was going to be the best student, that I was going to be the most successful one." I wiped at my face. "Of course they didn't care about my grades."

"Jordy." Roger reached out and took both of my hands in his. "Don't ever let anyone make you feel bad about yourself. You have no idea how special you are. Being different is hard, I know, but don't ever let anyone convince you it's better to change and to be like everyone else. You're smart, funny, and you have a core of natural kindness within you that most people don't have." He scowled. "Most people only pretend to be kind, you know, because they want something from you—and as soon as they get whatever it is they want, they can't be bothered with you anymore. The reason why people don't necessarily open up to you is because you're not like everyone else and they don't know how to handle that. But what it means is you'll never have to deal with all the superficial nonsense. When you make real friends, they'll be *real* friends." He smiled. "I'm your friend, Jordy."

I bit my lip. "Really?" I could feel tears welling up in my eyes. I felt a lot more emotional than usual; it must've been the pot.

"Really." He waved a hand. "I don't fit in here, either. Oh, sure, everyone's nice to me on a basic level because I'm a brother, but I don't have any real friends in the house. Nobody really makes an effort to get to know me. That first night when I saw you at Rush, I knew you were one of the special people. Like me."

"I don't understand." My head felt hollow. It was kind of nice—I could almost hear air rushing through my head. "Why did you join Beta Kappa in the first place? I've wondered about that for a while. You don't seem happy here."

"I'm not unhappy here." He picked up the joint and relit it. "This sure as hell beats living in the dorms. As you know, I'm an anthropology major. I kind of study the group dynamics around here. It's fascinating, to tell you the truth." He grinned. "Take Chad York, for example." His face darkened. "He is the personification of evil."

"Chad?" I was puzzled. "But he's so nice, and he's so good looking."

"Stay away from Chad York," Roger insisted. "You have to trust me on this, Jordy. Listen to your big brother. Chad is not attractive at all."

"Yes, he is," I insisted. "He's even better looking than Jeff Morgan."

"Don't be fooled." Roger took a big hit from the joint. "The outward exterior is just the packaging. Inside, he has a dark and twisted soul."

"May I have another hit?" I asked. Roger laughed a bit and passed me the joint. This time it didn't burn so much, but I did cough again. I passed it back to him. The hollow, empty feeling inside my head was getting stronger. It was nice. "Why do you hate Chad so much, Roger?"

"I hate all three of them—Chad, Brandon, and Rees. Brandon and Rees aren't as bad as Chad—no one is—and maybe if they got away from him they could turn from the dark side. But Chad—" He shook his head. "There's no chance for redemption from him."

"You're wrong." The empty feeling was going away. Now it was like my mind was kicking into overdrive. Thought after thought tumbled through my mind, a new one springing from the previous one. "It's just like *Star Wars*. No matter what anyone's done, no matter how beyond redemption they may seem, they can always change and save themselves. Darth Vader was able to."

"Chad makes Darth Vader look like a pussy," Roger spat out. "Besides, that's a movie. It isn't reality." He peered at me. "You have a crush on him, don't you."

Even stoned, I knew better than to tell the truth. "I just think he's sexy."

"Don't ever go there. Trust me."

"Why? What aren't you telling me?"

"Maybe someday. But not now." Roger crushed the joint out. All that was left was a tiny bit, which he placed inside a jar. "Just listen to your big brother. It's my job to take care of you during your pledge semester. And I will always, *always* watch out for you."

I was touched. I looked at him and felt overwhelmed by emotion. *Roger is my first real friend*, I realized. *He actually cares about me and wants to take care of me.* I bit my lip to stop myself from crying. "Can we get some fresh air?" I asked. I was feeling a little woozy.

"Sure." I followed him out of the room, down the hall,

and out into the parking lot. He led me around to the back-yard, and we sat down at the picnic table. We could hear the shouting and cheering coming from inside the party room. I smiled. It was a beautiful night. There were no clouds, and the sky looked like dark blue velvet. The stars winked at me, and I smiled back up at them—until I heard a loud moan coming from the direction of the house. "What's that?" I got up and walked over to the bushes just outside the downstairs windows. All of the rooms were dark except one, and the curtains were open.

I got closer and caught my breath. It was Chad moaning. He was bent over his bed, naked. My eyes widened. I wanted to look away but couldn't—and looked at the guy behind him. It was Jacob. He was holding onto Chad's hips, driving deep inside him. His own eyes were closed. I stood there, in shock, and wanted the earth to open up and swallow me whole.

My eyes filled with tears.

He'll never want a loser like you. Not when he can have guys like Jacob.

"Stupid Jacob," Roger said bitterly from beside me. I hadn't heard him come up. "He's going to regret that for the rest of his life."

Chapter 5

"Hey," Roger said as he stepped out of his room, "there you are. I haven't seen much of you lately." He frowned. "I'm beginning to think you're avoiding me."

"Oh, I've been around," I replied guiltily. "I haven't been avoiding you." It wasn't completely a lie—I just hadn't been looking for him when I came to the house. I hadn't even given him much thought, honestly, since Big Brother Night.

After seeing Chad getting fucked, I'd gotten sick again. Roger had been great—he led me back to the bathroom and washed my face, got me some more bottled water, apologizing over and over for pressuring me to get high. I finally told him to stop, and we'd gone back to his room. I curled up on the floor with a pillow and a blanket and pretended to fall asleep. He left the room shortly after, and I opened my eyes and stared at the ceiling. Alone, I allowed myself to cry from the bitter disappointment the night had turned into. *Just get over it,* I finally said to myself, wiping my face on the blanket. *You need to just accept the fact that Chad doesn't want you and is never going to want you.* And finally I'd fallen asleep on the hard floor.

When I woke up, it was morning. Roger was in his bed, snoring. I folded the blanket and stood up. I felt like crap. My head hurt and my teeth were all fuzzy. I got a piece of paper out of his desk drawer and wrote him a brief note, thanking him for taking care of me. All I wanted to do was go home and go back to sleep in my own bed. I walked out of his room, closing the door as silently as I could, and walked into the bathroom. I washed my face and used a paper towel to wipe off my teeth. It didn't help much. With a sigh, I pushed my way out through the saloon doors just as a door opened down the hall. For a split second, I debated running down the hall and out through the parking lot door, but my pledge training kicked in. I had to greet the brother, whoever it was, and shake his hand. As I started to turn around I heard Chad say, "Jordy? Is that you?"

I wished I had the ability to teleport. He was the last person I wanted to see—and of all times to run into him! I knew I looked like hell—but on the other hand what difference did it make? He didn't care about me. I was just glad Jacob wasn't with him. I was still in Roger's sweats, and my hair was undoubtedly sticking out in all directions. "Good morning, Brother Chad. How's your day going?" I stuck out my right hand. I forced a completely neutral expression on my face.

Chad walked toward me with a big grin on his face. You'd never know he'd had a late night. Every hair was perfectly in place, he looked rested and refreshed, and he was already dressed in khaki shorts, a pale blue pullover, and penny loafers. "My day is going pretty well so far, thank you for asking," he said as he gave my hand a strong shake. "But you look like you've had a rough night."

You don't know the half of it. "I was about to head home." I tried unsuccessfully to stifle a yawn. "I slept on the floor in Roger's room. And my head really hurts."

"Your first hangover," he replied with a smile that made my knees feel weak. "I was about to go see if anyone wanted to go grab breakfast." He let go of my hand. "What do you say, pledge? Want to go have breakfast with a brother?"

There was nothing I would rather do, but I had fur on my teeth. "I'd really like to, but I need to shower—"

"No problem," Chad replied. "Do you have your car here?"

I nodded.

"You can drive. We can swing by your place first and you can get cleaned up." He shrugged. "I don't mind waiting." He turned me around toward the door. "And I think it's high time we got to know each other better, don't you?" I didn't say anything as we walked through the parking lot to my car. The sun was incredibly bright, and I narrowed my eyes to try to cut down on the glare. Another wave of nausea rolled through my body as I fumbled for my keys and unlocked the car.

Chad whistled. "This is a really nice car."

"Thanks," I replied, sliding behind the wheel and starting it up. I turned the air conditioning up to high, and the cold air felt great against my hot skin.

"You're Roger's little brother, right?" he asked as he buckled his seat belt. "You know we were pledge brothers, right?"

"Yes, last fall," I replied as I put the car into gear and backed out of my spot. "And you're Jacob's big brother?"

"Yes." He frowned a bit as I pulled out onto Shaw Avenue and headed for my apartment. "What do you think of Jacob?"

"He's really nice," I replied, trying to keep my mind on what I was doing. He was sprawled in the seat next to me, his legs spread wide. His left hand was resting on the armrest between the two seats, and my arm kept brushing against his as I drove. I was getting aroused, despite how rotten I felt, and stupid thoughts kept rushing through my mind. *He's coming to your apartment, you're going to shower, maybe he's going to make a move on you, maybe when you're in the shower he'll join you in there, pressing his hard muscular body up against yours under the spray of hot water, and he's going to apologize for taking Jacob instead of you, maybe he took Jacob because—oh, stop it, Jordy, you're living in a fantasy world. He doesn't want you and he is never going to want you. He just didn't want to have breakfast by himself and you just happened to be there.*

"He seems to be," Chad went on. "Not particularly smart—just an observation, not being mean or anything, but he seems like he needs a lot of guidance." He touched my arm. "I'm sure you're wondering why I took Jacob for my little brother instead of you."

"Oh, no need to explain, Chad," I said hurriedly. "I'm fine with Roger. Really. He's a great guy."

"Oh, he is that," Chad replied. He turned and looked out his window. "You see, Jacob—how do I say this? Jacob needs guidance. He's not as smart as you are. I'm sure you've noticed he stumbles over his lessons a lot. When Eric told me both you and Jacob had chosen me, well, my first instinct was to take you." He started drumming his fingers on the armrest. "But then Eric said Jacob had picked me, too—and Roger was your *second* choice."

I shrugged. "Okay."

"I hope you weren't hurt." He patted my arm again. I took a deep breath and willed my hard-on to go away. "But Eric reminded me how introverted Roger is, and this might be the only chance he ever got to have a little brother—and that Jacob needed a big brother like me, to help him out."

He gave a little shrug. "So, what choice did I have? I couldn't deprive Roger, could I?"

Relief flooded through my addled brain, and it was all I could do not to shout with joy. *See?* I said to that nasty little voice in my head. *There WAS a good explanation for him not taking me. I am not a loser. He did want me. Eric talked him out of it!*

Believe that if you need to, the voice sneered back, *if that's what you need to feel better about yourself.*

"It's okay, really," I said as I pulled into the long drive to my apartment complex. "You don't owe me any explanations, Chad. I'm glad it worked out the way it did. Roger's a really great guy."

"This is a nice place." Chad whistled as I swiped my entry card at the gate and it swung open.

"I like it here," I replied, driving through the gate and turning to the right. "It's going to be weird moving into the house after living by myself for a year."

"Living in the house can be a bit of a challenge." Chad laughed. "There are some definite drawbacks—the lack of privacy is one"—I felt myself flush, wondering if he'd seen me and Roger watching him and Jacob—"but the advantages far outweigh the negatives, you know?"

"I'm sure," I said as I pulled into my designated parking place. We got out and headed upstairs. I kind of hoped we'd run into Blair or Jeff—I hadn't seen much of them since Rush Week—but there was no sign of them as I unlocked my apartment door and we walked inside.

Chad whistled again. "Damn, this is gorgeous."

"Help yourself to anything in the fridge and make yourself at home." I tossed my keys on the kitchen counter. "I'll get cleaned up as quick as I can."

"Do you have coffee?" He gave me a sad smile. "I really could use some."

"Of course I have coffee." I smiled at him. I quickly started a pot. "That should be ready in about a minute. I'll hurry."

"Take your time." He plopped down on the couch and picked up the remote from the coffee table.

My heart was pounding as I went into my bedroom and undressed. I'd completely forgotten how tired I was, how much I'd wanted to come home and go back to bed. It might just be a friendly breakfast, but it might also be our first date. I stared at myself in the mirror and groaned. *If this is a first date I've already blown it,* I thought. My eyes were bloodshot, there was crud in the corners of my mouth, and my hair looked like I'd been electrocuted. I started the shower while I brushed my teeth. Then I climbed into the shower and stood under the hot spray, moaning a little as the water washed the sleep and beer off my skin. I started lathering up my body. As I soaped my crotch, an image came to my head of Chad sitting on my couch stark naked. Or of me, walking out of the bathroom with the towel around my waist and finding him lying on my bed, naked. My dick started getting hard, and I kept lathering it. I closed my eyes, and the image of Chad bent over his bed flashed through my mind, only it wasn't Jacob fucking him from behind, it was me, and it wasn't Chad's bed, but it was mine, it was me fucking Chad, driving my cock deep inside of him time after time, and Chad was moaning and pushing back against me, trying to get me as deep inside as he could, and he was saying, *fuck me fuck me fuck me . . .*

And I came, drops of white shooting out of my cock and mingling with the hot shower water.

He's out there waiting for you and you're in here jacking your cock while you think about fucking him. Classy.

I turned the water off and grabbed a towel, cursing myself as I dried off. I hung the towel on the rack and walked into the bedroom, half expecting to see him naked on the bed—

He wasn't there.

I threw on a pair of underwear, grabbed a pair of jean shorts, and slid a CSUP tank top on over my head. I walked back down the hall and grabbed a Coke out of the refrigerator, taking a long swallow. I looked into the living room through the bar window.

Chad was sitting on my couch, paging through an issue of *GQ* Blair had loaned me. "This coffee is really good." He smiled at me, putting the magazine down. "I somehow didn't have you pegged as a *GQ* reader, though."

I nodded. "Blair loaned it to me. He thinks I need to learn how to dress better." I could have bitten my tongue off as soon as the words came out. *Nice move, why don't you make yourself out to be an even bigger dork than he already thinks you are?*

He looked me up and down. "Well, no offense, Jordy, but you could really use some help." He reached out and ruffled my hair. "What happened to that really cute hairstyle you had during Rush?"

He was touching my hair! "Oh." I bit my lip as he pulled his hand back. "Blair helped me with it, but I couldn't figure out how to do it myself, so I stopped trying."

He shook his head, still smiling. "Do you have any product?"

I nodded.

"Then come on, I'll show you," he said, pulling me back down the hall to my bedroom. He pulled my desk chair into the bathroom, plopped me down in it, and showed me how to style my hair. The entire time I was so conscious of how close his body was to me it was all I could do to remember to breathe. I could sense his body heat, and every once in a while he brushed against me. *Was that deliberate? No, someone like him likes guys like Jacob, remember? Not guys like you. Forget about it. He's just being nice.*

"There," he said, stepping back when he was finished. "Now, doesn't that look better? And you saw how easy it was to do. You can do it yourself from now on."

"Yeah." It did look better, a lot better. When Blair had tried to show me, it hadn't made sense to me. But the way Chad explained it, it made sense. It *was* easy. I *could* do it myself. "Yeah, I can. Thanks, Chad."

"Not a problem." He smiled at me. "Now, do you have any other shorts besides those?"

"Shorts?" I looked at myself in the mirror. "What's wrong with these?"

"Darling, they aren't *flattering*." He shook his head. "Don't you want to look your best?"

"Well, yes."

"Then you need to *burn* those shorts." He turned me around. "Now look at your butt in the mirror."

I looked over my shoulder. "Yes?" I wasn't sure what I was supposed to see. My butt looked like it always did.

"Those shorts make your ass look like a billboard," he said. "Don't get me wrong, those shorts are in style—and expensive—but just because something's in style doesn't mean you should wear it. The whole point of clothes is to enhance the way you look, and if something isn't flattering you shouldn't wear it. Even if you are the only person in the world who isn't." He raised the back of my T-shirt. "See? The cut of these shorts makes the rolls around your waist look even bigger—and your ass look shapeless and wide.

That's a major, *major* no-no for a gay man, Jordy." He winked at me. "You're selling your ass, so you want it to look as good as it can. Where do you keep your shorts?"

"They're in the bottom drawer of the dresser," I said absently, staring at my reflection. He was right. My ass looked gigantic, and the way my waist rolled over the waistband was really unappealing. But it had always looked like that. How could anything make it look different? I sighed. I was a dumpy, lumpy guy. I shook my head and walked into the bedroom. He was on his knees in front of my cabinet, the bottom drawer pulled out as he rifled through all my new shorts.

"Here." He pulled out a different pair of jean shorts. He held them up and pursed his lips. "These should do the trick. Put these on," he commanded, "and take those awful shorts you're wearing and throw them out in the trash where they belong. Promise me you'll never wear that cut again."

I hesitated. I didn't want to undress in front of him. I didn't want him to see my erection.

"Don't be shy!" He snapped his fingers. "Come on! Off with those shorts! You heard me! We're wasting time!"

I took a deep breath and pulled the shorts off. He looked away until I had pulled the new pair on. He smiled, then whistled. "That's so much better. Go look at yourself in the mirror."

I went back into the bathroom and looked over my shoulder at the mirror again. He was right. The cut of these shorts gave my ass shape and made it look smaller. I pulled my shirt up, and the roll was still there—but it didn't look nearly as bad as it had in the other shorts.

"I told you so," he said from the bathroom door, before tossing me another shirt. "Try this shirt."

I changed shirts, and almost whistled myself. Once I'd

tucked the shirt into my shorts, my waist looked smaller and my shoulders wider. "Wow." I couldn't get over how much better I looked.

"See?" He grinned. "Your clothes should flatter you and make you look better. They should play up your good points and hide your flaws."

"That's easy for you to say." I couldn't stop staring at myself. "You don't have any flaws to hide. Me, I have to hide almost everything."

He rolled his eyes. "Trust me, I have plenty of flaws. I just know how to hide them, is all." He ran a hand through his hair. "And you're being much too hard on yourself." He stood behind me, looking over my shoulder into the mirror. "You've got lovely skin, and when your hair's styled properly, it looks great. You've got a nice frame—nice broad shoulders, and strong legs." He smacked his own. "I really have to work on mine. I was cursed with my father's chicken legs. And this great big huge ass."

"You have a nice ass," I replied.

"That's very kind of you." He smiled at me in the mirror. "Come on, I'm starving. Let's go get something to eat."

"You're so lucky," he said when we were back in the car and heading out to breakfast. "I can't imagine what it must be like to come from money. I grew up kind of poor." He made a face. "My dad makes good money, but he resents spending every cent, and won't spend one if he can possibly help it."

"Wow," I replied, not sure what to really say.

"My dad's a prick," he said angrily, his face flushing for a moment, "but my mom's great, and so are my brothers and sisters. I'm the first one in my family to go to college. You'd think my dad would be cool with that, but he thinks I think I'm better than everyone else. As if I could be *worse* than him," he said, his voice dripping scorn. "I don't go back there very often. I always stay here on breaks. Polk is my home now." He shook his head, blond hair flying. "And he just hates the gay thing. Are your parents cool with it?"

"I haven't told them yet," I admitted. "I don't know how to bring it up. But I'm sure they'll be okay with it. My dad's assistant Lars is gay, and he's like a member of the family."

"My dad likes to pretend I'm straight." Chad sighed. "He refuses to even talk about it. When I came out to my parents—he just ignored me. He's never acknowledged it."

"I'm sorry," I stammered, not sure what else to say.

"Oh, don't be." He waved his hand. "It doesn't bother me. Turn into this parking lot here. Have you ever eaten here before?" He grinned at me. "It's great."

The Iron Skillet was packed with college students, but a hostess led us to a booth in the back right away. I didn't see anyone I recognized, but Chad waved at a number of guys and girls on our way back to the booth. She left us with menus, then disappeared. Within a moment a harried-looking woman in her late forties placed glasses of water on our table. "Hey, Marge." Chad winked at her. "Rough morning?"

"When you get to my age, Chad, every morning is a rough morning." She shrugged, resigned. "It's a usual Saturday morning. Everyone needing grease to kill their hangovers. You want your usual?"

He nodded, and she turned to me. "Um, what's his usual?" I asked as I looked over the menu. I'd never been much of a breakfast eater. I usually just had coffee and a piece of peanut butter toast.

She sighed. "Egg white mushroom omelet, wheat toast dry, coffee, and orange juice."

"I'll have that, too." I smiled back at her as she took our menus and hurried back to the kitchen to put our orders in.

"You eat healthy?" Chad asked with a slight smile.

"Not really," I admitted, feeling my face start to color. "It just sounded good."

"You should start thinking about what you put into your body," he replied. "You're never too young to start taking care of yourself. My father is a fat pig," he snapped. "I'll never end up like that." He paused as Marge brought our coffee. He thanked her and she walked away with the pot. "I'm serious, Jordy. I mean, you should start thinking about things like that. I mean, you have potential—a lot of potential, and it's a shame you're wasting it."

"Potential?" I took a sip of my coffee. "What do you mean?"

"You have a good face." He scrutinized me. "And a pretty good frame to build on—those wide shoulders and big legs. But you're out of shape. If you dropped a few pounds, ate right, and started working out—and dressing better, why, every guy would want you." He winked at me. "And no offense, but you have a really big dick."

I gaped at him.

He shrugged. "I couldn't help but notice when you were changing. Gay guys always notice." A smile played at his lips. "Seriously, if you started working out and got into shape—a nice-looking guy with a great body and a big dick? You could have anything you wanted, trust me."

"I'm not really into exercise," I admitted. Physical Activities classes at St. Bernard had been one of the banes of my existence there. I wasn't terribly coordinated, and my attempts to be athletic had earned even more scorn from my horrible schoolmates.

He put his hands up. "Okay. Just trying to be helpful."

We talked about a lot over that breakfast. Chad opened up to me about many things, not just his family, but his hopes and dreams for the future. I felt honored. He was confiding in me his own dark secrets. He told me his fears about never finding someone to fall in love with, about growing old alone, not being a success, and winding up like his own father. I listened to him, and the more he talked the more convinced I was that the two of us were meant to be together.

And he *was* interested in me. He listened to my horror stories about St. Bernard, shaking his head at the cruel indignities I'd endured at the hands of my savage classmates. It was nice.

For the first time, I felt like I had a real friend.

And when I dropped him off at the house, he'd invited me to join him on Wednesday night. "Me, Brandon, and Rees go out every Wednesday. It's so much fun, Jordy—you'll love it. It's fifty-cent-drink night at Fusions, this great gay dance club downtown. It's always crowded on Wednesday nights. Hot, hot, HOT guys! It's a blast." He smacked his forehead with the heel of his hand. "We'll have to get you a fake ID."

I walked on air all the way back to my apartment. I had another date with him! Oh, sure, Rees and Brandon were going to be there, too—but he was going to get me a fake ID. He'd invited me and wanted me there. It was beginning.

All of my dreams were going to come true.

I couldn't stop thinking about going to my first gay bar. I wanted to talk to Blair and Jeff about it, but I never ran into them—and even though they always said I could call whenever I wanted to, I didn't want to bother them. They were both so busy, and I could always tell them about it later.

Chad took me shopping Wednesday afternoon to pick out something for me to wear, and that night the bouncer just glanced at my ID and waved me in.

It was only nine, but the place was already crowded with

young gay men. One or two I recognized from around campus, but I couldn't stop staring. There was every type of gay man imaginable in there. I followed the boys to the bar. The bartender was gorgeous, wearing a yellow singlet that hid nothing. "Get Jordy a vodka cranberry," Chad instructed Brandon, who was ordering. I started to protest that I didn't drink, but Chad put his arm around me. I was conscious of how close he was to me. "So, what do you think?"

"It's unreal," I replied as a guy in tight jeans and no shirt walked by, checking Chad out. Chad winked at him.

Brandon pressed my drink into my hand. I sipped it. It wasn't bad.

"Finish that drink," Rees said in my ear. "And we'll go dance."

"Oh, I don't dance," I demurred.

"You don't dance?" Brandon made a face. "What kind of gay man are you?"

"I don't know how."

"It's okay." Chad chugged down the rest of his drink, tossing the plastic cup into the trash. "Just watch us."

I followed them to the edge of the dance floor. Someone was singing about a bad romance, and the dance floor was crowded. The three of them made a semicircle and started dancing. They took their shirts off and tucked them through their belts. I couldn't help but smile. They looked beautiful out there on the dance floor under the flashing lights as they started moving to the music. Chad was the best dancer of the three. The other two moved to the beat but looked a little clumsy. The music seemed to channel through Chad. Every movement he made was in sync to the music, from the hip movements to his steps to how he placed his arms. He tossed his head at the right moment in the music. I stood there, transfixed, unable to take my eyes off him.

He was just so beautiful.

A few drinks later, they managed to drag me out there, but I kept my shirt on. Some woman was wailing about a halo, and I tried to do what Chad did. I tried to sync my body to the lyrics and the music, and lost myself. It was fun. I was a little dizzy from the liquor, and everything seemed lost in time, somehow, as though this was where I'd always been meant to be. In that moment I felt loved and accepted. St. Bernard was my past, and I was never going back there. I had a great friend who was helping me with discovering my potential, and his two friends were nice, and out there on the dance floor I felt at home with all of them in a way I never had before. In that moment I loved everyone on the dance floor, but most of all Chad for showing me this, for sharing this with me.

I thought my heart would explode from joy.

"You're a good dancer," Brandon said in the car on our way back home. "Really, Jordy, you surprised me."

"I told you he'd be a good dancer." Chad reached over in the backseat and squeezed my shoulder. "I'm so proud of you."

Whenever I wasn't in class or doing some pledge duty, I seemed to fall into the habit of hanging around with the three of them. They made me laugh, and they were so nice. I didn't mind helping them with their homework, or with their papers, because it meant the sooner they were done the sooner we could go have some kind of adventure.

Brandon and Rees sometimes picked up guys when we were at Fusions, but Chad never did. I wondered what had happened between him and Jacob—but never had the nerve to ask. Jacob was never around, it seemed, and Chad seemed to like that just fine. I was still sorry he hadn't picked me for his little brother, and I sensed he was, too.

Every so often at a pledge meeting, I thought about asking Jacob—but it wasn't any of my business.

And now, it was Wednesday again—and the reason I was even at the house in the first place was to meet the guys and head out to Fusions. I'd been heading down the first floor hall to the stairs when Roger opened his door.

I don't have time for this. I'm going to be late meeting the guys, I thought—and promptly felt ashamed of myself.

Roger folded his arms and leaned against the doorframe, not saying anything.

"I haven't been avoiding you," I said again. "I've been kind of busy."

"Uh-huh." His face was expressionless.

"Roger, I—"

"Oh, there you are, Jordy!" Chad called from down the hall. Brandon and Rees were with him. They walked toward where we were standing. "Are you ready?"

"You're going somewhere with them?" Roger asked, raising an eyebrow.

"We're just going off to fifty-cent-drink night at Fusions." Chad gave him a brilliant smile, draping an arm around my shoulders. "Jordy loves to dance, don't you, Jordy."

"It's a lot of fun," I admitted. An idea hit me. "Why don't you come with us?"

"Oh, Roger doesn't want to go with us," Chad said before Roger could say anything. "It's not his kind of place, is it, Roger?"

"No, I guess it isn't," Roger said slowly. He looked at me, his face completely blank. "Have fun, Jordy."

The guys were already walking out the house's back door. "Roger, let's do something soon, okay?" I said. I felt bad. "Dinner and a movie, maybe?"

"Come on, Jordy!" Chad called from the parking lot.

Roger looked at me sadly. "No, Jordy, I don't think so."

"Why not?"

"JORDY!"

Roger just shook his head. "Your friends are waiting for you."

"Roger—"

His door shut in my face. I put my hand up to knock when Chad called me again. *Well, if that's the way you want it, Roger, then that's how it's going to be.*

And I walked out the back door to join my friends.

Half an hour later, I was on the dance floor.

I'd completely forgotten about Roger.

Chapter 6

Hell Week was aptly named.

It started on Sunday evening, and the rules were stringent. We lined up at the far end of the parking lot underneath the basketball hoop in nice dress clothes, complete with jacket and tie. Once the brothers led us inside, everything changed. We changed into white T-shirts and jeans—which we had to wear whenever we were in the house, and the only excuse to not be in the house was class or work. They replaced our pledge pins with bricks, which we had to carry with us everywhere. Knowing that Hell Week was modeled on military boot camp did not help in the least. By the end of the first day I was completely exhausted. I'd had a slight inkling that the brothers of Beta Kappa had a sadistic streak, but what surfaced that week was nothing I could have imagined. Gone were the smiling, friendly faces—replaced with reddened faces with their mouths open wide as they yelled at us, spittle sometimes flying into our faces. I learned to dread the sound of a whistle, because it came to mean more torture to be endured. We were required to run everywhere inside the house. We camped out in the Chapter Room with sleeping bags and pillows—on those rare occasions they let us sleep. We weren't allowed to eat or drink, and by the end of Monday my stomach had progressed from hunger to a dull regular ache. The sound of the whistle meant running at full speed into the Great Room and leaning against the wall with our knees bent at a ninety-degree angle until the whistle blew again to let us up. My legs ached, and I could barely think clearly. Several times I thought about just giving up and walking out of the house. But I didn't want to let my pledge brothers down. They were enduring it all with me, and so I gritted my teeth and kept enduring. When they let us head back into the Chapter Room to sleep around three in the morning, I would put my head on my pillow and ask myself, *Is this worth it?* I sat through my classes with my mind asleep and my eyes open. I prayed every day that the torture would end. I found myself fantasizing about food. I promised myself that when it was all over, I was going to treat myself to the best meal I could find in Polk.

And finally on Thursday morning before dawn we cleaned the Chapter Room and snuck out of the house, not leaving a trace behind to show we'd ever been there.

As I drove home, despite being bone-achingly tired and sleepy, I was elated. I'd done it. I'd survived Hell Week.

I walked into my apartment and made myself a peanut butter sandwich. I brought down some ground sirloin from the freezer to the fridge for later. After finishing the sandwich, I staggered down the hall to my bedroom and collapsed on the bed without bothering to undress. I slept for nine hours, not waking up until about three in the afternoon. I was still worn down but felt almost human. I'd slept through all of my classes but didn't care. I started a pot of coffee and got into the shower. As I showered, I wondered what they had in store for us that night. We were to avoid brothers all day—if we saw one we weren't supposed to meet his eyes. We were supposed to be lined up under the basketball hoop at six p.m.; all they told us was we'd be meeting with Beta Kappa's national examiner.

I was on my second cup of coffee when I opened my front door to get the newspaper just as Jeff and Blair walked out their front door.

"Oh!" I started to step back inside, but they stopped me with a laugh.

"Relax, you're not on campus or at the house," Blair said. "We're not going to report you or haze you." He winked at me.

"So you made it through Hell Week." Jeff smiled and shook his head. "Man, I don't think I could go through that again. No offense, but you look *terrible*."

"No worse than you did when you went through it." Blair playfully punched him in the arm. "How was it?"

"Awful," I said with a grin. "But I survived. Hey, I was about to make something to eat. I'm *starving*."

"How much weight did you gain?" Blair asked as they followed me inside. "I gained three pounds during Hell Week."

I walked into the kitchen. "How did you gain weight?" I asked, puzzled. "We weren't allowed to eat."

They exchanged glances. "No one fed you?" Blair said slowly. "I know it's a rule, Jordy, but you can be honest with us. It's over now. You did eat, right?"

"No one fed me." I was confused. "They told us we weren't supposed to eat or drink all week. I've never been so hungry in my life."

"So you turned down food?" Jeff asked. "Really, Jordy, you didn't have to do that."

"No one offered me anything." I shook my head. "What are you guys talking about? You're not making any sense." I turned on the stove and got the thawed pack of ground sirloin out and put it on the counter.

"Seriously, Jordy, you don't have to cover for anyone," Blair insisted. "Did you or did you not get fed this week?"

I started making patties. "No, I'm not covering for anyone. No one fed me." I got a skillet down and placed the patties in it. "Were they supposed to? I'm confused. I thought we weren't supposed to eat."

"I hate to break it to you, but yes," Jeff explained. "It's a rule, yes, but brothers break it all the time. It's all a part of the game. They kidnap you off campus and take you to Carl's Jr. or something. Or they sneak you into their rooms and give you food. You're not *supposed* to go all week without being fed, Jordy—you're just not supposed to get caught."

The burgers began sizzling. I sprinkled salt, pepper, basil, and thyme on them and covered the skillet with a lid. "I don't understand." I shook my head. "My brain is fried, frankly. So you're saying brothers were supposed to feed us this week?"

They nodded in unison. "Hell Week is a game," Blair went on. "There are rules, sure, but the brothers are supposed to help the pledges through the week."

"Your big brother didn't feed you?" A muscle worked in Jeff's jaw. "That's his *goddamned* job. You're not supposed to starve!" He slammed his fist down on the bar. "Christ!"

"I fed Jeff so much during Hell Week he actually *gained* weight." Blair grinned, tousling Jeff's hair playfully. "And like I said, I gained three pounds during mine."

"No, Roger didn't feed me at all." I flipped the burgers and salted that side. "You guys sure you don't want one?" My mind was racing. *Roger was supposed to feed me? To take care of me all week?*

I was starting to feel a little sick. Roger had been distant—friendly and polite but never rude. I'd asked him to do things with me, but he always turned me down with a very polite smile. True, I'd been spending a lot of time with Chad, but it wasn't like I'd been blowing Roger off.

They both nodded. "I thought Roger would make a better big brother than that," Jeff said, taking a swig from his bottle of Coke. He sighed. "I thought he'd make a great big brother."

"Roger hasn't spoken to me in weeks," I said, getting out the hamburger buns and putting two in the toaster. "Well, not really since Big Brother Night." I shrugged. "I try, but he just won't have anything to do with me, and you can only slam your head into a brick wall so many times."

"That's weird," Blair commented. "Did something happen on Big Brother Night?"

I shrugged as I started slicing an onion. My eyes started watering. "I thought we were friends, but he really hates Chad York." I cut the onion into thick slices. "And when I started hanging out with him—"

"Stop!" Blair interrupted me. He looked at Jeff. "I guess we should have been paying more attention. You've been hanging out with Chad?"

I nodded, getting out the jar of pickle slices. I flipped the burgers again, placing slices of cheese on them. "Yeah, right after Big Brother Night. I ran into Chad when I was leaving the house and we wound up going to the Iron Skillet for breakfast. We started hanging out. He's really nice. He's been taking me to Fusions." I started spreading ketchup on the buns. My stomach growled. "But I guess Roger doesn't want to be friends with me if I'm friends with Chad." I rolled my eyes. It sounded kind of juvenile.

"But your buddy Chad didn't feed you, either, did he?" Jeff asked angrily.

"Well, no," I admitted. I'd hardly seen Chad all week. "Some friend."

"Look, guys, what's going on here?" I asked crossly. My stomach growled again. "My brain is kind of fried right now, so you're going to have to be a little less obtuse." I took a bite out of my burger and moaned in pleasure.

It was the best cheeseburger I'd ever had.

"This is our fault." Blair sighed. "We should have been more honest with you."

"But in our defense, it's not really cool to talk bad about brothers to pledges." Jeff shrugged. "That whole brotherhood thing?" He shook his head. "The rules really suck sometimes. But, Jordy, you really need to stay away from Chad York. He's not what you think."

"You sound like Roger," I said stiffly, taking another bite of the cheeseburger. Juice dribbled down my chin. "What is the deal, anyway? Why are you guys so down on Chad?"

"Did Roger ever tell you why he doesn't like Chad?" Jeff asked. "You know Roger is my little brother, don't you?"

"Yes, I knew that." I rolled my eyes. "It's one of the questions on the interviews we have to do. What difference does that make?"

"Because Roger doesn't speak to me, either," Jeff replied. "When I was his big brother, I blew it. I wasn't there for him during Hell Week, or really any time he needed me." Jeff rubbed his eyes. "I'm not proud of it, Jordy. But that semester was when Blair was doing an internship in London, and I wasn't really paying attention to what was going on."

"You fed him at least," Blair pointed out.

"That isn't the point," Jeff replied. "The point is, Chad was horrible to Roger that entire semester, and I didn't do anything."

"What are you talking about?" I started wolfing down my

second burger. My stomach was growling for more food. "You're not making any sense."

"Chad's a horrible person," Jeff said venomously. "If I'd known what was going on, I would have blackballed him. He doesn't deserve to be a brother. Brothers don't treat brothers the way he treated Roger."

"What did he do that was so awful?" I finished the second burger and sighed in relief.

"This is going to sound mean," Jeff replied. "But I can't tell this story without sounding mean. Roger, if you hadn't noticed, isn't exactly the best-looking guy."

"So? Neither am I." I turned on the hot water spigot and started placing the dirty dishes in the sink. "What does that have to do with anything?"

"Chad, on the other hand, is really good looking," Jeff went on.

"If you like that type," Blair snapped. "I personally don't."

Jeff smiled at him. "Never mind, Blair. Do you think Chad is good looking?"

I nodded. "I think he's perfect."

They exchanged another glance. "Roger was attracted to Chad. The way I figure it, Chad liked the attention—"

"He's an attention whore," Blair interrupted.

"And so Chad really led Roger on. He pretended like he was trying to help Roger—you know, helping pick out his clothes, helping him with his hair—"

My hand flew to my hair.

"—and letting him hang out with Chad and his buddies Brandon and Rees. Brandon and Rees aren't bad guys really—"

"Just stupid," Blair snapped. "Incredibly stupid."

"—and they used to take him to Fusions on Wednesday nights—"

My God, Fusions. They used to take Roger to Fusions?

I remembered Chad saying teasingly to Roger, *"Fusions isn't Roger's kind of place, is it, Roger?"*

"—and then, after they were initiated, after leading him on for months, Chad told Roger he wasn't interested in him that way, and because of Roger's feelings for him, it was probably for the best they not be friends or hang out anymore. He cut Roger off at the knees. He told him on Initiation Night, which should have been a really happy night for Roger. Instead, Roger was devastated." Jeff's face set angrily. "I spent the whole goddamned night picking up the pieces. And the next day I confronted Chad. He just laughed in my face." Jeff's voice shook. "I should have punched him in the face, is what I should have done. Brothers don't treat brothers that way."

"Okay." I bit my lip. "So Chad was mean to Roger." Even as I said the words, I thought, *But you only have Roger's word for it. You don't know what happened, and you never asked Chad for his side of the story.* "I don't see what this has to do with me."

"It has *everything* to do with you," Blair went on. He reached over and grabbed one of my hands. "I know I haven't been around much, or had time to do anything other than say hi in passing, but I've noticed you've been dressing better. Has Chad been helping you pick out clothes?"

"Yes, he has." I nodded, sticking out my lower lip. "So? So what if he has? Is it so hard for you to believe he's just being nice? Because he cares about me?"

He kept on, ignoring what I'd just said. "And your hair, too, right? He helped you with your hair, didn't he?"

"Yes. He taught me how to do my hair. But it's not the

same thing." I felt nauseated. *They're wrong, they have to be wrong. Chad loves me.* "I agree there are similarities, but—"

"Has Chad ever kissed you, or touched you in any way that could be construed as a pass?" It was Jeff's turn now. He folded his arms. "Has there been anything other than a friendly hug, or a peck on the cheek?"

"We've never kissed, and he's hugged me a few times, yes. But—"

"It's the same thing all over again." Jeff shook his head. "It's exactly the same." He leaned forward. "Please, *please*, Jordy, tell me you aren't in love with him. Please."

I looked from one to the other. I didn't want to have this conversation with them. It was obvious they weren't going to believe anything I said and were all too willing to believe the absolute worst about Chad. I was on the verge of tears. "I know it might be hard for the two of you"—I said, my voice shaking—"to imagine that someone like Chad might actually be interested in me, but—"

"No, that's not what we're saying," Blair soothed. He got off the bar stool and came around into the kitchen. "What we're saying is that Chad plays these kinds of games with people. He hurts people on purpose, Jordy. He's going to hurt you, and we care too much about you to let that happen." He tried to put his arms around me, but I pushed him away.

"Of course you're good enough for Chad," Jeff insisted. "You're *too* good for him. He's not good enough for you. You deserve better than him. Listen to us, Jordy, please."

"I think it might be best if you left," I said, trying to keep my voice from shaking.

"Jordy—"

"Please." I turned my back on them.

I heard the door close behind them.

I wandered back into my bedroom and looked at the clock. I had to be at the house in two hours.

I grabbed my cell phone and started to call Chad.

Contact with brothers was forbidden before tonight.

Why would they lie to me? Why would they tell me all that stuff if it weren't true?

Why hadn't anyone fed me? All week?

It was St. Bernard all over again.

No one likes me. No one cares about me. No one wants me to be a Beta Kappa. My big brother hates me, and Chad—

No, I wouldn't believe that.

Chad did care about me.

Chad *loved* me.

But he's never really touched you, has he, other than a sexless hug or kiss on the cheek?

I started shaking. I sat down on the bed.

They know him better than you do. There's no reason for them to lie to you. Jeff and Blair have been nothing but kind to you since the day you met them. If they'd known about you and Chad, they would have said all of this to you long before today. And you've blown off Roger how many times? For Chad? You chose Chad over your big brother—and if what they said was true, can you blame Roger for not wanting to be your friend?

"It's not true," I whispered, willing myself to believe. "Chad really does care about me. He knows I'm a virgin. He knows I don't have a lot of experience. He just doesn't want to rush me into something I'm not ready for."

How many times had someone really hot hit on Chad at Fusions, only to be turned down? How many times had Chad just shook his head and said, "No, thank you, I'm here with Jordy" as he slipped his arm around my shoulders?

That had to mean something. It had to.

By the time I was standing in the parking lot lined up with my pledge brothers I was a complete emotional wreck. I couldn't even think about what might be in store for us as Eric Matthews walked across the parking lot to greet us at precisely six p.m. Once we were inside and they ordered us to change back into our Hell Week clothes, screaming and yelling at us as we fumbled out of our dress clothes and put on the filthy, nasty clothes we'd worn every moment we'd been in the house all week, I was disconnected. Chad wasn't in the crowd of brothers screaming at us. Chad wasn't there as they blindfolded us and the final, most horrible night of our pledge semester began.

The night seemed endless. The blindfolds never came off, as we were led around the house and screamed at almost constantly. At some point I just went numb. I just didn't care anymore. I spent most of the night sitting on the floor while weird music that sounded like whales fucking blared in my ears. And my interview with the national examiner, who would make the final decision as to whether I would be a Beta Kappa or not, was horrible. He called me names. He asked me if I thought I could buy my way into the brotherhood because I was rich. He called me lazy, stupid, and mean. He accused me of blowing off my big brother.

My God, everyone in the house has noticed.

"Get this spoiled brat out of my sight!" He spat the words at me, and someone helped me to my feet and took me out of the room. I was returned to the room with the loud music and seated on the floor.

It was all I could do not to cry.

On and on the night dragged.

And then, someone was whispering in my ear. "Stand up and come with me." I didn't recognize the voice. I just wanted to get away from the horrible room I was in with the horrendous loud noise that sounded like a cross between whale song and the screaming of an animal being slaughtered. I heard a door shut behind me, and I sensed I was in a room full of people.

"Take off your blindfold."

I did. I was in the Chapter Room, facing a room full of the brothers. Roger stood directly in front of me. "I'm so sorry, Jordy. We tried everything. But the national examiner just doesn't think you're Beta Kappa material."

I couldn't look him or any of the others in the face. I looked down at the floor.

"But we like you, Jordy." Roger's voice shook. "We think you are Beta Kappa material. We want you to come back and pledge again next semester. Will you do it?"

I looked up into Roger's face. I looked around the room at the faces of the other brothers. They all looked sad.

I wanted to scream *no* and walk out of the house for good.

But I looked at Roger. There were tears in his eyes. And I thought about how shitty I'd been to him, how I'd blown him off over and over again to hang out with Chad, and how he didn't deserve that. Not after everything Chad had already put him through. And I knew the national examiner was right.

I didn't deserve to be a Beta Kappa yet. And I would do it all over again—only this time, I would do it right.

"Yes," I said, my eyes filling with tears.

Roger threw his arms around me as the entire room cheered. "Congratulations, you passed the final test," Roger whispered in my ear.

I was too dumbfounded, too shocked, to say anything as Roger pulled me through the crowd of brothers who were slapping me on the back, saying congratulations, and grinning. When we reached the door to the storeroom in the back, Roger whispered, "Get back in there and be quiet. We have a few more pledges to get through." He opened the door and I walked through.

Jacob was standing there, his face streaked with tears. He was holding a bottle of champagne, and handed me one. He was about halfway done with his bottle. "Dude, we made it!" He grinned, weaving a little bit.

I popped the cork on mine and took a swallow. We were alone. I steeled my courage. It was now or never. "Jacob, what happened with you and your big brother?"

"Chad?" He made a face and took another drink. His face darkened. "We're not supposed to say bad things about brothers."

"It's just me," I whispered. By the sudden increase in volume of that horrible music, I knew they'd just brought in another one of my pledge brothers. "I won't say anything, Jacob, I promise."

"He only picked me to be his little brother because he wanted me to fuck him," Jacob whispered back, winking at me. "I thought he wanted me to be his boyfriend, but all he wanted was to get fucked." He shrugged. "Whatever. He has a nice, tight ass, so I'll fuck him whenever he wants me to."

My heart sank. "I saw you two through his window on Big Brother Night."

Jacob hiccuped. "I shouldn't have done it anymore after that night." He swayed again, and I grabbed him before he could topple over. "I want a boyfriend. I want to be in love." He winked at me. "But he's a good fuck, and he was a brother so I couldn't say no." He giggled. "The last time was last night. He took me to his room and he fed me, and I fucked him. But that's the last time 'cuz now I'm a brother."

A loud cheer from the Chapter Room let me know another pledge had passed the final test, and before I knew it Phil Shea had joined us. I gave him a hug, but my mind was elsewhere.

All along Chad had been getting fucked by Jacob. And he FED him *during Hell Week.*

My mind was reeling. I alternated between anger and pain, hurt and rage, even as I put on a good face for each of my pledge brothers as they passed the final test. I knew I should be more excited about finally making it into the brotherhood, but all I could think about was Chad.

What game had he been playing with me?

And even as the brothers led us out to the parking lot to burn those nasty T-shirts, I couldn't help but look for Chad. I was drunk, half of my bottle of champagne downed in toasts with my brothers in the storage closet. We sang the alma mater as our shirts burned, as brothers hugged us and congratulated us, called us "Brother" for the first time. I kept looking for Chad, but there was no sign of him anywhere.

And as the fire flickered out and the party moved back inside the house, I saw the light in his room was on.

I left the others and went to his room.

I knocked on his door. "Come in," he said from inside. When I opened the door, he smiled. "Hi, Jordy. Welcome to the brotherhood."

"Thanks." I took another swig from the champagne bottle. "Why weren't you there?"

"After Jacob passed the test, I came back to my room." He shrugged. "I did my part and was bored."

"It would have meant a lot to me to have you there."

"How sweet." Chad shrugged. "But your big brother was

there, wasn't he?" When I nodded, he added, "I'm actually kind of glad you came by. We need to talk."

"Really?" I swallowed, keeping my face neutral. I heard Jeff saying in my head, *"He told him on Initiation Night."*

"I'm afraid you may have gotten the wrong impression." Chad gave me a phony-looking smile. I'd seen it before, when someone Chad thought was gross hit on him at Fusions. "And I wanted to clear things up. I mean, I might be wrong."

"Well, that's good, right?" I replied. I was amazed at how level my voice sounded, because my heart was pounding. "It's always better to clear things up, make sure we're on the same page. What might you be wrong about?"

"About us, Jordy." Chad sat down on his desk chair. "I hope you haven't gotten the impression that we're dating or anything, or that we could ever be more than friends."

"And why is that?" I heard myself saying. My heart was pounding so loud I was surprised he couldn't hear it.

"Well, you know, you're funny and sweet and a lot of fun to be around, but you just aren't my type, if you know what I mean."

It felt like my soul was being pierced and shattering into a million pieces. My mind split. There was a part of it that was screaming in agony, in pain, but somehow the loud beating of my heart was drowning out the screams, shoving them behind a door in the back of my mind. Another part of me floated free, disconnected from my body, and floated up to the ceiling where I could watch and listen to what was going on.

"No, Chad, I don't know what you mean." My smile was frozen in place. "Could you be a little more clear?"

He sighed. "Oh, Jordy, why do you make me say this?" He shrugged. "I like guys who are in shape, have muscles—you know, who take care of themselves. Not like you."

Each sentence was another punch in the jaw. I was being pummeled, thrown back into the ring corner and being worked over mercilessly. I heard myself laugh as I struggled to keep control of myself. No one at St. Bernard had ever seen me cry, no matter how cruel they'd been.

But their cruelty had never hurt this much.

He was not going to see me cry. He was never going to know how much this hurt.

"Well, I didn't think that, Chad, so you don't have anything to worry about," I heard myself say. "I can't think why you had that impression in the first place." I watched his face as it relaxed into relief.

I wanted to punch him in the face. I wanted to kick him in the balls and stomp on him as he writhed on the floor in agony.

"Well, I wasn't sure, so I wanted to be clear." He mock-wiped his forehead. "Whew. I'm so sorry, Jordy. I didn't want to seem mean or anything. I'm glad I was wrong, and now we've got that awkwardness out of the way. I really am glad we're friends, Jordy."

And I want to see you die in excruciating pain.

"Me too." I forced a smile on my face. "You have no idea how happy I am we're friends." I had to get out of there. I was close to losing it completely, and he was never going to see me cry. As long as there was breath in my body, Chad York would never see me cry. "Well, I'm—I'm going back to the party."

"I'll be there in a sec." He gave me a hug, a weird one where he leaned forward and barely touched me. He gave me a cool peck on the cheek and patted me on the back again.

Somehow I walked out of the room and shut the door behind me before my breath started coming in gasps. I could-
n't catch my breath, and my eyes began watering as I held
on to the wall for support. I had to get out of there. I wanted
to get to my car and just drive. I wanted to get as far away
from Polk as I possibly could. I wanted to forget I'd ever
come here, that this whole thing had been a huge mistake—

"Jordy?"

It was Roger.

"Leave me alone, Roger," I said, my voice shaking as I
struggled to control the sobs. I would not cry in front of
him. "I want to go home."

"You're in no condition to drive," he replied. "Come on
into my room and tell me what's wrong." He peered at me
in the dim light of the hallway. "It's Chad, isn't it?"

I nodded, and he put his arm around me, leading me
down the hall to his room. He unlocked the door and
pushed me inside. He shut the door behind us and I sat
down on the bed. I started sobbing, and the story came
pouring out of me. "I am *repulsive* to him. I am fat and ugly
and gross." I wiped at my face. "I don't know what I was
thinking. I must have been crazy to think someone like him
would want me."

"There's nothing wrong with you, Jordy," Roger said
softly as he rolled a joint. "You have to get that out of your
head. Chad's the one with the problem."

"No, he was right." I forced a weak smile on my face.
"Look at me. Who in their right mind would want me?"

"You need to stop beating yourself up about this." He lit
the joint. "Trust me, I know."

"And I've been so shitty to you." I buried my face in my

hands. "I wish I was dead." I waved the joint away. "How could I have been so stupid?"

"I tried to warn you," he said simply. "But I've never wished I'd been wrong more in my life."

His words, his kindness, made me cry even harder. "He needs to pay for treating people like this," I blubbered. "He can't get away with this."

"Forget about him," Roger said, sitting down next to me and putting his arm around me. "You're worth a hundred of him."

I put my head down on his shoulder. "He needs to pay."

Roger kissed me.

I kissed him back.

He pushed me gently back down on the bed and unbuttoned my shirt. He started kissing my chest, my stomach, and then undid my pants. I put my hands behind my head.

Stop him, don't let him do this, you aren't interested in him.

But I didn't stop him, because it felt good. He put his mouth on my cock, and I closed my eyes. His mouth felt incredible on my cock. He started swirling his tongue around the head, and I started moaning. But even through the pleasure, no matter how good it felt as he sucked my cock, I couldn't get Chad's face out of my head.

You need to make him pay for this humiliation.

And as I came, my entire body going rigid with the incredible feeling of my first orgasm induced by someone else, the answer came to me.

Yes, I would make Chad pay. If the only thing wrong with me was my body, well, I could *fix* that. This ugly duckling would turn himself into a swan. And I would make Chad want me.

And as Roger fell asleep in my arms, a smile crossed my face.

No one will ever make me feel like this again. Ever. And I'll make Chad want me. I'll work on my body and make myself physically beautiful. And when he wants me, finally, I'll have my chance.

I would make him pay.

Interregnum

"So, the very next day I went to work." Jordy smiled a little sadly. "I was very determined. Once I make up my mind, there's no stopping me."

"So, you're telling me you weren't attractive," Palladino replied dubiously. "No offense, but I find that a little hard to believe." As soon as the words came out, he regretted them. *Slow down there, cowboy, you're letting the fact he's good looking affect your professional judgment.* But they were true. Sitting there looking at the handsome young man, it wasn't possible to believe he had ever been unattractive. The face was so handsome, for example. You don't change your face through diet and exercise.

Without saying another word, Jordy got out of his chair and walked over to the scroll-top writing desk pushed up against a far wall. He started rummaging around in the top drawer, moving aside papers and envelopes and a roll of stamps. Palladino couldn't stop staring at his ass inside the tight shorts. The shirt had crept up again, exposing the two dimples just above the curve. It was an exceptional ass, and Palladino considered himself to be a connoisseur of the male ass. He pictured what it must look like naked. He imagined it was white and smooth, the untanned skin contrasting with the deeply tanned torso and legs above and below.

I knew I was gay when I saw an amazing ass, he remembered.

It was in high school, at Polk West. He'd been a freshman and gone out for the freshman football team. He hadn't wanted to, but his father had played football in high school and so had his older brothers. There wasn't any real pressure put on him, it was just expected. And on the first day of practice, bruised and exhausted, he'd stripped down to shower. He'd carried his towel over his shoulder, and when he reached the communal shower area he'd stopped dead in his tracks. Right in front of him, another player was standing with his head under the stream of water coming out of the showerhead. His broad tanned back rippled with muscle, and it tapered down to the biggest, hardest, roundest ass he'd ever seen. He just stood there for a moment, gawking at it, before someone flicked him with a towel and startled him out of his frozen state. He got under his own shower but kept stealing glances over at Jim Delevan's extraordinary ass. He wondered what it would feel like to put his dick in there, or what it would taste like. And later that night, at home, he jacked off remembering Jim Delevan's magnificent ass, with the hot water cascading down over it.

For the next four years, his crush on Jim Delevan never abated. He took every opportunity he had to stare at Jim's naked body in the locker room. Whenever he ran into Jim in the halls, he couldn't help but watch that mighty ass encased in jeans. He never had the nerve to talk to Jim, but he fantasized about him every night before he went to sleep, using Vaseline on his cock as he stroked himself and dreamed about what it would be like to be Jim's boyfriend.

Jim got a football scholarship to San Diego State, and Joe never saw him again.

But this kid's ass rivaled Jim's, and that was saying something.

Jordy found what he was looking for and shut the drawer, standing up and walking back across the room. "Here," he said, holding out a photograph. "This is what I used to look like."

Startled out of his reverie, Palladino took the picture and stared at it. "This is you?"

"From a car wash we did as pledges to raise money to buy the class gift." Jordy stood there, his arms crossed and his legs spread, his left eyebrow slightly raised as he waited for Joe to look at the picture and agree with him.

Palladino struggled to keep from smiling as he looked at the picture. Granted, Jordy now had an absolutely amazing body, but he was hardly the fat, unattractive loser he'd been describing. "Jordy, there was nothing wrong with you." He looked up and met his eyes.

Joe wasn't lying. The picture was actually quite adorable. Jordy was soaking wet, because someone out of the picture had trained a hose on him. The water glistened as it soaked him. He was wearing a white T-shirt that clung to his body, and his soaked jeans shorts were sliding off his hips. Sure, he wasn't in as good physical condition then as he was now, but he wasn't disgusting to look at.

"Are you *blind?*" Jordy's eyes widened, his lip curled in scorn. "Look at those spaghetti thin arms! Can't you see the belly and the saggy boobs?" He shook his head, curls bouncing. "It was no wonder no one wanted me then."

"What I see is a really cute young man," Palladino said, putting the picture down on the coffee table, "who had absolutely no reason to be down on himself."

"That's nice of you to say," Jordy replied. "But it isn't true."

Joe shrugged. "Just because you don't see it doesn't mean it isn't there for others to see." He smiled to himself. Someone had told him that once, a long time ago, back when he was Jordy's age. "We are all our own worst critics, Jordy. Sometimes we need to give ourselves a bit of a break, you know?"

Jordy's mouth opened, but no sound came out. After a moment, he said, "Well, that's very sweet of you to say, Detective, but I wouldn't have wanted me, either. I can't blame Chad for not wanting me—but I did then." His smile was brittle. "Besides, if you don't find yourself attractive, how can anyone else?" He shrugged. "And I was used to people looking right through me whenever I went to Fusions. I'm not making that up, Detective." He shook his head again. "There was this one guy—I really thought he was cute. Chad introduced me to him three times. I was so repulsive he forgot about me every time. Each Wednesday it was like meeting him for the first time. You know how soul-destroying that is? And if I wasn't with Chad, the guy wouldn't even say hello." He made a face. "And Chad found me repulsive. He'd told me so. It was the only reason we couldn't be together. So, I needed to change. I made up my mind." His face tightened. "No one was ever going to make me feel like that again, Detective. No one was ever going to make me feel like a worthless loser ever again."

Joe stared at the pretty young man. *It's what's inside that matters*, was what he wanted to say, but he didn't. It might be true, but it wasn't always. Hadn't he himself complained regularly about the shallowness of the gay community, how muscles and bodies and handsome faces were the only currency that mattered, while personality and intelligence ran a far second? Didn't he go to the gym himself regularly, to keep his own body fit and trim? It would be hypocritical to argue about the value of inner beauty with this kid. It wasn't his inner beauty that had drawn Sean to him, after all. Sean thought he was a hot daddy. But deep pockets had proven more desirable to Sean than a hot body.

"This was all, what, six months ago?" Joe glanced down at the picture again. The boy in the picture was adorable, with his big smile and water dripping off of him. But the physical transformation was extraordinary. Sure, his face wasn't quite as fleshed out as it had been—there were no dimples in that face, or visible cheekbones, but it was quite obviously the same person. The warm eyes, the shape of the jaw, and the full lips hadn't changed. "That's pretty amazing." The arms in the picture were not "spaghetti arms" by any stretch of the imagination, but they weren't tanned or developed, either. He glanced back at Jordy.

"Thank you." Jordy inclined his head slightly. "But like I said, the morning after Hell Night I went to work. I came back here and cleaned myself up, and I took a good, long look at myself in a full-length mirror. Naked. Clothes can hide flaws, but nudity is the great equalizer." He laughed. "I took notes on all of my physical flaws and started doing research. I joined a gym and hired a trainer. Two hours a day, five days a week. I hired a nutritionist, and she designed a bodybuilding diet for me, designed to build muscle and burn fat. And I kept doing research—supplements, workout programs." He smiled faintly. "When I put my mind to something, I can become a bit obsessed. I wanted to know about the latest developments in muscle-building technology, whether it was exercise programs or supplements. I read everything I could, and of course my trainer was the best that money could buy here in Polk." He laughed. "While everyone else was studying for finals I was working on myself. Finals were just a slight distraction for me."

"You didn't have to study?"

"Of course not." He gave Joe a strange look. "I had so many points in some of my classes I didn't even need to take the final to get an A. I knew my coursework inside and out. I just reviewed everything an hour or so before the tests, and I knew I could ace them. And I did. I made the dean's list that semester—and I will again this semester." He shrugged. "This isn't a hard school, Detective. Anyway, I also had the five-week Christmas break to get myself into shape. So I had almost two full months before the next semester started to transform myself into a new person."

"You didn't go home for Christmas?" Joe knew he was letting the interview get off track and was glad his partner wasn't with him. Grace Rivera was a great partner, and the two of them got along well. Grace was a "just the facts" kind of detective, though, while Joe veered more along the "let the subject talk" school. Joe theorized it was a better methodology—you got a lot more insight about people by letting them talk, letting their prejudices and weaknesses come out in conversation. That way you could get a better sense of how trustworthy they were. And Jordy's story was captivating him. *It's not just because he's beautiful,* he told himself again as he waited for Jordy to answer. *This is a deeply damaged young man.*

"My parents wanted me to join them in Africa, but I told them I wanted to stay here and get a jump on next semester." Jordy shrugged. "It's not like we ever had a traditional Christmas with lights and a tree and all that, anyway. Mom and Dad are always somewhere exotic. They were bummed, but they were cool with it. I knew they would be, and I didn't mind being alone at Christmas."

"Really?" Joe couldn't imagine not spending Christmas with his family. He also couldn't imagine his parents being okay with him skipping out on the holidays, for that matter.

"There were times when I was at St. Bernard when I couldn't get to where they were. It's not a big deal. It's just another day, really. But two weeks in Africa would have fucked up my schedule, and I couldn't afford to lose that time. My life became highly regimented. Up every morning at six, eat breakfast, head to the gym for two hours with my trainer, then another hour of cardio, and then a post-workout snack, high in protein. I stuck to my eating program—five small meals a day, low in fat and carbs, high in protein. And what was really strange was that after that first week—which was hell, I might add, I've never been so exhausted in my life—I started loving working out." He got a faraway look in his eyes. "My off days from the gym—I felt like I wasn't myself on those days. I also started getting a weekly massage to keep my muscles loose and ready for more work. Even now, it's my favorite part of the day, you know. I love going into the gym, putting on the head-phones, just going deep inside myself and pushing myself really hard. You work out, don't you?"

"Yes." Joe nodded. He knew exactly what Jordy was talking about. He cleared his throat. "And where was Chad during all this?"

"Chad went home for the break. Most of the brothers were gone, and I didn't go anywhere near the house. I wanted my return to the house to be dramatic. I wanted to walk in and have everyone's jaw drop. And after a couple of weeks I started to see changes. My pants were getting looser. I was starting to see bigger muscles, more definition, even my abs were starting to show—and that convinced me to work even harder, to stay focused. Chad was going to see me and he was going to want me. But I couldn't wait." He cracked a smile. "I wanted to see how people—gay guys—would react to the new me. So, I decided to give my body a test run."

"What did you do?" Joe asked, but he suspected he knew the answer.

"I went to Fusions on New Year's Eve, to see how people would react to me." He smiled again. "I bought a new outfit. Boy, was I nervous! I had my hair styled and had the highlights put in." He ran a finger through his curls. "I'd gotten contact lenses, too." He inhaled deeply. "And so, the new Jordy strolled into Fusions that night."

"And?"

"It was like I owned the place." Jordy's eyes softened as he remembered. "I walked into the bar and couldn't believe it. Hot guys who'd looked right through me all the other times I'd been there were checking me out. It was crowded. I walked up to the bar. Usually Chad got drinks for us because it took forever for the bartender to wait on me. As soon as I stood at the bar, the bartender was right there. I couldn't believe it. He actually *flirted* with me. And while he was making my drink, another hot guy came up to me and started hitting on me. It was *incredible,* and I knew I was doing the right thing, had made the right decision. The whole night was amazing. That first drink was the only one I paid for all night long. I went out on the dance floor and took off my shirt. Guys kept checking me out, touching me, kissing me, dancing with me. I had *power* for the first time in my life, and it was awesome." He shook his head. "I got picked up for the first time. I think his name was Matt, I don't remember. But he was gorgeous, and we went back to his place. All he could do was tell me how beautiful I was. I fucked him senseless. He had a great ass." Jordy shot a glance at Joe. "I'm sorry, does that bother you?"

Joe shook his own head. "Doesn't bother me in the least," he replied in a monotone.

"It was awesome." Jordy's face lit up with a smile. "I mean, being with Roger was okay, but sex with a hot guy? It was like every fantasy I'd ever had came true. Matt had no body fat." His eyes got a distant look as he remembered. "His abs looked like they'd been carved from stone. His arms were huge. And that ass . . . my God, he did like getting fucked, and I loved fucking him. I was worried, you know, that I wouldn't be any good at sex, but turns out I was a natural." He winked. "And I discovered I really enjoyed sucking cock."

Joe swallowed, trying to keep his own face expressionless, trying not to imagine what it would be like to have this hot young man on his knees worshipping Joe's cock. *I need to get laid,* he told himself. *I'm horny and it's been too long. That's why this kid is having this effect on me.*

"I liked it a lot," Jordy went on. "I couldn't get enough of it. I went back out the next night and went home with someone else. I discovered how easy it was to find someone to fuck on the Internet. For the last three weeks before school started, I was having sex sometimes two or three times a day. I was like a kid in a candy store. . . . I couldn't get enough. Sure, some of the guys from online weren't as hot as their pictures, but I didn't care. They all loved me, wanted me, wanted to feel my muscles and lick me, kiss me, worship me." He frowned. "I know how bad that sounds . . . but you have to understand, it was all new to me. I wasn't used to it, and it did kind of go to my head a little bit. I couldn't believe the way men were reacting to the new me. It did bother me a little, you know. I mean, I was the same person I was before . . . the only thing that changed was the way I looked."

"The gay community can be superficial," Joe replied.

One of Jordy's eyebrows went up. "You're gay?"

Joe nodded, thinking *What the hell.* "Yeah."

Jordy smiled. "Well, damn, I'm sorry I never ran into you before."

Careful, Joe. Stay professional. "I don't get out much."

Jordy nodded. "You probably have a boyfriend, don't you?" He sighed. "Guys like you always do."

Guys like me? In spite of himself he was flattered. *Get a hold of yourself, Detective. This is an interrogation, not a god-damned pickup. Thank God Grace is not here. I'd never hear the end of this.* He cleared his throat. "Actually, I don't." He struggled to keep his voice noncommittal.

"Well, maybe after all this is over we could have dinner or something?" Jordy practically purred.

A gorgeous, sexy young man who also happens to be filthy rich and loves to have sex—what a serious slap in the face to Sean that would be!

An image of Jordy naked and lying on his back flashed through his head, a big smile on his face, cooing, *Fuck me, Detective, come on and give it to me, you big stud, I want that big fat cock in my ass, come on put me through the goddamned head-board, ride me you big fucking stud—*

He shook his head. "I don't think that would be a good idea."

"Why not?" Jordy sounded surprised. "I didn't push Chad out that window, no matter what my asshole brothers might have said. I mean, sure, I get that you're here on official po-lice business, but once you're done questioning me, there's no reason why we can't see each other socially, is there?"

I'm not entirely convinced you didn't push him.

A knock on the door kept him from answering. Jordy ex-cused himself and walked to the front door.

You're allowing your attraction to cloud your judgment, Joe chided himself. *Yes, he's a good-looking guy. It would be fun to fuck him. But it's clear he has strong feelings about Chad York. It's not impossible he pushed him. Sure, being rejected by someone you're attracted to is painful—God knows it's happened to you plenty of times, and will happen again, and it does suck—but it's hardly a motivation for attempted murder. But then again, you've investigated murders committed for a lot less. People are capable of anything—and he still hasn't told you what they argued about. In the heat of passion people do things they'd never do—and you can't forget this kid is really, really smart, and very emotionally vulnerable. He could have lost his head, shoved Chad out the window, and come back here to figure out how he was going to get away with it.*

"I'm sorry, Detective." Jordy walked back into the living room. "This is my neighbor—I told you about him. Jeff Morgan. Jeff, this is Detective Palladino with the Polk Police Department."

Joe stood up and shook hands with a handsome young man he recognized but couldn't place.

"It's nice to meet you," Jeff said with a slight midwestern accent. He frowned. "I'm sorry to interrupt, but I wanted to make sure Jordy was okay." He turned his attention to Jordy. "Eric called me and told me what happened."

"Some of the brothers think I pushed him," Jordy replied sourly. "Which is why the nice police detective is here."

"Well, Eric doesn't think so, and neither does anyone with a brain!" Jeff replied, his blue eyes flashing. "What a bunch of gossipy bitches." He turned back to Joe. "You can't believe Jordy did this!" He frowned. "I'm sorry, but you look familiar. Have we met?"

Joe stared at him, trying to place him. He was about to say Jeff looked familiar to him as well when an image of Jeff wearing a yellow thong, shaking his ass on the bar at Fusions, flashed through his mind. "I don't believe so," Joe replied, keeping his face immobile. Joe had tipped him more than once, managing to grope his legs and touch his perfectly chiseled chest. Sean had been crazy about him, unable to take his eyes off him as he moved around on top of the bar. *"Look at that package,"* Sean had said. *"It would be worth seeing if he's a hustler, don't you think, Joe? I mean, most of them are, right?"*

He pushed those thoughts out of his head.

"I just can't shake this feeling I know you from somewhere." Jeff shook his head.

Joe shrugged. "Maybe the grocery store or the gym."

"Maybe." Jeff frowned and turned back to Jordy. "Well, I probably should leave you two alone." Jeff touched Jordy on the shoulder. "Sorry, I wouldn't have interrupted had I known. . . . Jordy, come over when you're done. Are you going to be okay?"

Jordy nodded. "I think so. I mean, it's such a shock. . . ."

"Well, if you need anything, or just to talk, come on over. Blair's going to be home from rehearsal soon, and we should be home the rest of the night." He pulled Jordy into a big hug, and Joe bit his lower lip.

They're both so gorgeous, it would be hot to watch them—

"It was nice meeting you, Detective." Jeff shook his hand. "Just sorry it's under these circumstances. And if there's anything I can do to help, I'm just right across the hall." His face darkened. "I always knew Chad York was going to be more trouble than he was worth."

Jordy walked him to the door, and Joe could hear them murmuring to each other. He heard the door open and shut before Jordy came back and plopped down in his chair. "Sorry, Detective." He spread his hands sheepishly. "I wasn't sure if I should have just gotten rid of him."

Joe shook his head. "Not a problem."

"Jeff is a great friend," Jordy went on. "Him and Blair both. They've always been great to me." He grinned. "You should have seen the looks on their faces when they came back from Christmas break! They couldn't believe how much I'd changed...." His voice trailed off. "I guess that's where I left off, right?"

Joe nodded.

"The Saturday before the first Monday of school, the house always has a welcome-back party," Jordy went on, "and that's the first time the brothers saw the new me...."

Chapter 7

I got out of the car and took a deep breath.

I hadn't set foot in the house since Initiation Night. I'd skipped the end-of-semester party—I really didn't want to see or talk to anyone. The last time I'd walked into Beta Kappa I'd been fifteen pounds heavier, wore glasses, and looked like a total dork. I hadn't really known how to dress right, didn't have the slightest clue how to eat right, and had never set foot in a gym. As a pledge, I'd been a wide-eyed innocent just looking for a place where I could belong, make friends, and be myself.

I was a different person now, and my brothers were about to find out how much I'd changed.

I leaned back against the car. The house was all lit up for the party. The door to the backyard from the foyer was open, and I could see some brothers gathered around a couple of kegs. The deejay was lugging in crates of equipment, and some guys were seated at the picnic tables in the backyard. It had rained most of the day, and as the sun had gone down a thick fog had blanketed Polk. The street lamps glowed through the heavy mist. The parking lot was full, and I recognized some of the cars.

I almost got back in the car and headed back home. *Don't be an idiot*, I chided myself. *Remember how everyone at Fusions reacted to you that first time. Every time you've been back there you've met several guys, and you haven't gone home alone once. Chad is in for the shock of his life.*

That thought made me smile a little bit. In the six weeks since that horrible night when Chad dismissed me as beneath his notice, I'd replayed the scene hundreds of times in my head. I'd played it pitch perfect, never giving him the slightest clue how much he was wounding me. I was proud I'd not given him a single hint of how he was destroying me with a smile on his lips. I'd never forget that he'd been *smiling* as he cut me off at the knees and poured salt into the wounds. I would never forget those words as long as I lived.

"You're funny and sweet and a lot of fun to be around. But you just aren't my type. I like guys who take care of themselves."

My mouth twisted as I forced the humiliating memory out of my mind again. After all, he hadn't just come right out and called me a disgusting, fat pig unworthy of the great Chad York—but he might as well have.

I smoothed my red pullover down over my now-flat stomach. The sleeves had been rolled up to the top of my biceps, and my low-waisted jeans fit snugly and showed my new ass off beautifully. *Go inside*, I ordered myself. *You look great and you know it. Everyone is going to be amazed. Don't be so nervous, you're just being ridiculous.*

I must have changed my clothes about twenty times, trying to figure out what showed my body off to its best advantage. Should I wear a muscle shirt showing off my now-defined shoulders and arms? Or something with sleeves? Black jeans or low-rise blue? Unable to make up my mind, I'd finally called Jeff and Blair for help.

"I don't know what your problem is," Blair had drawled

after I showed them my third option. "You look amazing, Jordy. You look great in everything."

"You're sweet." I smiled at him. "But I want to look *perfect*. I want everyone to notice me."

"There's no such thing as perfect," Jeff replied, shaking his head. "You'll make yourself crazy that way. That's a path you don't want to go down. Trust me—you'll never be satisfied. You'll wind up with an eating disorder or juicing or something equally awful."

"Easy for you to say," I replied, pulling the blue shirt over my head and tossing it back on the bed. "It's effortless for you—for both of you."

"Effortless?" They looked at each other and laughed.

"Girl, you have no idea how much work I have to put into looking this fabulous," Blair replied. "And it's a never-ending struggle." He patted his flat stomach. "I gained so much weight in Europe over the break."

"You're not the only one," Jeff added. "I never should have let you talk me into going to Italy for that weekend. All that pasta!" He groaned. "I'll never be able to get back on the bar again if I don't get my definition back."

"Yeah, right." I rolled my eyes. The gods had gifted Jeff with a perfect body. "Stop fishing for compliments. You both look flawless, and what's more, you always do." I frowned at myself in the mirror. "You're sure these jeans don't make me look fat?"

"Stop freaking out so much." Jeff walked up to me and put his arm around me. "The point is, Jordy, we are all our own worst critics." He squeezed me. "We don't see ourselves the way others do." With his free hand, he reached down and pinched his waist. "See?"

"There's nothing there, Jeff," I replied, grabbing my own waist. "Look at this disgusting flab."

"Stop it, Jordy," Blair commanded. "For one thing, that's just extra skin from losing weight so fast. For another, those jeans look great on you and you know it. As for you, Jeff—there's not an extra ounce of fat anywhere on your body."

"And I know that." Jeff nodded, frowning down at the little bit of skin pinched between his fingers. "But no matter how many times I tell myself, I can't get it out of my head that it's fat."

"That's crazy," I replied. "You get up on a bar and dance in a thong, Jeff. People ogle you and give you money because you're hot."

"No crazier than you're being right now." Blair came up on the other side of me. "You look fantastic in everything you've shown us. I don't think there's anything you could wear that would look bad on you. But"—he gestured to the bed—"if I had to choose something, I'd wear that tight red shirt with the low-rise jeans. You look great in red. It's a good color for you. It also makes your shoulders and pecs look huge. And those jeans really show off your ass." He smacked my ass to emphasize his point and laughed. "You know your ass is hard as a rock, right?"

"I love you guys," I said, my lower lip trembling and my eyes filling with tears. "I don't know what I ever did to deserve two friends like you."

"Aww." They enveloped me in a big hug.

"Now get dressed and let's get going," Blair instructed.

So I put on the red shirt and the low-rise jeans, smoked a joint with them in the car on the way to the house, and now stood in the parking lot, looking at the house. They'd already gone in, and still I stood there summoning up the nerve. I could hear Lady Gaga blaring from the party room. The backyard was filling up with people drinking and laughing. I bit my lower lip. My stomach was churning.

You're being stupid. Remember how people react to you at Fu-
sions. Everyone at the house is going to be blown away by how you
look now.

But the only person whose opinion mattered was Chad.

You're beautiful now. His jaw is going to drop, and he is going
to want you. He's going to take you up to his room, and undress
you, and you're going to finally get to fuck that gorgeous ass.
You've had plenty of practice. You've learned how to drive a bot-
tom crazy with pleasure. Chad is going to have his mind blown,
and he won't be able to get enough of you, and he is going to love
you—didn't he say the only thing wrong with you was your body?
And you've taken care of that. You're perfect for him now.

I lifted my chin. "Come on, Jordy, let's go party."

I walked up the sidewalk to the back door. I paused at
the door and took one more deep breath, and walked
through the door.

"Wow!" Jacob Hinton did a double take as I walked up to
the keg. "Dude, you look amazing!"

I laughed and grabbed a cup. "Thanks. You look great,
too." I started filling my cup with beer. I had just lifted it to
my mouth when someone smacked my ass. I looked over
my shoulder at Jon Preston. "Christmas sure agreed with
you," he said, as he looked me up and down. "What the hell
happened to you?"

"I just decided to start taking better care of myself, is
all." I sipped my beer. The buzz from the joint I'd smoked
with Blair and Jeff was starting to wear off a bit. I couldn't
help but smile to myself. The reactions from the brothers
were everything I could have hoped for, and with each
compliment my confidence grew. I got another beer and
felt myself starting to relax. Some of the gay brothers were
checking me out, which was incredible. Jacob and Jon both
flirted with me, and I flirted right back with them. I kept an

eye out for Chad but didn't see him anywhere. I danced and got a third beer. I was developing a taste for it, even though it wasn't on my diet. *The hell with it,* I thought. *I'll just do another half hour on the elliptical tomorrow and that'll take care of it.*

I finished that beer and headed down the first-floor hall to the bathroom. Chad's door was closed, and I noticed the lights were off. I wondered where he was as I pushed my way through the saloon doors—

—and ran into Roger.

"Jordy!" His face lit up with a broad smile. He looked me up and down. "You look—I mean, *wow,* you look amazing."

My heart sank and my face flushed. He was the last person I wanted to run into. "Thanks," I replied, stepping up to a urinal. I unzipped my pants, hoping he'd leave.

He didn't. He turned to a sink and started washing his hands. I finished and zipped up my pants. "You want to smoke a joint?"

I considered it for a moment. I was getting a good buzz from the beer, but the high I'd enjoyed earlier was gone. *What the hell,* I thought. *I'm not going to let anything happen with him, anyway.* "Sure." I smiled at him. "That would be nice."

We went to his room and he locked the door behind us. I sat down at his desk chair while he rolled one. "I called you a few times, but you never called me back," he said, lighting it and passing it to me. "Why? Are you avoiding me?"

"Um, I was busy." I inhaled deeply.

He blinked slowly. "I wanted to apologize to you," he said. "And you don't have to worry about me trying anything again." He held up both hands.

"You don't need to apologize to me." I felt bad. He'd thought I was avoiding him because I was mad at him. I hadn't even given Hell Night a second thought. "I could have stopped it from happening." *And for God's sake, it was just a fucking blow job.*

"What happened between us on Hell Night was a mistake." He took the joint back from me. "I don't want you to feel awkward about it. It was totally my fault. And I'm sorry." He took a big hit, blowing the smoke out with a smile. "You're my little brother, and I want us to be friends. Just friends, Jordy. You don't have to worry about—"

"Oh, Roger, don't feel bad about it. It just happened." I shrugged. "It's not that big of a deal."

"No, I feel bad because I took advantage of you. You were drunk and upset about Chad, and I—"

I started laughing. "Let's just forget about it, okay, Roger? Really, it's okay." Impulsively I gave him a hug— which he held on to for just a moment too long. I pulled back and smiled at him. "Speaking of Chad, where is he? I haven't seen him at the party, and his lights are off."

"Chad moved upstairs," Roger replied. "I'm not surprised you didn't see him at the party." He made a face. "He doesn't seem to want to let his boyfriend out of his room."

"Boyfriend?" I couldn't have heard that right. "Chad has a boyfriend?"

"I know, right, can you believe it?" Roger laughed. "Poor thing has no idea what he's let himself in for." He shook his head. "He's hot, too." He touched my arm. "There but by the grace of God goes you, right?" He peered at me. "You are over Chad, aren't you? You don't still—"

"Don't be ridiculous," I replied, giving him my phoniest smile. I faked a shudder. "I can't even imagine how miserable I'd be. I don't even want to think about that." *A boyfriend? He has a boyfriend?* I felt like I'd been punched in the stomach. I somehow managed to keep talking, or rather responding, to Roger as a weird numbness crept over me. *Get ahold of yourself. Just because he has a boyfriend doesn't mean it's going to last, and you need to make sure he has no idea how you feel. You can do this. You can act like it doesn't bother you in the least.*

But part of me wanted to just get in my car and go home.

"He seems nice, too," Roger prattled on. "They apparently met at Fusions Wednesday night." I'd wanted to go but stayed home in case Chad showed up and spoiled my planned surprise, damn it all to hell, but on the other hand it would have sucked to have seen them meet and hook up. This was better. "Apparently he has a really good job, and seems smart, too. He graduated a couple of years ago and bought a house out in Avignon—"

"Avignon?" It sounded familiar, but I couldn't place it.

"It's a suburb just west of town," Roger explained. "Polk's one suburb." He laughed. "Chad of course enjoyed every second of introducing him to me." He shrugged, his eyes glittering with malice. "Of course this guy's only seen the *good* side of Chad and has no clue it's all an act. Chad is such a douche bag. I mean, they've been together what? All of three days? And Chad's already acting like they're ready to head to Canada and get married." He laughed again, rolling his eyes. "They barely know each other—once this guy gets to know him better he'll be heading for the hills fast enough—like all of Chad's boyfriends do."

It's only been three days, that's not really long enough to fall in love, they hardly know each other, I'm sure after they spend some more time together Chad will realize he's all wrong for him and be ready to move on, I can't believe this is happening, I should have fucking gone to Fusions Wednesday night, what the hell was I thinking, all of this work was for nothing . . .

"But I'm sure Chad will bring him out of his room. He'll want to show him off." Roger sighed. "I know I would."

"You'll meet someone, Roger," I replied absently, pulling myself together again. I couldn't hide in Roger's room all night, and I wasn't going to flee the party. So, Chad had a boyfriend? It was a temporary complication, that was all, and I just had to be patient. I stood up and patted his shoulder. "Thanks for the joint, but I've got serious cotton mouth now. I'm going to get a beer, maybe dance for a while." I smiled at him. "Promise me you won't just stay in here all night."

"I'll see." He shrugged. "If you want to smoke some more, just knock."

"Roger." I put my hands on my hips. "You've got to stop hiding in your room. Promise me you're going to come out to the party. You're never going to meet someone sitting here all alone. The perfect guy for you could be out there right now wondering where his perfect guy is—and you're trapped in here."

"That's really sweet of you—"

"I'm serious." I tapped my foot. "If we're going to be friends, Roger, you're going to have to listen to me."

He nodded. "Okay, you're right. I'll be out there in a bit." He looked down at his clothes. "I might want to change."

"If I have to I'll drag you out by the hair," I teased. I put my hand on the doorknob. "Got it?"

He smiled. "Thanks, Jordy, for caring. And you really do look amazing."

I closed the door behind me and ran to the bathroom. I turned on the cold water spigot and splashed water on my face, trying to get my breathing under control. I looked at myself in the mirror. "It wasn't all for nothing," I told myself. "This won't last, and I'll be right there to pick up the pieces when they break up, and Chad will see I'm the right one for him."

I felt a little better about the situation. I just had to be patient. It wouldn't last—Roger was right about that.

I smiled at myself. Of course it would happen.

After all, I was the right guy for Chad.

This guy, whoever he was, was just a momentary distraction.

I walked back to the party. The deejay was playing "Evacuate the Dancefloor" by Cascada, and I started dancing in place while I poured myself another beer from the keg.

"You're a good dancer," a guy said when I passed the tap over.

"Thanks." I smiled at him, thinking to myself, *Wow!*

He was short, maybe five foot six, but he had to weigh at least 190 pounds. He was wearing a faded pair of jeans that gripped his huge legs and a yellow, short-sleeved pullover stretched tight over a massive set of pecs. His waist was small, and he was cute with short, curly dark hair, blue eyes, a smattering of freckles across his snub nose, and an endearing smile. "Are you one of the new brothers?" he asked as he filled his cup. "I was studying in London last semester."

"You're Mike Van Zale!" I smiled, holding out my free hand to shake his. At the same time my heart sank a little. He was one of Jeff's little brothers and unfortunately was straight. He'd been dating the same girl since he was a sophomore in high school, and she was a sister at Delta Gamma. "I've heard a lot about you. Blair and Jeff are my next-door neighbors. I'm—"

"Jordy Valentine." Despite his small frame, his hand was

bigger than mine. "Jeff's told me a lot about you, too." He smiled, and I noticed one of his front teeth was chipped a little bit. "I'm glad we've finally met." He gestured around the room with his beer cup. "So, are you enjoying being a Beta Kappa?"

"Yeah." I took a big gulp from my beer. "It's great. I love it here. Smartest thing I've ever done in my life."

"You're supposed to be really smart, right?"

"I guess." I shrugged. "I made the dean's list last semester."

He winked at me. "Well, I might need help with one of my classes this semester." He rolled his eyes. "I fucking hate economics."

"Oh, well, it's really not that hard, it just takes a basic understanding—"

He held up his hand. "It's a party—we can talk about econ some other time, okay? But would you be willing to help me, if I need it? I really struggled with macro, and I'm really worried about micro."

"I'd be glad to." I grinned back at him. "Just get my number from Jeff and we can set something up."

"Great." He winked again and headed out to the dance floor.

I watched him go, cursing at myself. *He wasn't flirting with you, dumb-ass, he's straight. He was just being nice because he wants you to help him study. But Christ, what a waste of an amazingly hot guy! I hope his girlfriend appreciates what she has in him.*

I decided to go outside and get some air. As I walked to the door to the backyard, I saw them coming toward me. They were holding hands, and Chad hadn't noticed me yet. All of his attention was squarely on the guy he was with, and my heart sank even further when I got a good look at him.

I can't compete with that.

He was taller than Chad, which meant he had to be around six foot four at the least, and he had to weigh about 240 pounds. Chad had a great body, but this guy dwarfed him. His biceps were about the size of my head. He had bluish black hair; big, round brown eyes; and perfectly white, even teeth. His skin was olive, and his eyelashes looked dewy. He was built like a football player, and there was no excess fat anywhere. He looked like he could bend steel bars in his powerful hands. I tried to duck back out of sight before they saw me but was too slow.

"Jordy!" Chad's entire face lit up with a smile. He and his impossibly perfect boyfriend walked toward me, and I plastered a phony smile on my face.

I wanted to be anywhere else in the world at that moment—preferably a monastery high in the Himalayas.

"Hi, Chad." I tried to make my voice sound light and jaunty. "How are you?"

"Great!" His eyes flicked up and down my body. "I really like that shirt. This is Dante Bertucci." He smiled. "My boyfriend."

"Jordy, hi." Dante's voice was deep and his smile was genuine. "I've heard a lot about you."

"Don't believe a word." I smiled back in spite of myself. His grin was infectious. He grabbed my hand in one of his huge ones and pumped my arm.

"Oh, it was all good," he said, smiling at Chad. "Chad couldn't say enough nice things about you."

I'll just bet, I thought, still smiling.

"Will you two wait for me here?" Dante said. "I've really got to use the bathroom."

We said we would, and I watched him walk away. His tight jeans looked great on his big, hard ass.

"Isn't he *gorgeous?*" Chad whispered.

"Where did you meet him?" I somehow managed to keep my voice light.

"At Fusions on Wednesday," Chad replied.

Thanks for calling me. "I've never seen him there before," I observed.

"Oh, he broke up with his long-term boyfriend a couple of months ago, so he hasn't been out in years. I was just fortunate to be there the night he finally decided to get out of the house again." Chad lightly punched me on the shoulder. "If I hadn't been there, some other queen would have snapped him up like that." He snapped his fingers. "Can you believe my luck?"

Obviously there's no justice in the universe was what I wanted to say, but instead I just nodded.

"He's an architect," Chad went on. "You should see his house—he designed it himself. It's *gorgeous.*"

He kept talking, but I wasn't listening. The high from the pot I'd smoked and the slight buzz from the beers I'd drunk were both gone.

He hadn't even noticed that I looked different.

I might as well have been part of the furniture for all he cared.

I was stupid to think I could turn myself into someone Chad would want—he wants guys like Dante, and there's no way I can measure up or compete with guys like that.

All of my hard work had been for nothing.

Dante came walking back toward us. The music had switched again to the Black Eyed Peas' "I Gotta Feeling."

"I love this song. Let's dance!"

"Okay." Chad turned to me. "I'll see you later, okay?"

"Don't be silly." Dante smiled at me. "Come dance with us, Jordy. I'm looking forward to getting to know you."

Chad gave me a look I completely ignored. "Okay!" I

smiled back at Dante and followed the two of them out onto the dance floor.

We danced through that song and stayed out there through the next three. At some point, both of them removed their shirts. Dante tried to get me to take mine off, but I refused. There was no way I was going to stand next to the two of them and have my pitiful body compared to their godlike ones.

It was during the fourth song, "My Life Would Suck Without You," that I couldn't take it anymore. They started singing to each other, and put their arms around each other and kissed. I escaped, doubting they would even notice. I grabbed another beer and wandered away down the dark hall of the dorm. It was taking everything I had to not cry.

A door opened to my right. "Hey, Jordy!"

I turned. "Oh, hi, Mike."

"Are you okay?" He peered at me in the dim light.

"Fine," I replied, turning a bit so he couldn't see my face.

He laughed bitterly. "I'm not."

"What's wrong?"

"My stupid girlfriend dumped me." He wiped at his eyes. "We've been together five years, and tonight she decides to tell me she's not in love with me anymore."

"I'm so sorry."

To my horror he started crying. Not knowing what else to do, I put my arms around him and hugged him. His arms went around me and he pulled me in close. He put his head down on my chest and sobbed.

"Maybe we should get out of the hall," I said. "I mean, you don't want anyone to see you like this, do you?"

"Good point." He pulled me into his room and shut the door.

He had a single room, with a double bed pushed up against one wall. There was a desk on the opposite wall, and there was a poster of Pamela Anderson in her *Baywatch* bathing suit taped to the wall over the desk. The curtains were closed, and I could hear "Fergalicious" coming from the Great Room.

I sat down on the bed.

"Can I ask you something?" He sat down on the bed next to me, almost uncomfortably close.

I nodded. "Sure."

"Can I kiss you?"

"What?" I stared at him. "Mike, you're straight."

"I know it's weird, but I really need someone." He put his hand on my leg. "I like guys, I just like girls better." He sighed. "But right now I need to be with someone, okay, and I don't want to be with another girl." He slammed his other fist down on the bed. "I don't know if I want to be with a girl ever again."

He's vulnerable, Jordy, and a little drunk. You don't want to do this. He's going to regret this in the morning, and you're only doing this because of Chad and Dante.

But he's awfully hot.

I kissed him.

Our arms went around each other. We fell backward onto the bed, and he rolled over on top of me. My legs wrapped around his waist, and his tongue entered my mouth. Our crotches ground together, and I could feel he had a huge cock inside his jeans. I pulled his shirt up over his head. His chest was amazing. The pecs were perfectly formed and huge, and he had large pink nipples. I kissed one, and then the other. His body shuddered, and he started grinding his crotch into mine again. I put my hands on his big, thick arms. They were hard, no give to them at all. He pulled my shirt up and off, lowering himself back on top of me. He started kissing my neck while I fumbled with his jeans, finally undoing the button fly and pushing them down. He wasn't wearing underwear, and smiled at me as he got off me and kicked his pants off. He undid my pants, pulling them off and throwing them aside. I smiled at him as he pulled my underwear off—

—and put his mouth on my cock.

I put my hands on the back of his head.

He certainly knew how to suck a cock.

"Ooooooooooh." I moaned as he worked me with his mouth. He reached up with his big hands and started playing with my nipples. "Oh, God, Mike, that's awesome, don't stop, man. . . ."

He stopped and smiled at me. He got up and straddled my face. I found myself staring at one of the biggest cocks I'd ever seen—and he was uncircumcised. He leaned down and started sucking me again, and I reached up with my head and took him in my mouth. I licked the head of his dick and he moaned, but he kept working on mine. He tasted slightly of sweat and smelled faintly of urine. I reached up with my hands and gripped his ass, pulling it down as I swallowed his entire length. His ass flexed, and he pushed himself deeper into my throat as I swirled my tongue around it, gripping his ass tightly with both hands.

It tasted wonderful. I wanted it deep inside of me, and I felt my own load starting to build, and just as I was about to shoot he pulled his mouth off and stroked me until I came in a huge load that rained down on my stomach.

I could feel him stiffening, and he pulled his cock out of my mouth.

As soon as the head passed through my lips he started shooting his load down into my face. He moaned, his ass stiffening, his entire body going rigid, his eyes closed and his body jerking with each shot.

Finally, he was finished and he rolled over onto his side.

"Wow," he whispered.

I reached for a towel and wiped off my face, then my stomach.

"I don't fuck," he said as I started to get up. "Don't go."

"I—"

He lay back down on the bed and patted the pillow next to the one where his head rested. "Stay with me and cuddle, okay?"

I looked at him. *What the hell.* I slid up and put my head down on the free pillow.

His arms wrapped around me and he kissed the back of my neck.

I closed my eyes. It felt good there in his strong arms.

He wasn't Chad, but he'd do.

I fell asleep.

Chapter 8

Beyoncé's "Sweet Dreams" woke me up.

I opened my eyes and didn't know where I was at first. But the muscular arm draped over me brought it all back in a rush. I'd fallen asleep in Mike's bed, and I could feel his hard-on pressed up against my ass. On the nightstand, I could see it was his cell phone playing the chorus. He shifted and mumbled a bit against my back, and as I looked at the phone I could see Mike's girlfriend's face staring at me. *Perfect timing,* I thought, smothering a grin. After another moment, Beyoncé was cut off, and the phone chirped. I eased his arm off and slid out of the bed, sitting up on the side. I could hear guys talking outside the window, and the alarm clock on his desk read 9:47 a.m. I got up and grabbed my underwear, sliding it on.

"Where you going?" Mike mumbled, his eyes half open. "Don't go."

"Your girlfriend just called." I slid my jeans up, buttoning the fly. "I think she left a message."

He sat up in the bed, and I leaned over, kissing him on the cheek. "Thanks for last night," I whispered. "That was really hot."

He grabbed my arms and pulled me down on top of him, pushing my hand down to his erection. "You want to play some more before you leave?"

It was tempting, but I pushed myself back up. "I think you should probably call your girlfriend back." I picked my shirt up and slipped it over my head. "I bet she's sorry she dumped you and wants you back."

"Fuck her." He pushed the covers aside and started stroking himself. In spite of myself, I was getting hard. He winked at me. "You sure you don't want some more of this?"

"I'll stay," I said, putting my socks on, "if you let me fuck you." I reached for my shoes. "You've got a gorgeous ass."

"I don't do that." He stopped stroking himself and frowned. A drop of pre-cum oozed out the tip.

I slipped on my shoes, leaning over to kiss his cheek. "Mike, trust me. You are really hot, but you really want to call your girlfriend." I stood up, grabbed his phone, and tossed it onto the bed next to him. "Don't get me wrong, I'll be more than happy to be with you again—but what I really want is to fall in love and be with someone who really wants to be with me, not with his girlfriend." I reached over and rubbed the top of his cock. "Work things out with her one way or the other—but if you're not really into guys . . ."

I shut the door behind me as he dialed his phone.

Once I was inside my car, I started laughing. I couldn't help it. The whole thing was so absurd. I remembered Blair telling me once that "straight boys will put out if they're drunk enough—all it takes is a six-pack." I rolled my eyes and started my car. As I backed out of my space, I saw Chad walking Dante to his car. Chad was just wearing a pair of basketball shorts and sandals. His shorts were riding really low, and I looked away as I put the car in drive and headed home.

How long is this going to last? I wondered as I drove. I liked

Dante—he seemed like a really nice guy. But he was standing in my way. Somehow, I was going to have to get rid of him. The question was, how? I kept running through alternatives as I drove, but nothing seemed possible. *Maybe I'm going to have to let this run its course.*

As I walked into my apartment, I decided the best thing for me to do was wait and be patient. An opportunity would present itself, surely.

The first week of classes sped by. My classes all seemed really easy, and it was going to be another semester of making the dean's list without putting a lot of effort into it. My first meeting as a brother was Monday night, and the main item on the meeting agenda was the start of Rush the next week. I kept watching Chad, who spent the entire meeting doodling in a notebook in front of him, not participating in the meeting at all. He was sitting in between Brandon and Rees, and they seemed equally bored. When the sign-up sheet to work the Beta Kappa booth in the quad on campus went around, I signed up for as many slots as I could. I was proud to be a brother and wanted to contribute. When the meeting broke up, Mike came up to me. "Hey, can I talk to you for a second?"

"Sure," I replied, wondering if he was going to invite me into his room again.

"I wanted to say thanks." He stuck out his big right hand, and I shook it. "I called Leona when you left the other morning, and we talked everything out. We're back together again."

I smiled. "Mike, that's great. I'm really happy for you."

"I also wanted to thank you for Friday night," he went on. "I was a wreck, and it was nice of you to keep me company when I was so down about her."

I bit my lip. *It wasn't like I didn't get something out of it,* I thought. "Glad I could help. And I was serious about help-ing you with your econ class, if you need me to."

Later, as I was getting into my car after the meeting, I saw Dante pulling in. I sighed, and debated whether I should say hello.

You should—how else are you going to get into position to help them break up if you don't befriend Dante?

Instead, I started the car and left.

There was plenty of time for that later, I reasoned, and I wasn't ready to start playing the game yet.

It still hurt to see them together.

Besides, I still hadn't figured out how to do it.

I'd hoped my first Rush as an actual brother would give me something to focus on besides Chad and Dante. It was easier said than done. I ran into them everywhere, it seemed. When I went to the grocery store, they were there, shopping for a romantic dinner Dante was cooking that night. Every time I drove into the parking lot at the house, there was Dante's car to remind me. I went shopping for clothes, and sure enough, there they were, trying things on and laughing while I watched through slitted eyes. As if that weren't enough, it turned out that Dante worked out at my gym. As my trainer put me through my paces, I couldn't help but keep an eye on Dante whenever I could. He al-ways wore a loose-fitting tank top with spaghetti straps, ex-posing his mountainous pecs, and was drenched with sweat as he lifted weights I couldn't conceive ever being strong enough to move myself.

It just further emphasized my inability to compete with him.

And every time I got into bed and closed my eyes, I couldn't get the image of the two of them together out of my head. I'd get hard, imaging muscular Dante on top of

Chad, fucking him, his big ass clenching and unclenching as Chad screamed with pleasure.

And after I wiped my own cum off myself, I'd cry a little bit.

But at least I knew Dante wouldn't be around during Rush.

I managed to successfully avoid Chad during the first two nights, and I was pleased to discover I actually had a knack for rushing. Well, maybe part of it was knowing if I kept myself busy talking to prospectives I wouldn't have time to talk to Chad or wonder what he was doing or if he was going over to Dante's house the minute Rush ended. So I lost myself in talking to the prospectives and taking them on tours. My memory also came in handy. Being able to remember their names, where they were from, and things they told me impressed them. It also didn't hurt that I really believed Beta Kappa was the best house on campus with the most to offer pledges. I *believed* what I was telling them. I dragged Roger along on the tours, including him in my conversations with the prospectives. I was a little surprised when Roger dropped the surly mocking attitude he'd had when I'd gone through Rush and seemed to open up and enjoy himself. He was really making an effort, and I was proud of him. He was trying to change. Every once in a while, though, I'd catch him staring at me. It was like he was studying me, which kind of creeped me out a little bit—but then I'd just shrug it off.

It was just my imagination—which was working overtime.

Every morning when my alarm went off, my first thought was, *Maybe today's the day they're going to break up.* I wasn't proud of it. Dante seemed like he was a great guy—and every time I saw them together it was obvious Dante was really into Chad. I would look at Dante's massive muscles, his handsome face with the extraordinary smile, and think, *You don't have a chance. He's hot, he's nice, he's got a great job, he has everything you could possibly imagine going for him. Even if they do break up, Chad is hardly going to replace champagne with grape juice. He's never going to want you. You need to accept it and move on.*

Tuesday night, when Rush was over and I finished talking with the Bid Committee about some of the prospectives, I walked out into the parking lot and saw them kissing. They were leaning up against the trunk of Dante's Porsche, and they had their arms around each other.

It was like being punched in the face.

I stood there watching for a minute. They finished their kiss, and Dante opened the passenger door for Chad. A few moments later the Porsche roared out into the street.

I sat in my own car, my head down on the steering wheel.

What is wrong with you? You're wasting your time hoping for something that's never going to happen. You need to just get over Chad and be done with it once and for all. Even if they do break up, it's going to take years of working out for you to have the kind of body Chad's attracted to. You're never going to have him. Stop wasting your time. So what if he doesn't want you? Plenty of other guys do. You only sleep alone by choice. Let go of the revenge fantasy—the truth is, if Chad ever wanted you you'd never turn him down in a million years. Let go of all of it. Be friends with him, because that's all you're ever going to be. So what if he hurt you? Did he really lead you on, or did you just fool yourself?

I started the car. It made sense. It was time to move on.

I woke up on Wednesday morning in a really good mood. I went to my classes, did my time in the booth, and headed over to the house to help get things ready for that night. As soon as I got out of my car, Chris Moore called my name. "Can I talk to you for a minute?"

I bit my lower lip. What could the president want with me? Had I done something wrong? He clapped me on the back. "I have to say, Jordy—and don't take this the wrong way—but I was a little worried about you for Rush."

"Really?" I frowned.

"Really." He smiled at me. "I mean, you're kind of shy, and so I worried a bit you'd struggle with Rush. But man, was I wrong! You sure stepped up! I don't think I've ever seen anyone work as hard as you this Rush Week."

The praise felt good. "Well, it's important." I smiled back at him.

"We've already had ten bids accepted, and at least seven of them said how much they liked you." He clapped me on the back again. "That's seven pledges you're pretty much responsible for recruiting. And Eric told me how hard you've been working at the booth. I'm proud of you, man."

"Thanks, Chris." Praise from the president! As I watched him walk back to the house, I couldn't help but laugh to myself. I might have a talent for rushing pledges, but if Chris had known the real reason I'd thrown myself into it so hard, he wouldn't have complimented me.

I was standing there when a car pulled into the lot, almost blinding me with the headlights. I put up an arm to cut the glare, but it pulled into a spot and I started walking over to my car. I'd just put the keys in the door when someone called my name. I paused, with my hand on the door handle, and looked over.

Dante had just gotten out of his car and was walking over to me.

Great, I said to myself. *Just what I need right now.*

"Hi," I said when he got close enough to hear me.

"Hey, Jordy, how you doing?" He stopped and shifted his weight from one foot to the other uncomfortably. He was wearing a pair of plaid shorts and a muscle shirt.

"Tired, how are you?"

"I imagine Rush Week must be rough on all of you," he said, still shifting.

"It's tiring, a little draining, but you know, it's important."

"Can I ask you a favor?"

Alarms started sounding in my head. "Sure."

"Would you mind grabbing a cup of coffee with me? I need to talk to someone, and I figured you'd be the best person." He gave me a rueful smile. "And when I saw you, well, I just figured it was meant to be."

Okay, this is just strange. I started to say something about Chad but stopped myself. I was curious. What did he want to talk to me about? So I nodded and said, "Sure, you want to go to the Starbucks on Shaw?"

Relief flooded his face. "That's perfect. I'll meet you there."

I watched him walk back to his car and waved once he was inside. I got into my own car and followed him out of the parking lot.

All the way to Starbucks random thoughts ran through my mind. *What does he want to talk to me about? My advice on buying something ridiculously expensive for Chad? My help in throwing a surprise party or something?*

Once I had my iced mocha in hand, I sat down with him at a table in the corner farthest from the counter. We were the only people in the place, and that annoying Michael Bublé was singing on the speakers. "So, what's up?" I asked, adding Sweet'N Low to my drink.

"I don't know how to say this." He played with his straw.

"So just say it."

He looked at me, his face miserable. "I think Chad's going to break up with me."

My heart leaped in my chest. *YES!* I managed to plaster

a concerned look on my face. "Dante, why would you think that?"

"I don't know. It's a feeling I've gotten. The last couple of nights when he's stayed over"—my heart sank again—"I don't know, it's been different somehow. I hate to ask, but has he said anything to you?"

"How different?"

"He seems distant." He shrugged his massive shoulders, the muscles flexing and popping out. "Remote, somehow. I mean, he's never been like that before. It was like he didn't want to be there. I mean, the sex was just as hot as ever"—somehow I managed to keep smiling even though I wanted to throw my iced mocha in his face—"but afterward, well, he didn't want to cuddle anymore. Maybe it's nothing, but he doesn't seem to be as relaxed as he was at first. I don't know, maybe it has nothing to do with me. I thought it might be the pressure of Rush. . . ." He let his voice trail off.

"That very well could be," I mused, trying not to get up and start dancing on the table. "Rush is really draining."

"Has he said anything to you?"

I shook my head. "No, but he probably wouldn't. I mean, Rees and Brandon are his best friends. He'd talk to them before he'd talk to me about anything so personal." I shrugged. "I haven't really talked to Chad much since school started, frankly." I couldn't resist adding, "I mean, he's really spent most of his time with you."

"Rees and Brandon aren't his *real* friends," Dante replied. "He told me that *you're* his only real friend."

I didn't know what to say. I just stared at him.

"Rees and Brandon are just party buddies," he went on. "You know, people to go out with and hang with and get drunk with. He's never had a real conversation with them—and I can see why. I had them over for dinner one night and both of them were drunk before dinner was ready. They're shallow. But you?" He gave me a sad smile. "He really cares about you. You're his real friend."

I didn't know what to say, so I just picked up my coffee and took a big drink. A voice inside my head was urging me to take advantage of this opportunity to bury this relationship once and for all.

But Dante was so clearly miserable—I couldn't do this, could I?

But if you break them up, then Chad is free to finally see what he's missing in you. And you know you're the right guy for him. The only impediment was your body—and sure, maybe you aren't a great big hunk of muscle like Dante yet, but you're on your way. If he's out of the way—

I sighed. "I don't know what you want me to do," I said slowly.

"Can you talk to him for me?" Dante's big brown eyes pleaded with me. "Please?"

I pushed that voice out of my head and smiled at him. "I can't promise anything, but I'll talk to him, okay?"

"Thank you, Jordy, I really appreciate this." He scribbled his cell number down on a napkin and shoved it at me. "Call me anytime, okay?" He stood up and awkwardly hugged me.

I sat there for a while after he left. I looked at the napkin with his number on it. I pulled out my phone and entered it into my address book.

When I arrived back at the house, the first person I ran into was Chad. He was sitting at the picnic table in the backyard as I walked up from the parking lot, and I caught my breath. He wasn't wearing a shirt, and my heart started beating a little faster at the sight of his chest. He waved at me, and remembering my promise to Dante, I headed over there.

What do I say? I wondered as I drew nearer to him. *I should have just said no.*

"Jordy!" He smiled, but his eyes seemed a little sad. "I've hardly seen you this semester."

I sat down on the edge of the table. "Well, you've been busy." I shrugged. "It's cool, I get it."

"Yeah, well." He looked down at his hands. "I've missed you."

"I've missed you, too."

"Hey, you want to go to Fusions after Rush?"

"Sure." I wasn't exactly dressed for going out, but what the hell. "Will Dante be joining us?"

"No," he said quickly. He didn't look up, just kept staring at his hands. "I just broke up with him." He gave a slight shrug. "Was probably shitty to do it by text message, but—"

My heart almost jumped out of my chest, and it was all I could do not to jump to my feet and scream *"YES"* at the sky. Trying to keep my voice level, I said, "Oh, Chad! I'm so sorry! What happened?"

"It wasn't there." This time he did look up. "I mean, he was everything I wanted—hot, successful, had his act together, but I was forcing it. After the initial attraction wore off, I mean, I was trying to force it, make it work when I really wasn't feeling it at all." He tossed his head. "I don't know what's wrong with me. I mean, could there be a more perfect guy than Dante?" He sighed. "Gorgeous house, great career, and that body—oh, my God, that body." His lower lip came out, and he pinched it—a weird habit he had. "Well, the sex wasn't great."

"It wasn't?" I wasn't sure I wanted to hear this, but somehow I had to.

"He's a bottom." Chad looked into my eyes. "A total bottom."

"And that's a problem?"

Chad sighed, like he was dealing with someone incredibly stupid. "I like to get fucked, Jordy. I was *born* to be fucked." He ran a hand through his hair. "You know how they always say it hurts the first time, that it's something you have to practice and learn how to do?" He leaned forward. "Not for me. The first time I was with a guy, he went right in. All the way in, and it didn't hurt. It felt awesome. I was a natural. And I love getting fucked. But Dante? No interest in being a top at all. Nope, he just wanted to get fucked. And I need to get fucked, you know?"

My dick was getting hard. I swallowed. I opened my mouth to say *but I'm a top* but stopped myself. This wasn't the time to make a move. No, I was playing for keeps, for a lifetime together, and being a rebound fuck wasn't enough for me.

"I'm sorry, Chad." I put my hand on his bare shoulder. It felt cool to my touch, but a little electrical charge flowed from my palm straight to my stiffening cock. I crossed my legs to try to make it less noticeable. "I really liked Dante. We had coffee this afternoon."

His eyes narrowed. "You did?"

I nodded. "Yeah, I ran into him and he invited me out for coffee. He said he wanted to talk to me. I was curious so I went."

"And just what did he want to talk to you about?" His voice was terse.

"You." And in that moment, I knew I was doing precisely the right thing. The way his face twisted made me feel slightly triumphant. "He was worried about where your relationship was heading, and he wanted to know if you'd said anything to me."

Chad's face flushed. He stood up and started pacing

around, the words tumbling out of him. "That just pisses me off. He went behind my back and talked to my friends about me? Tried to get my friends to betray my confidences? Man, I did the right thing dumping him. That's just so—so *junior high*."

"I know." I nodded, trying hard not to smile. "I mean, did he want me to pass you a note in gym?"

"Exactly." Chad folded his arms, which made his chest and arms look even bigger. "I am so sorry he put you in that position, Jordy." He shook his head. "That's just so wrong." He blew out a deep breath. "Well, any doubts I may have had about dumping him are gone now." He patted my shoulder. "I'm so glad you told me. You're such a good friend." He glanced at his watch. "I'd better get some clothes on. Fusions later, okay?"

"You got it, bud." I watched as he walked back inside the house, waiting until he was inside before letting out a sigh of relief.

I didn't think the night was ever going to end. Chad stuck by my side almost all night, and I remembered Dante saying, *"You're his only real friend."* I couldn't help but give Rees and Brandon smug looks from time to time. *He likes me better than his pledge brothers. He likes me better than anyone else.*

And finally, the night was over and we were walking into Fusions.

"Get us some drinks, Rees," Chad said loud enough to be heard over Lady Gaga and "Paparazzi." Obediently, Rees went to the bar, and Chad put his arm around my shoulders. "It's nice for us to be out again," he said into my ear, his breath against my lobe sending tingles down my spine. "I really missed it."

"But didn't you and Dante—"

"He wasn't as much fun to dance with as you." He gave

me that smile again. "Didn't you notice? He had no rhythm *at all.*"

Rees brought our drinks, and I took mine, sipping it. The club was crowded, like fifty-cent-drink night always was. There was a crowd of guys on the dance floor, and an assorted drag queen here and there. When Brandon spotted someone he knew and vanished into the crowd, Rees was right behind him.

"Where are they going?" I asked, finishing my drink and putting it down on a table.

Chad rolled his eyes. "See that guy over there?" He pointed. "The one in the wifebeater?"

I followed the direction he was pointing. "The guy with the tattoo?"

Chad nodded. "They had a three way with him a couple of months ago and have been looking for him ever since." He made a face. "I think that's creepy."

"Creepy?"

"Not three ways—those can be a lot of fun. But to have sex with your friends?" His lip curled a little bit. "That's gross. It's like having sex with your brother."

I looked at him, but he was finishing his drink. *You think having sex with a friend would be like having sex with your brother?*

That didn't bode well for me.

But I wasn't going to be his friend, I was going to be his boyfriend.

"Come on, let's dance," he said, pulling me out onto the dance floor.

I followed him through the gyrating crowd until we got a space where there was actually room to dance, and we started moving. I started scanning the crowd of dancers when a chilling thought occurred to me.

What if Dante shows up?

I was starting to sweat, so without a second thought I pulled my shirt off and tucked it into the back of my jeans. Chad smiled approvingly at me. *He thinks I look good!* I thought as he did the same. "I'm so proud of you!" he shouted to me over the music, which was now changing to "TiK ToK" by Ke$ha.

I blushed happily. Finally he was noticing my hard work! "Thanks," I replied.

"Two months ago you wouldn't take your shirt off, and now look at you!" He beamed, and turned to watch a muscular guy who'd climbed up on one of the speakers.

He still hasn't noticed.

I felt my eyes well up, so I used my shirt to wipe sweat off my face and hide my tears. I suddenly became aware of a guy dancing behind me, grinding his crotch against my ass. I looked back over my shoulder and grinned at him. "You've got a great ass," he said into my ear.

"Thanks." I glanced down at his torso. "Nice pecs!" I turned around and faced him, still dancing. He put his arms around my neck and pulled my head down to his. We kissed on the dance floor, the lyrics of the song pulsing through my head as our crotches came together. My cock was already hard, and I could feel his through his jeans, which had crept down low enough for me to tell he wasn't wearing anything underneath.

"My name's Devon," he shouted once our mouths came apart.

"Jordy," I shouted back.

"I've never seen you here before."

"You just never noticed me."

"I would have noticed." He leaned forward and ran his tongue over my right nipple.

I smiled at Devon. "You want to get out of here?" Devon winked at me as one of his hands brushed against the crotch of my jeans.

I looked around for Chad but didn't see him at first . . . and then I saw him.

He was up on the speaker, grinding his ass into the muscle god.

"Yeah," I said to Devon. "Let's go. You want to go to my place?"

"Better." He grabbed me by the hand and led me off the dance floor to a darkened corner of the bar, and opened a door. It was a bathroom, one I'd never seen before. He locked the door behind us. There was a dim light over the mirror. He pushed me against the door and turned his back to me, grinding his ass into me. He reached back and grabbed my cock. "Oh, yeah, I knew you'd have a big one." His pants dropped and he bent forward a little. "Come on, fuck me, man."

I undid my pants while I dug a condom out of my pocket. I tore it open and slid it over my cock. He pressed a little brown bottle into my hand. "Take a whiff," he whispered.

I held it up to my nose and took a deep inhale. Within moments my head was roaring, I could hear my heart pounding, and I wanted to be inside him.

I grabbed his hips and slid my cock inside him.

He took the bottle back. "Oooooh, yeah." He pushed back against me. I started pounding at him. It felt amazing, like his ass was gripping me and not going to let me go until—

He cried out, his body shuddering.

He slipped forward and my cock popped out of his ass.

He turned around and licked my face.

He peeled the condom off and spat on his hand, and started stroking me.

It didn't take long before I came.

He pulled his pants up and unlocked the door. "Thanks, man." He winked, and opened the door and was gone.

I shook my head. *Did that just happen?* I pulled my pants up and fastened them. I walked back out onto the dance floor. Chad was dancing by himself, the muscle god he'd been on the speaker with nowhere to be seen. "Where have you been?" he shouted over the music.

"Bathroom."

He put his arms around me. "Man, I've missed this." He kissed my cheek. "I've missed you."

And even though I knew better, I started believing again.

Chapter 9

"**Y**ou're really turning into a bit of a whore," Brandon Benson said, opening his eyes wide as he took a sip of his iced tea. "Chad's kind of worried about you. And so are we."

I stopped, a forkful of cucumber halfway to my mouth, stunned. I couldn't have heard that right, could I? It was completely out of left field. One minute we were talking about the new pledge class and which ones we might want for little brothers. And then WHAM! A shot right between the eyes—and a cheap shot, at that, given who it was coming from.

"No, I'm not," I replied, putting my fork back down. "Why would you say that?" *Yes, pot, I am black* ran through my head as I sat there staring at him. I looked from him to Rees, who just gave me a little helpless shrug and a rueful smile, as though to say, *This wasn't my idea, sorry.*

We were sitting in the food court in the Student Union. It was crowded, and the noise level made it hard to hear. I'd run into them as I was heading home from my last class. They'd invited me to join them for lunch in the Union, and it was time for my next meal. I'd just planned on going home and making a protein shake, but maybe something solid was in the cards. I'd only had a shake for breakfast and a protein bar for my second meal of the day, and there was a decent salad bar in the Union. I had about two hours before I had to meet my trainer at Body Quest, and I rarely got a chance to talk to either of them without Chad around. I'd always gotten the sense they only put up with me because of Chad, which was more than fine with me. I kind of only put up with them because of Chad. But the friendly request made me curious, so I'd agreed.

Being told I was a whore wasn't what I'd been expecting.

"How many different guys have you slept with in the last couple of weeks?" Brandon asked, raising his eyebrows, a slight smile playing at his lips. "Seriously, Jordy."

"I don't know. I don't count them," I said, giving my attention back to my salad. *Maybe the same amount as you, give or take?* I thought, getting irritated. "It's not like I'm trying to break a world record or something. I don't see what the big deal is. I use condoms."

"Chad's just worried, is all," Rees said. He took a bite of his grilled cheese sandwich. "He thought we should have a talk with you." He gave me a nervous little smile.

"I don't understand." I speared a mushroom, trying to push down my rising anger. "If Chad is so damned concerned, why isn't he talking to me about this?" *And you'd be surprised if you knew what he thought about YOUR behavior, you idiots.* "I mean, it's not like you guys—" I stopped and took a deep breath. *Don't argue with them, find out what this is all about. It's coming from Chad. What is he up to now?* I felt a little surge of triumph. *He couldn't be jealous, could he?*

"Oh, we offered." Brandon gave me a smile.

I smiled back at him. He really was cute, I decided, with the gap in his front teeth and the big jug ears. I'd never paid much attention to him before—why was that?

Because he's one of Chad's inner circle, that's why.

"Yeah," Rees chimed in. "We care about you, Jordy, and you know, we don't really get to hang out with you that much." He gave me a wide smile. "I mean, you're not just our fraternity brother, you're a part of our circle, you know?" He touched my hand.

"Circle?" I popped the mushroom into my mouth. "That's sweet. You know, I always kind of got the impression you guys didn't like me very much." *There, what have you got to say to that?*

They exchanged glances. "I don't know why you'd think that," Rees said slowly. He touched my hand again. "I can't speak for Brandon, but I like you, Jordy." His hand stayed on top of mine for maybe a beat longer than it should have. "You're smart, and you're funny."

"Thanks." I studied his face. He seemed sincere, but I wasn't sure if I could trust him.

"Besides"—Brandon leaned in and lowered his voice— "we're the hottest four gay guys at Beta Kappa—probably in the whole Greek system—and so we have to look out for each other. We owe it to each other to watch out for each other. You know what I mean?"

It was all I could do not to laugh. Sure, it felt good to hear him say it, but *seriously?* My body had really been chang-ing—the hard work at the gym and the diet and supple-ments were creating a true miracle, and I'd had to buy some new clothes because my shirts were getting too small—but I was hardly in the league of Chad, or Jeff, or Blair. For that matter, Rees and Brandon were hot guys, but they weren't, either.

"Well, I appreciate it, but nobody needs to worry about me." I took a sip from my water bottle. "What's the big deal? I meet a hot guy, we hit it off, we go have sex. Isn't that what we do?" I shrugged. "You guys certainly do."

"Within limits, sure," Brandon went on. "But—" He looked at Rees for help.

"Every single time you go to Fusions you go home with someone," Rees finished. "You don't want people to start thinking you're a whore, Jordy. Once you have that reputation, you can *never* walk it back."

I looked at him. *You should know* was on the tip of my tongue, but I didn't say it. As I sat there looking at them, another idea began to form in my head. Brandon and Rees were the Supremes to Chad's Diana Ross. Was it possible to turn them against Chad? If Chad didn't have them, he'd be even more dependent on me ... divide and conquer. It made sense to turn them into allies—and then drive a wedge between them and Chad. And *they* were making the first overture. *So, Jordy, use this as an opportunity.* "You guys are right," I said. "And now that I think about it, I have been kind of whorish lately." I gave them both my most genuine-looking phony smile. "I so appreciate the two of you taking the time to talk to me about this. I promise to dial it back a bit." I touched Rees's hand. "You have to understand, I'm not used to this. It's all new to me." I shrugged. "You guys have been hot your whole lives. Me, I was always the fat kid no one noticed. So, the attention kind of goes to my head."

"I wasn't always hot," Rees replied.

I frowned at him. "Oh, come on, Rees. You were a jock in high school, weren't you?"

"Yeah," he replied, looking down at his hands. "I was. But I was carrying some extra weight. Chad pointed it out to me when we were pledges, so I started watching what I ate and doing more cardio."

Interesting.

"I was skinny," Brandon added. "Really skinny."

"I don't believe you." I speared another cucumber.

"Chad told me to eat more protein and lift heavier weights," Brandon went on.

"It's worked." I gave him a big smile. "You both look amazing. Chad really looks out for us, doesn't he?" I pushed my plate away. "If it weren't for him, I'd still be fat."

"You weren't ever fat, Jordy." Brandon made a face. "Sure, you weren't in the best shape, but you were always cute. I know I thought so."

"Me too," Rees added. He winked at me. "I mean, yeah, now you look amazing, but you were always a cute guy. You always had a nice ass." He giggled. "Seriously."

I bit my lower lip. I could hear Chad saying, *"Those shorts make your ass look like a billboard and make that roll around your waist look even bigger than it is."* I swallowed. "Thanks, guys, I appreciate it. And thanks for the advice."

"See, Brandon?" Rees finished his grilled cheese. "I told you he wouldn't get mad." He smiled at me. "Jordy's a great guy." He frowned. "I don't know why we don't hang out with you more."

"Because Chad monopolizes him," Brandon snapped.

Interesting, I thought. *Could there be dissension in the ranks?* I looked from one to the other. There was definitely something going on with Brandon and Chad, but what? Brandon most likely wouldn't say anything in front of Rees. *Divide and conquer—must get Brandon alone sometime.*

Rees looked alarmed at Brandon's disloyalty. "No, I'm sure that's not it. We're all friends and brothers."

"He does kind of keep us apart," I mused, trying really hard not to laugh out loud. The whole thing was so absurd. There wasn't anything stopping either Brandon or Rees from ever calling me or making plans with me, and Chad certainly wasn't—unless there was something they weren't telling me. Could Chad really have that kind of power over them? But if they wanted to think that, I wasn't about to stop them. "I wonder why?"

"Because Chad always has to be the center of attention," Brandon replied. "Haven't you noticed?"

"Brandon!" Rees warned.

"It's true, Rees, and you know it, even if you're too big of a coward to admit it," Brandon snapped. He turned back to me. "You might as well know, since we're being all friendly now." His face twisted into a sneer. "Chad's not that wonderful. Nobody could be as wonderful as Chad thinks he is."

Oh, trust me, I already know that.

"It has to be all about Chad or he won't be a part of it," Brandon went on. "He's not that much hotter than I am, no matter what he thinks."

"Brandon!" Rees stared at him, his mouth open.

Brandon gave him a long look. "Sorry," he mumbled to me. "Forget I said anything."

I definitely have to get Brandon alone sometime. I stood up. "Well, this was fun. Thanks, guys—I enjoyed this." I picked up my tray. "But I really need to get out of here. I've got to meet with my trainer." I glanced at my watch. "I'll be late if I don't get going."

"You really do look amazing," Rees said. "You've done a great job."

"Call me later, guys, and we'll do something." I walked away from the table, dumped my trash, and headed outside.

It's working!

I wanted to break into song in the middle of the Quad.

Chad was *jealous.*

He was beginning to realize what he was missing.

* * *

My workout went really well—even Jay, my trainer, noticed my good mood. I worked hard for two hours—it was chest and back day. "You're really getting big," Jay said as I stepped onto the scale after we were finished. "You've gained another three pounds since last week." He smiled at me. Jay was about forty. He'd competed as a bodybuilder when he was in his twenties and still was in remarkable shape.

"Three pounds?" I frowned, stepping off the scale and looking at myself in the mirror. I pulled my loose shirt tighter around my waist and made a face. "I don't want to get fat again."

"You aren't fat, Jordy." Jay shook his head. "Muscle mass is heavier and more compact than fat tissue, how many times do I have to tell you that? If anything, you were getting too thin for a while there. What's your waist size now?"

"I'm wearing 29s." I kept staring at myself and the pesky roll at my waist.

He laughed. "And you're worried about being fat?" Playfully he punched my shoulder. "Dude, I wear 32s." He shook his head. "You need to really work on your self-esteem. Now hit the showers."

There was no one in the locker room when I undressed. I grabbed a towel and headed for the steam room. I stopped in front of the full-length mirror by the steam room door and stared at myself. Was Jay right? I wondered, looking at myself from every angle. Was I being too hard on myself? I reached down and grabbed the roll at my waist. My stomach was flat, and in the overhead lighting I could see the abdominal muscles. I flexed them, and they popped out. I stuck a finger in between two of them. I still needed to drop some fat weight, I decided. I grinned at myself and opened the steam room door. It was empty, and I plopped down on the lower bench. Steam hissed as I leaned back, relaxing. I closed my eyes.

What a great day, I thought as I sat there sweating, my heart dancing. *My hot trainer gave me a compliment, Brandon and Rees both thought I was hot—hell, they'd thought I was cute before I started working out, and Chad—Chad is noticing the changes, too. Chad is starting to get jealous.*

I'd known it was just a matter of time before Chad noticed the attention I was getting when we were at Fusions.

Being beautiful was better than anything I could have ever imagined. People treated me differently—and not just at Fusions. I got better service in restaurants, and people were a lot friendlier to me. It was *nice.* It was nice having attractive guys come up to me and tell me I was sexy and hot. It was awesome being an object of desire. I'd never dreamed it would turn out this way—but it was working. Chad didn't like me going with other guys. He was starting to realize he'd made a huge mistake.

And when he made his move, I would shut him down the way he'd shut me down.

As I sat there, I went over it again and again in my mind.

Maybe it would happen tonight at Fusions.

I could see it so clearly. I'd be on the dance floor with my shirt off, dancing with some really hot muscle guy. We'd be touching each other, kissing underneath the disco ball, and Chad would interrupt.

Can I talk to you? he'd say, and lead me off the dance floor.

I love you, Jordy. You're so beautiful, so sexy. You're the perfect guy for me. You're smart and rich and funny and sexy, and you're everything I could ever possibly want in a boyfriend. I am so sorry I didn't see it before. I was being shallow and stupid. Can you ever possibly forgive me? I blinded myself to what was right in front of me the whole time. Can we go back to your place and start over?

Sure, I'd say, and we'd go back to my place.

And I would fuck that big, hard, muscular ass.

Afterward, we would lie there in bed together, and he'd say, *I am so glad we're together now.*

Together? I'd reply. *What do you mean?*

I smiled broadly as I imagined the look on his face when I would say the words that would make him feel the way he made me feel, when I would pull the rug out from under him and make him suffer the way he'd made me. *I don't think it's a good idea for us to date, Chad. I mean, you were probably right when you said it was a bad idea. I don't think it would work. You're sexy and a great guy and all, but you're really not boyfriend material.*

It would be *classic*.

The steam room door opened, but I kept my eyes closed, lost in my reverie. "Hey, Jordy." It was Jay, my trainer.

I opened my eyes. "Hey." I nodded to him. He was naked, not even a towel wrapped around his waist. I'd never seen Jay naked before. I knew he had a great body—he always wore shirts that exposed his upper pecs, shoulders, and arms—but his definition was unreal. His pecs were two thick slabs perched above deeply cut abdominal muscles. He trimmed his pubic hair and obviously shaved his thick balls.

"You mind if I turn up the steam?" he asked.

"Nope." He walked over to the controls and turned the dial up. His back was thickly muscled, and just above his ass was a tribal tattoo. "I want an ass like yours," I said, closing my eyes as more steam hissed into the room.

"Squats and lunges," he replied, sitting down on the bench next to me. "Which you're already doing."

"Cool," I replied. A few seconds later I felt his left leg brush up against mine. I opened my eyes. The steam room was filled with fog. I couldn't see the door or the glass panes. I looked at Jay, sitting next to me. He was pressing his leg against mine, and with his right hand he was stroking himself.

"What are you doing?" I asked, even though it was obvious.

He smiled at me, placing his other hand on my inner thigh. "You're very sexy, Jordy." He moved his hand farther up, until it reached my towel. He paused for just a moment and then slid his hand under the towel. His fingers closed around my cock, which was getting hard.

"Is this a good idea?" I gasped out as he started rubbing the head of my cock with his thumb.

"I'm not looking for a boyfriend," he replied. "If you want me to stop, I will."

"As long as this doesn't fuck up our—*oh*." He opened my towel.

He whistled. "Man, I knew you were hung, but that's just beautiful." He slid down to his knees and pushed my legs farther apart. He licked the head, and I closed my eyes and leaned back. "And, no, it won't interfere with our business relationship, unless we let it." His tongue darted out and licked me again. "What's a little head between friends?" He took me into his mouth.

I can't believe my trainer is giving me a blow job in the steam room in my gym, I thought, smiling to myself.

He started moving his mouth up and down my shaft.

"Oh, Jay, that's nice," I whispered as he kept working me. He slid one of his hands between my ass cheeks and started fingering my asshole.

The steam continued to hiss and swirl around us as he sucked my cock. My skin was drenched in sweat, water rolling down my face and chest.

I reached down and started pulling on his nipples. He took my cock out of his mouth and smiled up at me. "Oh, yeah, baby, that's nice, work them nipples. Harder." I twisted them and pulled. He moaned and then put his mouth on my cock again. He was stroking himself with his other hand as his right hand kept playing with my asshole. He started moving his head faster as I yanked on his nipples so hard I thought they might come off in my hands.

And I could feel my cum starting to rise in me.

"Oooooh, I'm going to come!"

He pulled his head back just as I shot. I came in his face and hair, thick ropy strings of white cum shooting into his smiling face . . . and he moaned as he came, his eyes closed as I pulled on his nipples, his entire body trembling.

Finished, he smiled at me, grabbing my towel and wiping his face.

"Go shower," he whispered, "and thanks."

I am a whore, I thought to myself as I walked out to my car. *I just had sex in a public place with my personal trainer, for God's sake. Maybe Chad is right—I need to slow it down some.*

That was the part about my "whorish" behavior that was so funny. Chad had no idea what I did outside of Fusions.

My cell phone chirped as I climbed into the car. I checked my text messages. There were three from Chad, *Call me when you get this, we're still going to Fusions tonight right,* and *CALL ME!*

There was also a new one from Jay.

That was amazing, Jordy. Do you want to have dinner sometime?

I smiled to myself, typing back, *If I get to fuck that hot ass, hell yeah.*

Oh, hell yeah was his response. I laughed as I started my car.

I might not have been good enough for Chad, but no one else seemed to think so. My personal trainer was into me. The hot guys at Fusions liked me, wanted me.

Jay was right. I needed to seriously work on my self-esteem.

I drove home.

I got to Fusions shortly after nine.

Chad, Brandon, and Rees were standing at the bar when I walked in. Brandon's face looked thunderous, and I wondered what was going on. I got a drink and walked over to them. "Hey guys, what's up?" The bar was crowded, and a hot muscle daddy with tattoos all over his chest smiled at me. I smiled back.

Brandon shrugged. "Oh, we're getting a lecture on conduct." His face was twisted in anger, his arms folded in front of his chest.

"Conduct?" I looked at their faces, one at a time.

"If you want to be a slut, Brandon, no one's stopping you," Chad snapped. "But don't come crying to me when—"

"Don't worry." Brandon cut him off. "You're the last person in the world I'd come to." He walked away, and Rees shrugged before going after him.

"What was that all about?" I sipped my drink, trying not to smile. *I'd been right—there was dissension in the ranks.*

Chad shrugged. "I'm just sick to death of Brandon's attitude, is all." He smiled. "I like that shirt. It's really flattering. Can I borrow it sometime?"

"Sure," I replied. Brandon and Rees were standing by the dance floor, arguing. "Do you think I'm acting like a whore, Chad?"

"What?" Startled, he looked at me. "Why would you ask that?"

"Well, Brandon and Rees and I had lunch today, and—"

He set his jaw. "Let me guess. They told you I said that, right?" A muscle in his jaw pulsed. "Damn it to hell, I'm going to kick his fucking ass."

"It's not a big deal—"

"I've about had it up to here with the two of them," Chad went on like I'd said nothing. "Last Wednesday when you left with that guy, I said something, but it was just a joke. I can't believe they repeated that to you." His eyes narrowed. "They're both just jealous of you, is all."

"Jealous? Of me?"

"They think you're taking their place." He rolled his eyes and then froze. "Oh. God."

I turned to see what he'd seen, and my heart sank. It was Dante, looking amazing in a white wifebeater and a pair of cutoff jeans. *Damn it!* I swore to myself. *This is all I need.* He saw us, smiled, and walked over. "Hey guys." He leaned in and kissed me on the cheek. "Hi, Chad."

My eyes went back and forth between them. I was torn between leaving them alone or staying and watching. I didn't want to watch them go through a mating dance—but maybe Chad wasn't interested. . . .

"How are you?" Chad asked stiffly, his face tightening.

"Doing good." Dante smiled, flashing his perfect teeth. "I just bought a new car."

"Cool. What did you get?" I asked when Chad didn't say anything.

"A Mercedes. Maybe I'll take you for a ride sometime." Dante brushed against me.

What's going on here? I wondered. My body was reacting,

and I gulped down the rest of my drink. I smiled. "Excuse me, guys, I need to get another drink."

"I'll get it. What are you having?" Dante flashed his teeth at me again.

Is he flirting with me? In front of Chad?

"Vodka cranberry."

"Be right back." He turned and headed for the bar without asking Chad if he wanted anything.

Chad's eyes narrowed. "He's being awful friendly to you." He sniffed. "I suppose he's trying to make me jealous."

"Because of course he couldn't possibly be interested in me," I said before I could stop myself.

Chad gave me a weird look. "I didn't say that."

"Forget it."

"No." Chad crossed his arms. "Why did you say that?"

"Well, you always act like I'm a leper or something," I replied, cursing myself for saying anything. "I'm not."

"Here you go, Jordy." Dante handed me my drink.

"Thanks, Dante." I took a big gulp. Chad was still staring at me.

"I can't get over you," Dante said, looking me up and down. "I haven't seen you in what? Three weeks? And look at you. You look incredible."

He is flirting with me, I thought, trying not to get excited about it. *This was too, too perfect.* I glanced at Chad, whose face was turning red. He was furious. And in that instant, I made up my mind.

Because of course, Chad, anyone who'd ever been interested in you couldn't possibly ever want ME, right? Because I'm just a loser, right? Well, I'll show you loser, you fucking asshole.

And I saw everything with perfect clarity in that moment. I could lose weight, I could build muscle, I could build the kind of body an underwear model would envy—but to Chad I would always be that loser who wasn't good enough for him. He was never, ever under any circumstance going to want me. I was never going to be "his type."

It was all I could do not to throw my drink in his arrogant face.

I turned to Dante. "You want to dance? I love this song."

"I'd love to."

We left Chad standing there and went out onto the dance floor. I took my shirt off and tucked it into the back of my jeans as I started moving. Dante was dancing with me, and our chests brushed against each other. "You're a great dancer," he breathed into my ear as he came up behind me and rubbed his crotch against my ass. "Very sexy."

I laughed. "Well, you're a god."

His big arms snaked around my waist, and he pulled me back against him. I turned my head back over my shoulder and we kissed. Out of the corner of my eye I could see Chad watching us with no expression on his face. His arms were folded, and if he could, there was no doubt in my mind he would have shot laser beams out of his eyes at us.

We danced for a couple more songs, and Dante excused himself to go to the bathroom.

I walked over to Chad, using my shirt to mop sweat off my face.

"What do you think you're doing?" Chad said angrily.

"Dancing."

"You're breaking the code."

"Code? What code?"

"You don't sleep with your friends' exes," Chad hissed through clenched teeth.

"Who said I was going to sleep with him?"

"You're practically fucking on the goddamned dance floor!" Chad snarled. "You don't want to get on my bad side."

"You need to calm down," I replied, not allowing myself to get angry. "We're just dancing, Chad. What is your problem?"

"You're right." He shook his head. "I'm sorry, Jordy. I—you know what? I think I'm just going to leave."

"Why?"

"I'm just not into this anymore." He looked at me. "You want to go grab something at the Iron Skillet?"

He looked so sad my anger melted away. "Sure. What about Rees and Brandon?"

"We came in Brandon's car. You drove, right?"

I nodded. "Yeah."

"Come on, let's go."

The Iron Skillet wasn't very crowded. I ordered a club sandwich without mayonnaise, Chad a grilled cheese. I was going to regret the sandwich, but I figured I'd do an extra ten minutes on the elliptical machine the next day.

"I'm sorry I was being such a bitch," Chad said as we ate our food. "Brandon just really pissed me off, and then seeing Dante—" He made a face. "It just kind of threw me off."

"He probably was just trying to make you jealous," I replied, keeping my voice even. "Very junior high school."

"Well, Jordy, maybe, maybe not." He gave me a sad smile. "I hope you don't think I think you're unattractive." He swallowed. "It's amazing the way you've transformed. You look completely different."

But you didn't say I looked good.

"I'm so glad we're friends," he went on. "I mean, Rees and Brandon are good guys, but they're not like you." He looked down at his food. "Sometimes I think you're my only real friend."

In spite of myself I was touched. "You mean that?"

He nodded. "I mean, Rees and Brandon are fun, but

that's all they think about—partying and getting laid. You're different. You're serious."

He touched my hand.

Here it comes, I exulted.

"I'm so glad we never slept together," he went on. "That would spoil everything. You can't stay friends with someone after you've slept with them."

My heart shattered. "I know," I managed to say.

I dropped him off at the house and headed home.

As I pulled into my parking space, my phone beeped. I flipped it open. There was a text from Dante.

Hey, man, where did you go? I was enjoying dancing with you. Some other time?

I smiled to myself. *Fuck you, Chad*, I thought as I got out of the car.

It was time for a change in plans, and strategy.

Chapter 10

I hesitated for a moment, my hand poised to knock on the president's office door. I wasn't sure why I was there—but I doubted it was something good. I'd gotten the e-mail that morning, asking if I could stop by at three. No explanation, no hint as to what the meeting was about, so I'd wondered about it all day. Now it was three on the dot. *Don't be a pussy, Jordy,* I chided myself, and knocked.

The door opened almost immediately, and I wondered if Chris Moore had been standing there waiting for my knock. He smiled, which relaxed me a little. "Thanks for stopping by." He stuck out his hand and gave me the fraternity hand-shake. "Come on in and have a seat."

"I haven't been in here since I accepted my bid," I said. Chris's room was just on the other side of the office. His door was open, and I could see how messy his room was. I sat down in the very same chair I'd sat in to get my bid. Then I was too nervous to pay any attention to the room. It was really small, and there was another door behind the desk. A group photo of the brothers in tuxes was the only decoration on the white walls, and it was captioned SPRING BETA KAPPA FORMAL. I crossed my legs and waited.

Chris closed the office door. "We're getting a little concerned about you, Jordy," he said, walking around and sitting down behind his desk.

"Who's we?" I asked, shifting uncomfortably in my seat. "I can ask, right?"

"Of course you can ask, Jordy." He gave me a smile. He made a steeple with his fingers on the desktop. "This isn't an interrogation. You don't need a lawyer or anything."

"Good to know," I replied, forcing a smile on my face. "So, who's getting concerned about me, Chris? And what about?"

"The Executive Council." He put his elbows on the desk and leaned forward a bit. He gave me a reassuring smile. "And don't feel singled out. You're not the only brother I'm having a chat with this week." He shrugged. "We've noticed that you've missed a couple of Monday night meetings, and you weren't around at all last week for Little Sister Rush." He waved a hand. "I know, you're gay and you don't care about women, I get that, but Little Sister Rush is *important,* even if it's not mandatory."

"But if it isn't mandatory—" I shrugged. "It shouldn't be held against me if I didn't come." I thought about making an excuse—a term paper or something—but kept silent. I'd gone to Fusions on Wednesday night with Chad and the guys, and Chris probably knew. It wasn't easy keeping secrets at Beta Kappa.

He leaned back in his chair and sighed. "I know, I know, but Monday night meetings are mandatory. And when you miss a few of them, and then skip Little Sister Rush..." He spread his hands helplessly. "If you miss another meeting you're going to be placed on social probation. You know what that means, right? You can't come to parties, you can't come to the formal. And you don't want that, do you?"

I bit my lip and shook my head no.

"Which leads to another problem," Chris went on. "As you know, Big Brother Night is this Saturday. Attendance is mandatory. And you've been chosen."

I gulped. "Seriously?" I hadn't been expecting that. Since Rush Week, I'd had little interaction with any of the pledges I'd helped recruit. I hadn't even given them a second thought. I'd been so wrapped up in my revenge fantasies—and I could hardly explain *that* to Chris.

"Seriously," Chris replied. "And I don't know if you *should* be allowed the privilege of having a little brother. You've really been shirking your responsibilities to the house, Jordy." He shook his head. "What's going on with you? You were such a *great* pledge."

"I've been dealing with some personal shit, Chris." I looked down at my hands. I just couldn't look him in the eyes. I shook my head. "I'm sorry. I shouldn't let my own bullshit interfere with my commitments to the brotherhood."

"I'm probably going to cross a line here." He narrowed his eyes. "But I'm sorry, I feel like I have to, Jordy. Believe it or not, I am really worried about you." He wiped his eyes. "As president, I feel like I have a responsibility—not just to the brotherhood as a whole, but to every brother here in the house." He began drumming his fingers on the desk, and I realized he was actually rather nervous. He barked out a mirthless laugh. "I haven't gotten to know you well, but I like what I do know. You know we don't have a problem with your sexuality, right?"

I bit my lip and nodded. "Diversity is our strength."

"Beta Kappa used to be just as homophobic as every other house on the mall," he went on. "Sure, there were brothers in the house who were gay, but as long as they kept it quiet there wasn't a problem." He shrugged. "I consider myself to be straight, but I've been with guys before. I just prefer women. So, I guess you could say I'm bi or whatever. It's only been a couple of years since we made the house more open to people with alternative sexualities, and I still believe that's a good thing. But there's still an undercurrent of homophobia here in the house. It's closeted, if you'll forgive the expression, but there are brothers here who don't like gays. But they deal with it, and at least on the surface don't act on it. Overt homophobia, just like overt racism, is grounds for being expelled from the house."

"I know." This had all been part of our pledge training, and I wasn't sure why he was going over all of this with me again.

"I don't know if you were out before you pledged, but one of the things we all take pride in—as a whole, and me certainly as an individual—is the fact Beta Kappa is here for all of our brothers whenever things get tough for them. Some brothers have issues with their coming out process." He sighed. "How has it been for you?"

I blinked at him a few times. I opened my mouth to say, *Everything's been just fine,* but I couldn't bring myself to say the words. He sat there patiently watching me, waiting for me to say something. A flood of emotions rushed through my mind. But the one thought I kept coming back to was, *He's talking to me because he cares.*

I felt like crying.

"It's been hard," I replied finally, trying to keep my voice steady. "I had no idea it would be this hard." Tears started filling my eyes. "I mean, Blair and Jeff have been great . . . but . . ."

Chris sighed. "It's Chad York, isn't it?" He got up out of his chair and walked around behind me, putting his hands on my shoulders. "I know you two have gotten close."

"I don't know that I would call it *close*." I wiped at my eyes. "I care about him, but sometimes..."

He started rubbing my shoulders. "Let it all out, Jordy. You can trust me."

"I just don't know." I hated myself for being so close to tears. "I love him and I hate him at the same time." It felt good to say it aloud. "And I don't have anyone to talk to about it. I mean, what am I supposed to do?" A tear slipped out of my right eye. "I mean, sometimes he's so sweet and nice—and then two minutes later he's just so fucking mean." I wiped at my eyes. "He's been so nice—I mean, he helped me figure out how to dress, and..." I let my voice trail off. I waved my hand and struggled to get ahold of myself. "And then other times he just makes me feel like I'm *worthless*."

"You aren't worthless, Jordy." Chris patted me on the shoulders and sat back down again. "You have to know that, believe it. You're a great guy. You have a kind heart—I mean, how many brothers have you helped with papers? All someone has to do is ask you for help, and you never say no." He folded his hands. "You're an asset to the house. You've got a great sense of humor—everyone likes you." He gestured at me. "And you've changed so much physically. You don't even look like the same person who pledged last semester."

"Chad told me he—" My eyes welled up again. "He told me he could never be interested in someone who didn't—"

A muscle worked in Chris's jaw. "So you started working out." He sighed. "Look, Jordy, I don't have all the answers. But it seems to me you'd be better off with someone who appreciates you for who you are."

"I'm in love with him." It felt good to say it out loud. "Chris, please don't tell anyone."

"What we talk about in here is no one's business," Chris

replied. "Your secret is safe with me. Besides, I kind of suspected." He sighed. "I've been watching you, Jordy—and the way you look at Chad—"

I closed my eyes. "Believe me, Chris, I don't want to be. I love him, but I don't like him very much. Does that make sense? Can you love someone without liking them?"

"Apparently you can." He gently smiled. "That's got to be hard, Jordy. Chad's a hard person to get to know. I should know—he's my little brother. Sometimes I wonder if I failed him somehow, you know? He was *different* when he was a pledge. So eager to please, so committed. . . . I don't know if something happened to him between his initiation and the next semester, but he was different when he came back." He sighed. "Maybe when he was a pledge he was acting, and he didn't need to act anymore when he was initiated . . . but I thought we were close. I was wrong, I guess. Maybe that's who he was all along." He peered at me. "You've changed, too, Jordy—and I'm not talking about just physically, either. What's with you and Roger?"

"Roger?" I wiped my eyes and got control of myself. "What's Roger got to do with any of this?"

"You two started out really strong, and now it seems like you barely speak." He nodded. "Did Chad have something to do with that?"

I wanted to say *yes*, but it would have been a lie—and I didn't want to lie to Chris. "No, it's my fault. I chose Chad over Roger."

"I see." He looked at me. "Look, I don't know what's going on with you, but you're not the same guy who pledged the house. I know you're going through some stuff, but you're a good person, Jordy—don't ever lose sight of that. I know you'll get through this and you're a lot stronger than you give yourself credit for."

"Thank you."

"But you can't allow yourself to lose sight of the brotherhood and your commitment to it." Chris shook his head. "Ordinarily, I wouldn't allow you to take a little brother, given your sporadic attendance this semester, but I also think the responsibility is something you need right now, and it might help you to realize how important the house really is to you. Are you willing to take on that responsibility?"

I thought for a moment. "I think so."

He smiled. "The pledge who's chosen you is Galen Donovan."

I gulped. "Galen? Seriously?"

"Seriously." Chris leaned back in his chair. "I don't want to sound condescending, but I know Galen is a good-looking kid. I don't know if he's gay or straight—you know we don't ask—but it's your responsibility to see him through this semester, to teach him about brotherhood and to watch out for him. That means—"

"I can't sleep with him."

"At least not until after initiation." Chris went on. "Sex complicates things—as I'm sure you've already found out. I would advise against it."

I nodded. "I understand." I stood up and reached across the desk to shake his hand. "Thanks, Chris. I'll be a better brother, and you won't be sorry you let me take Galen."

"If you need to talk, my door's always open." He sat back down. "The brotherhood is always here for you, Jordy. Never forget that. Beta Kappa for life."

"Beta Kappa for life," I replied, shutting the door behind me.

I stood in the hallway for a moment, a little shaken.

I've been a shitty brother this semester, I thought, *and I'm lucky Chris's decided to give me another chance. I've let all this idiocy with Chad change me for the worse, and it's consumed me. It's not healthy. I've been obsessed.*

I looked at myself in the mirror across from the office door.

I didn't like what I saw—and for once, it wasn't the way I looked.

You've been so consumed with trying to get even with Chad you've let everything else slide. You've let it affect your relationship with Roger, with Blair, with Jeff, with everyone else in the house for that matter. And for what? Because Chad didn't want you? So what? There are plenty of other guys out there who do want you, who do see what you have to offer, and Brandon and Rees were right. You've been acting like a whore, and that doesn't reflect well on you. Let it go, Jordy. Let it all go. You can still be friends with Chad. You know he's not evil, he's a good person—you've let everything you feel for him be colored by the fact he wasn't attracted to you and just wanted to be friends.

I smiled at myself.

Let this be the start of a new Jordy. Recommit to the brotherhood, recommit to the house, patch things up with Roger, and start fresh with Chad, too. Let go of the negativity and focus only on the positive.

I heard someone coming down the stairs at a gallop and turned to see who it was. "Hi, Brandon!" I grinned. "How's it going?"

"Jordy!" He enveloped me in a hug. "Dude, about yesterday—"

"It's okay, bud." I smiled at him. "Really, I appreciated it."

He sighed in relief and flashed his gap-toothed grin at me. "I'm so glad. Rees and I were both worried—especially after last night at Fusions—we thought you might be mad—"

"No, it wasn't that." We started walking down the hall. "I was just caught up in some Chad drama."

Brandon rolled his eyes. "There's *always* Chad drama, isn't there?" He grinned again. "Well, let's do something soon." His face darkened. "After I finish this damned Modern European History paper, anyway." He sighed. "Man, this is a *bitch*."

"What are you writing about?"

"He assigned me the Thirty Years' War. I'm on my way to the library now to get some books." He sighed. "If I don't get started now, there's no way I'll ever finish."

"Tell you what—why don't you come over to my place tomorrow night and I'll help you with it?" I smiled at him. "I did a paper on it in high school—I may even still have it on my computer. I mean, I won't let you plagiarize it, but you can look it over and maybe it'll give you some ideas on how to do yours."

"Seriously?" He stared at me. "You'd do that?"

"Of course I would."

He grabbed me in a bear hug, lifted me, and spun me around. "Dude, you're the best!" He kissed me on the cheek and set me down. "Okay, I'll come by tomorrow night around six, is that cool?"

I nodded, and grinned as he ran down the hallway and out into the parking lot.

I felt better already.

I walked down the hallway and paused in front of Roger's door. *Why the hell not?* I said to myself. *Might as well get started making amends—there's no time like the present.* I started knocking.

There was no answer. I tried again, and then shrugged. *I can catch up to him later.*

I walked out the back door. Some of the brothers were playing basketball at the far end of the parking lot. I walked over to my car, and was about to unlock it when one of them yelled, "Hey, Jordy!"

I stopped and saw Chad walking toward me. He was drenched in sweat and wasn't wearing a shirt. The sunlight gleamed on his wet torso. He was wearing a pair of long gray fleece shorts that almost reached his knees. In spite of myself, I felt a stirring in my groin.

Down, boy, I said to myself. *Out with the negative, in with the positive. A fresh start with everyone, right?*

"Hi, Chad." I grinned at him. "What's up?"

"I'm so glad to see you," he said, slightly out of breath. "I wanted to call you later. I owe you an apology."

"Really? For what?" I replied, thinking, *See? When you start thinking positive and get rid of the negative energy, everything starts getting better.*

"I was kind of bitchy to you last night," he said, running a hand through his hair. Drops of sweat flew as he shook his head from side to side. "About Dante, I mean."

I waved my hand. "You don't need to apologize."

"No, I do," he went on. "I mean, obviously Dante was using you to try to make me jealous, and I took it all out on you. I mean, it wasn't your fault he was acting so junior high."

"It's okay, really, Chad—"

He laughed. "I can't believe I let him get to me that way." He rolled his eyes. "I don't know what I ever saw in him. I mean, really." He tossed his head. "And it was so obvious—I mean, like he would ever be interested in someone like you."

It was like being slapped across the face. I froze but somehow managed to keep my face neutral. I didn't say a word.

He looked at me. "You know what I meant," he said, nonchalantly dismissing his hateful words.

"Yes." I smiled. "I know exactly what you meant. Thanks for the apology." I turned and clicked my key fob to unlock the car. "I've got to run. I'm going to be late for my trainer."

"I'll call you later!"

I started the car, then backed out of the spot. I shifted the car into drive. He was still standing where I'd left him. He shrugged and started walking back to the basketball game. I sat there, my car idling, and watched him walking. But rather than admiring the muscles in his back, or fantasizing about his ass, I thought, *I could run him down right now.*

It would be so enormously satisfying.

I imagined pushing my right foot down on the gas pedal.

I heard the thump as the front of the car hit him.

I could hear his startled cry as he rolled up onto the hood, the shocked look on his face as it hit my windshield.

I put my foot on the gas pedal.

I shook my head and drove out of the parking lot.

But as I turned out of the lot, I reached for my cell phone. I clicked through the address book until I reached DANTE, and hit the send button.

It rang twice. "Dante Bertucci."

"Hey, Dante, this is Jordy Valentine."

"Hi, Jordy."

"I just wanted to call and apologize for last night," I said smoothly. "I was wondering if I could make it up to you somehow?"

"There's no need to make up anything." He laughed into the phone. "I was a little surprised that you disappeared, but I figured Chad had something to do with it."

"Yeah, well." I laughed. "I still feel kind of bad about it."

"Tell you what—why don't you come over to my place tonight around seven? I'll make you dinner," he purred into the phone.

"If you're just trying to get back at Chad—"

"Chad has nothing to do with this," Dante replied. "That's over. Come on over tonight and I'll show you what I mean." He gave me the address.

"See you tonight," I replied.

I closed my phone and smiled. *Dante would never be interested in someone like me, right, Chad? Obviously he would only use me to try to make you jealous—as if someone as beautiful and perfect as you could ever be jealous of a loser like me, right?*

So much for getting rid of the negativity and starting over.

Dante's house was in Avignon, a separate township just over the city line. I plugged his address into my car's GPS and headed out at a quarter till seven. I chewed on my lip as I drove. My workout with Jay that afternoon had been strange—he'd acted weird through the whole two hours—distant and unfriendly. This was a change. This was our first workout since our steam room adventure, and several times I'd wanted to ask him if something was wrong. When the session was over, I'd grabbed my bag and left the gym, not showering there like I usually did.

I shouldn't have done anything with him. That was a mistake. Obviously, it changed things, even though he said it wouldn't.

I shook my head as I turned into Dante's subdivision. *Maybe I should just find a new trainer. I'm not paying him to be rude to me.*

The GPS directed me into the driveway of a beautiful, two-story brick house. I turned the car off and sat for a moment. I was a few minutes early. I looked at the lawn, which was perfectly manicured. Rows of rose bushes lined the front porch. A fountain bubbled in the center of the lawn. Behind the house, palm trees towered over the roof. I got out of the car and started up the walk, thinking, *This is crazy, I shouldn't be doing this. Remember positivity, no more negativity. Look at how fucked up things are with Jay now. Do I really want to go down this path?* I climbed the steps to the porch. *I'm not really interested in Dante, I'm only interested in getting even with Chad, and that's really unfair to Dante.*

I started to turn to go, but then I heard Chad's voice in my head.

"He wouldn't be interested in someone like you."

"We'll just see about that, Chad," I muttered, and knocked on the door.

The door opened, and Dante stood there in a yellow Speedo, wiping water from his chest. "Sorry." He smiled. "I was taking a swim and lost track of time. Come on in."

I walked into the house and gasped. The entryway went all the way to the roof, and there was a skylight. The entryway opened into a huge sunken living room, and as I walked down the steps I couldn't get over how beautifully decorated it was. The floor was covered in a deep plush carpet my feet sank into. The walls were painted a soft coral, and the entire back wall was glass, with a stunning view of a swimming pool landscaped to look like a grotto. I walked over to the wall of glass. "Wow." The entire backyard was lush with vegetation. "It looks like a jungle out there."

"That was the idea," Dante said from behind me. "Why don't you go on out and have a seat? I'll put some clothes on and meet you out there."

I started to say not to bother but bit my tongue. "Okay."

"There's an open bottle of red wine on the table out

there," he said, turning to walk down the hallway. "Help yourself."

The yellow bikini barely covered his backside, and I watched him go. *Get a grip, Jordy—don't even go there.* I opened the sliding glass door and stepped into the backyard, then closed the door behind me. There was a picnic table just outside the door, and the patio was covered. I poured myself a glass of wine and sat at the table.

A cool evening breeze stirred the wind chimes, and the waterfall at the near end of the pool splashed soothingly. It was very quiet back there, and all the stars were out in a dark purple sky overhead. *If I didn't know better, I'd think I was out in the country somewhere,* I thought, taking a sip of the wine. It was a Chilean pinot noir, and was quite good. *Excellent taste in wine, a gorgeous home—Chad was crazy to walk away from this.* I turned to the sound of the glass door sliding open again. Dante smiled at me. He'd put on a white cotton guayabera shirt and loose-fitting surgical scrub pants. He gestured at his clothes. "I hope you don't mind, but when I'm home I like to be comfortable."

I refilled my glass. "I don't mind at all. This is really good wine."

"Glad you like it." He filled a glass for himself and we clinked glasses. "And I'm glad you're here."

"Why am I here, anyway?" I asked, setting my glass down on the picnic table.

Dante flashed me his perfect white teeth. "I like you. I want to get to know you better." He shrugged his powerful shoulders. "Is there something wrong with that?"

"Chad thinks you're trying to make him jealous."

"Chad thinks everything's about Chad," he countered evenly. "Do we need to talk about him? It's a beautiful night, don't you think, and I would rather talk about you."

"Me?" I was flattered, in spite of myself. "What do you want to know, Dante?"

"Do you really speak three languages?" He got up and walked over to the house, and flipped a switch. Pachelbel's Canon began playing softly through concealed speakers. He sat back down, raising his eyebrows.

"Four, actually." I took another sip of the wine. "If you count English."

He laughed. He had a nice laugh, and I smiled back at him. I turned and looked back at the jungle. "It's very peaceful back here."

"That was the idea," he replied. "I work really hard, and my job can be pretty stressful, so I wanted a tranquil space where I could come relax when I got home." He shrugged. "The whole house is designed to be relaxing, so every place you go is comfortable. Every room, every chair, every couch, everything is in harmony and balance. Would you like a tour?"

"Maybe later." I laughed. "I'm just so relaxed back here I don't want it to ever end."

"Life getting you down?" he asked, an eyebrow arching as he reached for the bottle to refill his glass.

"A little." I wrapped my arms around myself. "But sitting back here, I feel like I can take care of everything. Nothing seems important back here." I smiled at him. "Thanks for inviting me over."

"My pleasure." He glanced at his watch. "Dinner won't be ready for about another hour. You want to get in the hot tub?"

"I didn't bring a suit."

"I can loan you one."

"You just dried off." I shrugged. "Maybe later?"

"You spoil all my fun," he teased. "Now I'll have to come up with another way to get you out of your clothes."

I stood up and pulled my shirt up over my head. "All you have to do is ask," I replied, tossing my shirt to him. He caught it, folded it, and placed it on the table. I kicked off my shoes and started to undo my pants.

"Wait a minute." He got up and walked around to me. He put his big arms around me and pulled me in close. I could feel his heart pounding as he pressed his thick chest against me. "I like you, Jordy. I like you a lot." He looked me deep in the eyes. "And yes, I want to take you to bed. But I don't want a one-night stand with you."

"What *do* you want?" I replied, leaning my face toward his until we were bare inches apart.

"I want to get to know you. I want to date you." His hands slid down my back and cupped my ass. "Is that something you want, too?"

I slid my hands inside his shirt until they rested on his big pecs. His skin felt hot to the touch. "I think I could want that, yes."

He leaned in and kissed me. It was chaste, a sweet kiss, just our lips pressed against each other as we stood there. He tasted of the wine and mint. He slowly started moving me around in a slow dance, there under the stars, to Pachelbel's Canon. And when he undid my pants, I didn't resist as he slid them down. I stepped out of them and pulled his shirt up over his head, kissing him at the base of his throat. "You have such a beautiful body," I breathed into his ear as he started kissing my neck.

"Not as beautiful as yours," he whispered back, and he swung me up into his strong arms as effortlessly as if I weighed no more than a feather, and carried me back into the house, kissing me the entire time. He set me down on the couch and stepped out of the scrubs. He was naked underneath them, and he sat beside me on the couch. He lay back and pulled me down on top of him. I traced his lips with my right index finger, and we kissed again.

It was like nothing I'd ever experienced before. Usually sex was rushed, hurried, and frantic—an animalistic need to sate desire. But this—this was gentle, and slow, and loving. We explored each other's bodies with hands, mouths, and tongues in a slow ritual of pleasure. And when I finally entered him, it was like we became one with each other. I didn't want to slam into him, pound away at him until he gasped with pleasure and screamed when he came. Instead, I gently moved into him, not pressing, not forcing myself into him. Rather, I waited for him to slowly open to me, slowly sliding back and forth until his breathing came faster and I went deeper into him.

I couldn't take my eyes off his incredible body as I made love to him, as I kissed his neck, as I stroked his magnificent chest.

And when he came, just before I did, tears slipped out of my eyes. And when I was finished, I collapsed on top of him, and he kissed the top of my head.

"That was beautiful," he whispered. "I could lie here with you for the rest of my life and never get up." He smiled. "Hey, you're crying." He kissed my wet cheeks. "Why?"

"I don't know." I snuggled against him. "I've just never felt so close to someone before." I felt safe lying there, in his arms, like nothing in the world mattered.

He squeezed me a little tighter. "It's been hard on you, hasn't it."

I nodded. "I've been so lonely." I forced a laugh. "I had no idea just how lonely until now."

"You don't ever have to worry about that anymore." He kissed my cheek again. "You're a special guy, Jordy. I could see that the first time I met you." He started stroking the back of my head. "Forget about Chad. Forget about everything in your past. Start over. You can't do anything about the past, but you can do something about the future. Don't let your history poison your future."

Chad was an idiot to walk away from you, I thought.

"You're a good person," he continued. "That's what matters. The outside is just wrapping paper. You can wrap a pile of shit in the most gorgeous paper, but it's still a pile of shit." He kissed me again. "Now wipe those tears away. No more crying, you got it?"

"I'm okay." I smiled back at him. "Should we shower before dinner?"

He nodded, and I climbed off him. When he stood he wrapped his arms around me again. "Stay the night?"

I nodded. "I'd like that."

And he led me to the shower.

Chapter 11

Having sex with Brandon had been the last thing on my mind when he came over so I could help him with his paper. But it had been kind of a shitty day. I woke up in Dante's arms, and he made me breakfast before I came home. He'd sent me a few flirty texts in the morning, which made me smile, and I'd responded in kind. He wanted me to come back over that night, but I remembered agreeing to help Brandon with his paper so had to beg off—and the next night was Big Brother Night and I'd be stuck at the house. So we made plans for me to come over for dinner on Sunday. *Make sure you bring a swimsuit ;)* was his last text.

I'd gone to my classes walking on air. I couldn't focus on the lectures. I just sat there and daydreamed about Dante, remembering what it felt like to have his arms around me, remembering how special being with him was. I'd always thought the term *making love* was stupid—but now I understood what it meant. There was definitely a difference between that and fucking. I was sorry I wasn't going to be able to see him again until Sunday. I couldn't wait—especially after he texted me a nude photo while I was sitting in my Art History class.

It was at the gym that the day started going downhill.

I showed up at Body Quest in my workout clothes. I checked in at the front desk, and the girl working there frowned at me. "Didn't Jay call you?"

"I don't think so," I replied, pulling my phone out of my shorts pocket. I checked the messages. Nothing from Jay. "Is there a problem?"

"You really need to talk to Jay." She sighed. "He doesn't work here anymore. He should have called his clients to let them know." She pushed a stray lock of hair off her forehead. "I'm so sorry."

"What?" I stared at her. "What happened?"

She looked around, then leaned over the counter. "I'm not supposed to say anything," she whispered, "but you were one of his clients so you should probably know. He had sex in the steam room with one of the members."

Oh, my God. "Seriously?"

She nodded. "One of the other members went into the locker room and saw him. He even recorded it on his cell phone and turned it over to the manager." She clicked her tongue. "The member is going to have his membership canceled, once Rosemary gets a chance to talk to him." She shook her head. "Can you believe it?"

"Thanks," I mumbled, and headed over to the elliptical machine to start my workout.

Somehow, I managed to make it through my workout. I drifted from machine to machine, crazy thoughts running through my head.

They're going to cancel my membership, I'm going to have to find another gym and another trainer, someone taped us in the steam room, I wonder who it was, I can't believe I let him do it, I wonder why someone would do such a thing, there's a video of me having sex with Jay, oh, my God, I wonder if anyone else has seen it, what if it gets posted on the Internet, oh, God, I need to talk to Dante, what am I going to do?

When I finished my workout, I headed out to the parking lot. I got into my car and sat there for a moment. I got my phone out of the console and texted Jay: *Just found out—dude, I'm so sorry.*

I didn't expect an answer, and didn't get one.

All the way home I fumed. There *had* to be something I could do. Sure, Jay and I had broken the gym rules, but it was still shitty. I made a call when I got home, and felt a lot better when I hung up.

Brandon showed up at six on the dot, wearing a pair of nylon sweatpants and a tank top showing off his broad shoulders and firm chest. He gave me a hug and a kiss when I answered the door. It was obvious he wasn't wearing underwear. "Thanks for doing this," he said, plopping down on my couch. "I appreciate it." He winked at me. "I promise to make it up to you somehow."

"No need. You want something to drink?" I asked, getting myself a Diet Dr Pepper out of the refrigerator. Soda makes you bloat, but I kept some on hand for a treat every once in a while. After the weird thing with Jay, I felt like I deserved some kind of treat.

"A Diet Dr Pepper would be great," he replied, removing reference books from his backpack.

I walked into the living room carrying his can of soda. He took it from me, and I sat down on the couch next to him. "Your topic is the Thirty Years' War? When is this due?"

He nodded. "Yes. And it's due on Monday."

"Nothing like waiting to the last minute," I said, and I laughed. "But you're not going to get a good grade on so broad a subject. I mean, historians write books on the subject and can't get everything in," I explained. "All you'll be able to do is oversimplify everything, and I'm sure your professor is sick to death of that kind of paper."

He grinned at me and shrugged. "That's why I'm here." He frowned, knitting his eyebrows together. "What do you suggest?"

"One of the most interesting dynamics to this religious war is the fact that Catholic France—led by a cardinal, no less—intervened on behalf of the German Protestants," I replied. "Cardinal Richelieu was one of the first modern statesmen; he was able to look past the religious question and realize it was in the best interests of the French to side with the Protestants, to break the power of the Catholic Hapsburgs. By doing so, he made France the preeminent power in Europe." I shrugged. "That should be your thesis."

"You sure know a lot about this." Brandon started bouncing his legs on his toes. His left knee brushed against mine.

"I wrote a paper about Cardinal Richelieu's contributions to the Thirty Years' War in high school," I replied. He stopped bouncing his legs and slid down on the couch a bit. He spread his legs out wide, and his knee came to rest touching mine. I picked up one of the books from the coffee table, glancing at him out of the corner of my eye. *Is he hitting on me? Or had it just been an accident since we're sitting so close?* I flipped the book open to the index and found RICHELIEU, CARDINAL. I marked the page with a Post-it note and scanned the entries. "At that time, it was truly shocking that France . . ." I let my sentence trail off. Brandon's hand had dropped to my inner thigh. I turned my head. "What are you doing?"

He gave me his gap-toothed grin. "Do you mind?"

I swallowed. "Well—" I licked my lips. "No, not really." His hand slid up my leg. I put the book down and leaned back into the couch. "Is this why you asked me for my help?" I swallowed. "It's not like we have a lot of time to work on this paper, Brandon."

His hand reached my crotch and he let it rest lightly on

my stiffening cock. He leaned into me and kissed the side of my neck. "I really need help with my paper," he breathed against my neck, "but I kind of need help with my hard-on, too." He took my left hand and pressed it against his hardness.

I choked down a laugh. It was like dialogue from a porn movie—a *bad* porn movie. But the hardness I could feel through the thin nylon was rather impressive. I closed my hand around it, and he moaned, closing his eyes. "Yes," he breathed, "oh, yes." He opened his eyes. "Can we go into your bedroom?"

"Okay." I stood up and started walking toward the hall, but he grabbed me from behind and swung me up into his arms easily. "Damn, you're strong." I put my arms around his neck.

"I've wanted you to fuck me since we came back this semester." He carried me down the hall and put me down on my bed. He smiled down at me and pulled his tank top over his head.

I'd seen him shirtless before on the dance floor at Fusions but had never paid a lot of attention—I had always been focused on Chad. I'd always thought Brandon was hot, but I'd never realized just how hot. His torso was hairless other than the path of curly dark hairs trailing down from his navel. I'd never noticed how broad and muscular his shoulders were, or how thick the muscles of his upper arms were. Veins bulged in his forearms. His stomach wasn't ripped but was completely flat, and two deep lines descended from his pelvic bones to disappear inside the waistband of the sweatpants. Just below his ribs, two abdominal muscles stood out above the flat plain beneath, but as he moved, the lower abdominal muscles popped out as well, disappearing again when he put his arms down. He kicked off his sandals, hooked his thumbs inside his waistband, and pulled the sweatpants off in one fluid movement. He placed his hands on his bare hips and just stood there for me to take it all in. His cock was long, thicker at the base, and narrowing as it reached his thick mushroom-like head. His pubic hair was trimmed short, and his balls were shaved hairless, nice and plump beneath the branch of his cock. His legs were also smooth—not defined but solid in their muscularity and the smoothness of his skin. I reached out with my right hand and stroked his left leg.

His skin was softer than I would have thought, and silky to the touch.

He climbed onto the bed, getting on all fours and then leaning down to kiss my neck. His tongue darted out and ran down my neck, making me shiver with desire. He undid the button of my shorts and yanked down. I lifted my ass, and my shorts and underwear slid down my legs. I pulled my shirt off and tossed it over into the corner.

"Wow," Brandon said, his eyes widening. "You have a *huge* cock."

"I do?"

He kissed the head of it, and a bit of pre-cum leaked. "Oh, yeah." He smiled up at me. "It's big, man, one of the biggest I've ever seen—outside of a porn movie, that is." He opened his mouth and took the tip inside, swirling his tongue around it.

"Oh . . . my . . . GOD," I moaned, putting my hands beneath my head as he started sliding his mouth up and down over it. His right hand came up and started pinching my right nipple, and involuntarily I thrust my hips upward.

He gagged a bit, letting me slide out of his mouth. A string of spit extended from the head to his mouth, and he wiped it away. He winked at me, and whispered, "Don't do that, man." He pulled on my nipple again. "It's too big—let me work it my own way. You won't be sorry, I promise."

"Sorry," I whispered, and I actually was. "It was a reflex."

"Just relax and let me worship this monster the way it deserves to be worshipped." His left eye slid shut in a wink.

He certainly knew what he was doing.

After a few moments, I stopped him. "I'm going to come if you don't stop."

"Don't want that." He licked the head of my cock one last time before straddling me. I handed him a condom, and he opened it, sliding it down over my cock. He grabbed the bottle of lube from my nightstand, squirted some into his hand, and slicked up my cock. He winked at me again as he maneuvered himself down on top of me. His eyes closed as I entered him. "Oh, damn, that's big," he muttered, inching down a bit more before stopping again. "Man, I don't know if I can take all that."

"Take it," I growled. I was already close, and this teasing with his tight asshole was going to make me come.

He stuck his tongue out at me and grinned. He took a deep breath, exhaled, and slid all the way down. "Oh, yeah," he moaned, and started riding me. He held me down so I couldn't move—he really was strong—not letting me arch up or try to take control. He started moving up and down, slowly. He would go all the way up until just the tip was inside him, and then slide down really fast before going up in slow motion again.

"Dude, I'm really close," I said again, and he opened his eyes.

"So am I," he whispered, and he slid down again.

He cried out when he reached the bottom, and he started coming. Warm drops shot out of his cock, hitting me on the face, on the chest, and all over my abdomen. He jerked spasmodically with each shot, an involuntary cry coming from his lips.

And as he ground down on me, the pressure on my balls broke and I felt my own eruption begin.

He was still holding me down so I couldn't move.

It was agony—a delicious agony. My back arched, my legs twitched, and I couldn't catch my breath.

"Wow," I whispered after the last spasm had passed.

He leaned down and kissed me, and slid me out of him. He collapsed next to me on the bed. "That was nice," he whispered.

I started to protest when Brandon lit a cigarette, but I closed my mouth and put my head back down on his chest and listened to his heart beat.

That was when he made the remark about me sleeping with Dante.

"And how did you know about me and Dante?" I asked, watching as his cock continued to stiffen as my fingers traced figures around his navel.

He put a hand down on top of mine, stopping my hand. He kissed the top of my head again. "Rees saw your car parked in front of his house last night," he said slowly.

"Rees?"

He laughed. "It's a small town, man." He inhaled on his cigarette. "Rees has a fuck buddy who lives down the street from Dante. Your car was still there this morning."

I closed my eyes. "Shit."

"I mean, I don't care, and don't worry—I'm not going to say anything to Chad." His voice hardened. "I'm pretty fucking sick of Chad, to tell you the truth."

That got my attention. *Careful, Jordy, you can't be sure if you can trust him completely,* I reminded myself. *He's been one of Chad's acolytes for a long time now. Chad might have put him up to this.* Inwardly, I shook my head.

I was getting *way* too paranoid.

"Why?" I kissed his chest. "I thought you guys were all really tight. Pledge brothers, and all."

"Oh, Rees and I have known Chad for years—long before we came to school here," Brandon went on. "We knew each other in high school."

"But you didn't go to the same high school."

"We lived in towns right next to each other," Brandon went on. "You didn't know that? Woodbridge and Salem are right beside each other. Our city limit ends where theirs begins." He kissed the top of my head again.

"Wow. What was that like?"

"Chad was different then." He sighed as I started rubbing my thumb over the head of his cock. "He was a really sweet guy."

"He still is," I lied.

"No, he isn't. He's changed a lot." Brandon dropped the cigarette butt into the soda can, where it hissed. "He really was different, you know." He laughed. "Nobody liked Chad at his school. Salem was a lot different from Woodbridge. Salem was pretty relaxed about things—more liberal, I guess you'd say. Woodbridge? Everyone in Woodbridge pretty much went to this awful church that kind of controls the town. They have a curfew for kids, you know—you can't be out past ten. Chad was this tall, skinny kid with bottle glasses, and he didn't really fit in. He got picked on a lot. And his dad?" He shook his head. "Mr. York is a real dickwad. Chad couldn't wait to get out of there. We used to talk about it all the time." He sighed. "Being gay was easier for me and Rees in Salem. It didn't hurt, I guess, that we were both jocks. I played basketball and baseball, Rees was on the wrestling team. But no one at our school cared we were gay, you know?"

"Uh-huh," I said, my heart pounding.

"But when we got here, Chad changed. I mean, yeah, Chad was kind of our leader. He could always come up with fun things to do. We made a pact to come here." He started stroking my hair. "And you know, when we were pledges, Chad was our class president. He's really organized, and he was great. The brothers all loved him. And it all kind of went to his head." He shrugged. "Maybe it was being a dork in high school. I don't know, really. But that's when Chad got to be controlling and so mean."

"Mean?"

"Oh, come on, Jordy, surely you've noticed he's got a mean tongue on him!" Brandon started laughing. "He's mean, but in a funny way, that's why it's so hard. You never know if he's just teasing you or being a bitch. And if he doesn't get his own way, he goes for the throat."

"Yes," I whispered.

"And he likes to use people. I don't like that," Brandon went on. "I mean, I remember the day you walked into Rush. You walked in—I was working the table, remember?—and as soon as I saw you I thought, *Oh, no, Chad's going to eat this kid alive.* And sure enough, when Chad came to the table and saw you, he said something awful to you—I don't remember what it was."

"I don't remember."

"You've got spinach in your teeth."

"And I remember after you walked away, I thought, *Chad's going to blackball that kid and not give him a chance.*"

I bit my lip.

Brandon laughed, and it was an unpleasant sound. "And then he saw your application, and how much money your parents were worth. He took off looking for you."

It took all of my willpower to keep my hand from shaking.

"I mean, how fucking shallow, right?" Brandon started stroking my back. "Only two things matter to him—looks and money. You had money."

I closed my eyes. My heart hurt.

"It was sickening the way he sucked up to you," Brandon went on. "Sickening. And all because you had money."

"I—I don't understand." Somehow, I managed to keep my voice from shaking.

"Sweetie, of course you don't." Brandon kissed the top of my head again. "Why do you think Rees and I didn't try to be friendly to you when you were a pledge? We both liked you, but what Chad was doing made us sick. Chad was being your friend because you had money, and then would make fun of you behind your back, to us."

I bit my lip and blinked back the tears forming. A rush of memories flooded through me.

"That's really why Rees and I talked to you yesterday in the Quad," he said. "Because we knew if we didn't, Chad would be so hateful to you."

"But he is my friend, right?"

"That's what I am trying to tell you, dear." Brandon laughed. "Don't *ever* think Chad is your friend. He isn't. He isn't anyone's friend."

"What did he used to say about me?"

"Used to?" Brandon stopped stroking my back. "You know what? I'm sorry, I shouldn't have said anything to begin with." His hand started moving again. "He just makes me so angry sometimes . . . and you're a really great guy, Jordy. Really. Forget the whole thing."

Stay focused, don't let him know how much it hurts—you have to find out!

I kept my voice light. "You think I'm a great guy? Or do you just like my big dick?"

He shifted onto his side and looked into my eyes. "Jordy. You're a great guy. You also happen to have a great big dick." He grinned at me. "And really, Jordy, I'm sorry I said anything. Forget about it. Don't think about it anymore.

Chad is so not worth it." He reached out and stroked the side of my face.

"I promise I won't be upset." I reached down and closed my hand around his erection, sliding my thumb over the head.

"God, that feels so good," Brandon moaned.

I pushed him over on his back and rolled on top of him, pushing his legs apart with mine. I started grinding my crotch against his and grabbed both of his wrists and held them down over his head. I put my mouth on his armpit and began lightly nibbling at the delicate skin just beyond the razor stubble. His hips started moving back and forth as a low growl escaped from his throat. His eyes went back in his head, which also tilted backward. I moved my mouth up to his ear, placing more pressure on his wrists. "You like when I dominate you, don't you," I whispered in his ear before licking his earlobes. He continued writhing underneath me. "You like being dominated, don't you, boy?"

His head nodded, his breath coming faster and faster as my cock ground against his.

I let go of his hands and rolled off him.

"Hey!" He pouted. "Why are you stopping?"

I rolled over onto my side and smiled at him. "Are you going to tell me what Chad said?"

His eyes widened, and his lips spread in a delighted smile. "Are you saying you won't fuck me unless I tell you?"

I raised my eyebrows.

"Oh, that's *evil!*"

I grabbed hold of his cock and started moving my hand.

"Jord-*eeeeeeee* . . ." he moaned. With my other hand I began pinching one of his nipples. I placed my mouth on his throat and started licking the base.

"Oh God oh God Jordy please fuck me please . . ."

"Tell me," I breathed into his ear, stilling my hands.

He opened his eyes. "Okay, man, but you wanted to know."

I kept rubbing the head of his cock as he talked, even though what he was saying sickened me. His words washed over me like acid, flaying away my skin. It felt like my soul was shriveling inside of me, my heart was shattering.

It hurt, oh, God, how the words hurt.

When he was finished, he closed his eyes.

I climbed on top of him, spread his legs wide, and slipped a condom over my cock. I grabbed the lube bottle and squirted some on myself, then shoved myself into him as hard as I could, as far as I could go.

His mouth opened and a loud gasp came out of him.

I started fucking him, raping him as hard as I could.

I pounded him, going deeper inside of him than I had the first time. He tried to form words, but couldn't. He could barely catch his breath as I pounded him, my movements so rough and powerful that his head banged against the headboard a few times. His eyes were half-closed, his breaths coming in gasps as I tugged at his nipples, bit them, all the while pulling myself almost completely out of him before ramming into him as hard as I could.

At some point he stopped being Brandon to me.

He became Chad.

And I wanted to hurt him as badly as he'd hurt me, as he'd hurt others and would hurt still more men in the future, men he hadn't met yet, men who didn't even know he existed, men whose lives he would wreck and damage, the way he'd wrecked me.

I heard Chad's voice sneering the words Brandon had repeated to me.

He's such a loser. All he has going for him is his money.
Wham!
No one would want him. He's so lame, such a loser.
WHAM!
He's acting like a whore, though why anyone would want to fuck him is beyond me. There's no accounting for taste.

His voice kept echoing inside of my head as my climax began to build inside of me, but I kept pounding him, deeper and deeper. I was slamming him hard, but all he could do was moan, louder and louder, and I kept fucking him. . . .

And then I came in a violent convulsion, an orgasm that wracked my entire body, and as I came, Brandon started to come with a loud scream.

And I collapsed on top of him, both of us trembling.

"Wow," Brandon said after what seemed like an eternity. "Just—*wow*. That was—*wow*." He pushed me off and sat up, turning to put his feet on the floor. He shook his head. "I—I don't know if I can stand up."

"Sorry," I said between gasps. "I—I don't know what came over me."

He looked back over his shoulder at me and flashed his gap-toothed grin. "Never, ever apologize for fucking some-one like that, Jordy." He stood up and walked into the bath-room, holding on to the wall. A few moments later, I heard the shower start running.

I rolled over onto my back and stared at the ceiling.

Now that I was alone, I waited for the tears to come.

But they didn't.

All I felt was anger.

My original plan of vengeance was too, too simple. It was predicated on the notion that Chad was a human being with a heart, feelings, and emotions. That would never work. He was evil, pure and simple. He was a user. He'd treated Roger like shit. He pretended to be my friend and laughed at me behind my back. I could even almost forgive him for dismissing me as not attractive enough—and even had been willing to do so. But this? No, this was far, far worse. He was a monster, and he always got away with it. Chad would *never* want me. To him, I was always going to be a sad, pathetic loser.

No, Chad's payback had to be bigger than what I'd originally planned.

I had to drive a stake through his rotten, foul heart.

Brandon came walking back into my bedroom, a towel wrapped around his waist. He sat down on the edge of the bed and pulled his sweatpants on. He looked at me. "You're not going to tell Chad, are you?"

I looked at him. "Why would I do that?"

"Good." He let out a sigh of relief as he pulled his tank top back on. He leaned over and kissed my cheek. "I guess we should get back to work on the paper."

"Screw it." I smiled at him. "You can just use mine, right? It's not like your professor would ever find out."

His eyes widened. "Really?" He leaned over and kissed me. "Can you e-mail it to me? When I get back to the house I'll put my name on it and send it in."

"Sure." I touched his back.

He put a finger over my lips. "Maybe I could come back over next Thursday and you could help me with some other things?" He smiled.

"Yeah." I smiled back. "That would be great."

"Okay. See you then."

I heard my front door close behind him.

I put my hands behind my head and stared at the ceiling. *So, I'm just a sad, pathetic loser, huh, Chad?* I thought to myself. *We'll just see who the sad, pathetic loser is, you worthless piece of shit. When I'm done with you, you'll be sorry you were ever born. Your days of using and abusing people are over. I'm going to see to it that you're punished, once and for all.*

I picked up my cell phone, and texted Dante: *Hey, babe, Brandon just left. You up for some company?*

He answered almost immediately: *Sorry, I'm tired. And something came up on Sunday.*

I stared at the message.

Was he blowing me off?

I got up and walked into my study. Tapping the phone against my chin, I e-mailed the paper to Brandon.

Jay was fired today. Now Dante's blowing me off.

Maybe I was just being paranoid, but—

I scrolled through my in-box. Most of it was junk, but there was one from one of the brothers—Bobby Dunlap. I frowned. Bobby was a nice guy, but we weren't exactly buddies. He liked to gossip too much. The saying around the house was "telephone, telegram, tell Bobby."

There was a file attached to it.

I clicked the e-mail open. The only message was *Have you seen this yet?*

My heart sinking, I saw it was a video file. I clicked to download it, and when it opened—

It was me and Jay in the steam room.

I clicked it closed.

Everyone at the house has probably seen this.

I fought down the panic.

Chad.

It had to be Chad.

My jaw set. *Okay, then, so that's how it's going to be, so be it.*

Let the games begin.

Chapter 12

Iwoke up the next morning feeling a lot better about everything.

I sat up in the bed and glanced over at my alarm. It was almost ten. I turned on my iHome and yawned as Lady Gaga's "Paparazzi" began playing. It was a particularly apt song, I thought, given as it was about stalking. The sun was shining in through my windows—it was a beautiful morning. My bed felt comfortable, and I thought about staying in bed and trying to go back to sleep for another hour or so, but dismissed it. I had a lot of damage to repair, and lying in bed wasn't going to get any of it done.

And I could smell coffee brewing. I'd set the automatic timer on my coffeemaker before going to sleep, and the aroma was too much to resist.

I got out of bed and walked into the bathroom, then washed my face and brushed my teeth. I looked at myself in the mirror and smiled at my reflection. "Today," I said to my image, "you're going to kick some serious ass, take no prisoners, and make some people sorry they were ever born."

It was a good feeling.

I shook my head, wondering at how worked up I'd been the night before. At first, I hadn't been able to fall asleep—which wasn't a surprise. As I'd lain there in bed, staring at the ceiling, with Brandon's smell still clinging to my sheets, I ticked off on my fingers everything that had gone wrong: a video of me messing around with Jay in the steam room at the gym circulating on the Internet, Jay getting fired, and apparently my fledgling relationship with Dante was over before it could begin. It was pretty safe to assume that Dante may have seen the video. It was also safe to assume that Rees had told Chad about Dante and me.

Chad, Chad, Chad—it always came back to Chad, didn't it?

How could I have ever thought I was in love with him? I'd sighed, resisting the urge to pound my head against the wall. I'd ignored the truth about him from the very beginning because I was so fucking attracted to him, overlooking his cruelties and bitchy little remarks. But in fairness, he'd played me. The question was, *why?* Brandon said it was because of the money, but that didn't make any sense to me. He'd never asked me for money. When we went out, we took turns buying drinks. When we went out to eat, we took turns paying. I'd been very careful to not make the difference in our financial situations apparent. Maybe that was it—maybe Chad had expected me to pay for everything and he resented that I didn't? But that didn't make any sense, either.

I'd kept tossing and turning, watching shadows from the moon dancing on the ceiling. *You'll never know what his motivations were,* I had finally told myself, *and ultimately, it doesn't matter. You never did anything to him to justify what he's done. And it was one thing when he was just pulling shit on you—but he got Jay fired, and that's unforgivable. Jay never did anything to him. He didn't even know Jay.*

And yes, we shouldn't have done it in the steam room. It was the first time I'd ever done anything like that, and maybe Jay did make it a habit—which logically meant he *should* have been fired.

But making a video of us and circulating it on the Web? That was bullshit—utter and complete bullshit. Maybe it seemed funny at the time, but that kind of shit could haunt someone for the rest of his life. That, I think, was what made me the angriest. It didn't hurt me in the long run. I was never going to have to worry about getting a job, and I certainly had no plans to ever run for public office.

But Jay was a personal trainer, and what gym would hire him knowing he had blown a client in the last gym where he worked? And even if they didn't know and hired him, he'd always have to worry it might turn up sometime.

Jay was a great guy. He'd turned me from an out-of-shape nerd boy into someone who turned heads whenever he walked into a gay bar. He'd always been nice to me, except for that last training session when he'd been so distant and cold—and maybe *that* was because he already knew about the video.

Chad has to pay, I'd thought, closing my eyes, *and tomorrow morning you can figure it all out. It was one thing to come after me, but destroying other people to get at me? No, that couldn't go unpunished. And you know exactly what to do, and how to do it.*

And with that enormously satisfying thought, I had been able to fall asleep.

I took a shower and then took my coffee out onto the balcony. I sat down on the wicker love seat and closed my eyes for a moment. It was very peaceful out there, and my mind flashed back to Dante's backyard. *I need to get some wind chimes here,* I thought with a pang. My heart hurt at the thought of Dante. I really liked him. It could have led to something special. *You're getting ahead of yourself,* I thought. *Just because he didn't want you to come over last night and canceled Sunday doesn't mean anything. Something else may have come up, and the timing with all the rest of this bullshit was just bad.* As much as I wanted to believe that, I knew.

I smiled. *Poor, stupid Chad was about to get it between the eyes—so enjoy your little triumph while you still can, you fucking bitch.*

I wasn't going to have my gym membership suspended, and I knew I could get Jay's job back. I picked up my cell phone and made the call to get the ball rolling. "As soon as possible," I instructed. "Preferably today. I'll be waiting for your call." I smiled as I disconnected the call. I stroked my chin with the edge of my phone.

Money, indeed, was *power.*

And that was it for the video. Who fucking cared if it went viral on the Internet? So what? It was just two sweaty guys in a steam room going down on each other. Big fucking deal. The picture quality wasn't that great, and in fact, you could barely tell it was me and Jay. The only people it would be of interest to would be people we knew. I sent Jay another text: *Jay, I'm taking care of everything. I will call you later once everything is fixed. Don't worry. Hope you're okay. Jordy.*

I got a second cup of coffee and was just sitting back down when my phone chirped. I clicked on the message from Jay: *Hey man, sorry about everything, this whole mess is my fault and I need to own up to it. I'm freaked out and don't know what I'm going to do, but I'm sure I'll come up with something.*

I shook my head and texted back: *Just sit tight, babe. I'm handling everything.*

My phone chirped again while I was answering him. I clicked on the new message and smiled. It was from Brandon: *Thanks again for last night. Man, that was some hot sex! And thanks for the paper. I just e-mailed it in.*

Another piece fell into place—one I hoped I wouldn't have to use.

I did like Brandon—and he'd told me the truth about Chad.

But if I had to, I would.

I called Dante, but he didn't pick up. "Dante, hey, this is Jordy, can you give me a call when you get a moment? We need to talk." I ended the call and sat there, watching the pool. There was someone lying out there on one of the reclining deck chairs, and I thought it might be Jeff, but I couldn't tell for sure. Blair's car wasn't in the parking lot. It was calm and peaceful on the balcony. There was a nice cool breeze blowing, the sun was shining, and the sky was blue. I appreciated the solitude—Dante was right. Having a place you could go and be peaceful was helpful. *Definitely need to get some wind chimes*, I thought again. I felt another pang about him. But maybe it wasn't too late to rescue that—and I reminded myself there was a slight chance Dante hadn't seen the video.

I stood up and stretched. *But if that's what it is—if Dante saw the video and wants nothing to do with you now—then he wasn't who you thought he was in the first place, and do you want to have a relationship with someone that judgmental?*

Definitely food for thought there.

I got another cup of coffee and sat down at my computer. I wanted to watch the video again, just to be on the safe side. I needed to know a few things before I made my next call.

This time, I clicked the video player to full-screen mode.

When it started playing, I watched carefully. Something had bothered me when I watched it the first time, but I'd be unable to put my finger on what it was. That was partly, I now realized, because I'd been in so much shock I hadn't been able to think clearly—to think anything besides *oh, my God*. But now, as it started, I was able to put my finger on exactly what had bothered me the first time I'd viewed it.

I distinctly remembered that the outer glass wall of the steam room, looking out into the shower area, had been fogged up. I hadn't been able to see through it. When I'd been sitting in there, I had no idea Jay was even out there until he opened the door and walked inside. So how had someone in the locker room seen what we were doing, let alone been able to tape it? The girl at the front desk had said someone had seen us from the locker room.

That wasn't possible.

And as the video started again, I smiled to myself.

At the start of the video, you could see me from above and behind. I was sitting on the first row of benches with my feet on the floor. There was steam swirling in the room, but you could see me relatively clearly. After about three seconds, the door to the steam room opened and Jay walked in, naked, and sat down next to me.

There had been no one else in the steam room when I had walked in, so whoever had taped this had *not* been in there. I clicked the video player closed—I was all too familiar with what happened next—and thought for a moment. I closed my eyes, leaned back in my desk chair, and tried to recall exactly what the back wall of the steam room looked like. Obviously, whoever had shot the video had some kind of peephole into the steam room. Unfortunately, I couldn't remember everything about the back wall—I'd never had any reason to pay any attention to it. That was a useless line of thought.

Well, then, what's behind the wall?

I pictured the gym again. It was a stand-alone building, with a parking lot in the front that continued around for more parking on either side and parking in the back. The front wall was all glass. The cardio equipment was lined up along the front windows so you could look out onto Shaw Avenue while you worked out. The front two-thirds of the building was devoted to the weight area. The front desk was located in the center of the weight area, and it was round with refrigerated cabinets below that stocked water, protein and energy drinks, and assorted protein bars. The locker rooms were in the back—the men's on the left side, the ladies' on the right. Separating the locker rooms were office spaces and the storage room.

I raised an eyebrow. Either the storage room or someone's office had a peephole into the men's steam room.

And I was pretty sure Body Quest's owners wouldn't want *that* to become public knowledge.

The next question was, who actually shot the video?

Someone who had access to the offices and the storage room. It had to be someone who worked there.

I laughed. I knew exactly who'd done it.

I picked up my phone and made the call I needed. I asked the right questions and got the answers I'd expected. I hung up and smiled again.

Money was indeed power.

I poured what was left in my coffeepot into my mug and walked back out onto the balcony. My father had once advised me, "Anytime you're in a situation where you get emotional or start to panic, the most important thing to remember is to calm down and put your emotions to the side—and think logically. Logical thought will almost always get you out of any situation. Logic never fails. Your emotions will cause you to make mistakes every time.

Don't shut them down completely—you don't ever want to become one of those people who don't feel anything. That's a living death. But you don't want to ever make a decision based on emotions. That only works out if you get lucky, but ninety-nine times out of a hundred you'll wind up worse off than you were before. Never forget that."

I sat back down on the wicker love seat on the balcony and picked up my phone again. I dialed Dante's number and got his voice mail again. I sighed, and then sent him a text. *I don't know what's going on but we need to talk.*

It was entirely possible I was overreacting, but it was weird how he'd gone from hot to cold so quickly.

Logic.

Bobby Dunlap had sent me the steam room video. I went back inside and pulled up my e-mail account. I clicked on his e-mail and checked. Yes, I'd been blind copied. The time stamp on the e-mail showed it had been sent around seven-thirty Friday night. I rolled my eyes and opened an Internet-tracking program. *Stupid, stupid people,* I thought. *My father wrote programs and had his own programming company. Do you honestly think I can't find out just about anything I want to through a computer? I was using computers before I was five. I've forgotten more about computers—and the Internet—than you'll ever know. And I have access to software your average Joe does not.*

It took me exactly four minutes to hack into Bobby Dunlap's e-mail—the university's e-mail service was "protected" by a security system that was laughable—and see who he'd copied on the message. As I scrolled through the addresses, I shook my head. He'd sent it to almost every single Beta Kappa—so everyone in the house had seen it. But one name was missing from the list: Chad York. Cyork@csupolk.edu wasn't on Bobby's list. I went to his in-box, and there wasn't anything there with a video attachment. I rolled my eyes and clicked on Deleted Mail. Like so many others, Bobby believed that deleting an e-mail got rid of it and didn't know he actually had to clear his deleted mail archive.

Typical.

And sure enough, there it was.

An e-mail from Chad with a video attachment, and the subject line read: *Check this out.*

I opened the e-mail and read the message.

> Bobby,
> Download this video. I am sure you will be as shocked as I was. For obvious reasons, I can't forward this around. Would you mind doing it? Everyone in the house has to see this.
> Xo Chad

I forwarded it to myself. I signed out of Bobby's e-mail account and switched over to mine. I opened the e-mail and hit print. I leaned back in my chair and thought while it printed. I leaned forward and opened another access program—one my father's company had developed for law enforcement. I logged in the IP address of Bobby's computer and crossed my fingers. If his computer was hooked up to a wireless network—which Beta Kappa had—I could access his computer like it was right in front of me.

Got to love wireless. I smiled to myself as Bobby's desktop came up on my computer. I clicked on his documents folder. *Oh, silly, silly Bobby,* I thought as I started dragging all his class notes to the trash. I opened a couple of files—term papers he was working on. *Pity,* I thought as I deleted them. *Sure hope none of these are due soon.* It was tempting to load a hard-drive-destroying virus, but I resisted that temptation. A corner of my mouth curled up into a smirk. *No virus*, I decided, *because while that might suck, it will drive him crazy wondering what happened to all his schoolwork.* I pictured him sitting in front of his computer, eyes wide in horror, as he tried to find his term papers and finally realizing they were gone forever.

Next time you'll think twice before doing Chad's dirty work, asshole, I thought as I emptied the trash, smiling at the pop-up warning ARE YOU SURE YOU WANT TO EMPTY TRASH? FILES WILL BE PERMANENTLY DELETED AND CANNOT BE RETRIEVED. I knew that wasn't strictly true; a ghost of the files would remain on the hard drive and an expert tech could retrieve them—but it would also cost a fortune Bobby didn't have. I clicked the *Yes* box, and the trash emptied.

Never should have fucked with me, Bobby. I'm smarter and richer than Chad. You picked the wrong side, now suffer the consequences.

I whistled as I deleted all evidence I'd tapped into his computer from his history files, and I logged out of his computer.

Even the best forensic computer expert wouldn't be able to figure out someone had hacked in.

For a brief moment, I considered hacking into Chad's laptop, but decided against it.

I had something much nastier in store for his sorry ass.

Someone started knocking on my front door, and my heart lifted for just a moment, thinking it might be Dante. But it couldn't be—security hadn't called me to let him in. *I really do care about him,* I thought sadly as I went to see who it was, and cursed Chad again.

I opened the door to see Jeff standing there in his white

Speedo, a blue towel draped around his shoulders. "You got any coffee made?" He gave me his dazzling smile. Beads of water speckled his firm chest. "We're out and I'm dying."

"Come on in. There's some in the kitchen," I replied, standing aside to let him in. "Where's Blair?" I asked as he took the last of the coffee.

"Do you mind if I make some more?" he asked, yawning. "Blair left for Palm Springs yesterday. His dad is being interviewed for one of those stupid magazines for a special on Father's Day, and they're doing a photo shoot, and they want Blair to be a part of it." He dumped the wet grounds and refilled another coffee filter. He took a big drink from his mug and sighed in relief as the coffeemaker started brewing. "On my own this weekend." He shook his head. "Was a shitty night at the bar last night—dead. I didn't even get a hundred bucks." He yawned again. "I don't know why I bother sometimes. I'm completely exhausted, and for what? Maybe it's time to stop dancing and get a real job." He plopped down on the couch. "I could make more at Starbucks."

"Would they let you work in a Speedo?" I teased, following him into the living room. "I'd certainly frequent that Starbucks if they did."

He laughed. "I don't think that would fly." He peered at me. "How are you doing this morning?"

"I've been better." I shrugged. "Last night was kind of rough, but I'm figuring it all out." I grinned at him. "Some things have gone down, but I'm looking at it as an intellectual challenge."

He set the mug down on the coffee table. "Listen, Jordy, I've got to tell you something." He cleared his throat. "I hate to be the one to tell you this, but this morning when I checked my e-mail—"

"You had a message from Bobby Dunlap with a video attachment," I interrupted him. "When you clicked it open, it was a video of me having sex with someone in a steam room."

"Oh, you know." His body sagged a bit. "I'm so sorry, man. Are you okay?"

I nodded. "Yeah, actually, I am. I freaked out a little last night when I saw it, but what can I do?" I shrugged. "It's already out there—Bobby sent it to the whole brotherhood. It's embarrassing, but I'm okay with it. I'll live, obviously." I gave him a brittle grin. "Hey, it might even get me laid. It's a good advertisement."

Jeff laughed. "Well, you've certainly got a great attitude about it. It's weird, you know, I made porn when I was a junior active, and the brothers found out about it. It was just that one weekend, but—" He sighed. "At least things have changed around the house since then. I was almost expelled from the house."

"Seriously?" I hadn't thought about that. I closed my eyes for a second and fought down the panic. *Remember, you've got an ace in the hole.* "You think maybe that's why Bobby sent it around? To get me blackballed?"

Jeff's eyes widened. "Oh, God, I didn't think of that." He shook his head, drops of water flying. "I don't think that's Bobby's style. He's a gossip—and he probably didn't think about that." He frowned. "If enough brothers complain, though—yeah, they could try. Conduct unbecoming a Beta Kappa, which is a fine line, you know. Being gay's not a problem anymore—that's why they tried to get rid of me, which forced the issue. Fortunately, the brothers decided to make the house open to gays. But yeah, it's a possibility."

"I'm not worried about it." I gave him a reassuring smile.

"Don't worry, Jeff. Trust me, I have the entire thing under control." I waved a hand. "I'm not worried." My phone rang. I saw who it was and smiled. I held up a finger. "I need to take this. Give me a second, okay?" I walked out onto the balcony. "Hello?" As I listened, my smile grew. "Excellent," I said. "Absolutely excellent. Go for it." I hung up just as my phone chirped. It was a text from Chris: *Hey, I need to talk to you before Big Brother Night. Can you come by my office around six?*

See you then, I replied. I walked back into the living room. "I just got a text from Chris—he wants me to come by his office at six."

"Uh-oh." He frowned. "That's not good."

"Don't worry." I put my phone down. "I'm not."

"Well, call me and let me know how it goes. You sure you're okay?"

"I swear."

"Cool." He got up and gave me a hug. "If you need to talk . . ."

"I'll call you." I squeezed him back. "If you'll excuse me, I have some things to take care of before I meet with Chris."

"Can I take another cup of coffee?"

I nodded. After the door shut behind him, I checked my watch. It was almost one. I retrieved my phone from the study and checked it. Dante hadn't answered my text.

Maybe he's just busy. Yeah, right.

I didn't have time to deal with Dante today.

I walked out to the car and drove over to Body Quest.

The parking lot was practically empty, so I parked close to the front door. I walked in and smiled at the guy working at the front desk as I approached. "Hi," I said as he smirked back at me. I'd been right. I'd seen him before—at Fusions. He was short, maybe about five seven, with red hair and freckles. I'd always thought he was kind of hot—had even thought about hitting on him once or twice. Now, I was glad I never had. "Hi," I said. "Is Rosemary in?"

He nodded. "She's in her office."

I glanced at his name tag. "Thanks, Robby."

I walked back to the office. Before I stuck my head in the door, I checked. The room behind Rosemary's office lined up with the steam room. I rapped on the door as I entered. "Rosemary, can I speak to you?"

She looked up. She was maybe about five feet tall and was of Hispanic descent. Her hair was a mop of disheveled curls, and she was about twenty or thirty pounds over-weight. She never wore makeup and had an abrupt, un-friendly manner. I'd never liked her—she was kind of a rude bitch, which was going to make this even more fun.

Her eyes narrowed. "Ah, yes. Jordan Valentine. I've been meaning to call you. Would you mind shutting the door?"

"Not at all." I slammed it and sat down in a chair in front of her desk.

She cleared her throat. "It has come to my attention you've engaged in conduct on the property that is unac-ceptable, and I'm afraid I am going to have to cancel your gym membership." She tapped a pencil on her desk. "You've been a really good member, and I'm sorry that it's come to this."

"And you've already fired Jay?"

"I'm afraid so." She bit her lower lip.

"And just how did you find out? About our conduct?"

She flushed. "I was e-mailed a video of—what you two did in the steam room. Obviously, I have no choice in this matter." She passed an envelope across her desk. "You'd paid for a year's membership in advance, and you'd also paid for three more months of training sessions with Jay. I've written you a check for the money you paid. I didn't have to do that—your conduct violated the membership agreement you signed, and so you were entitled to no refund. But I want this to be as amicable as possible."

I kept smiling. "I have absolutely no desire to make this amicable, madam."

Her face turned a darker hue of red. "You have no choice in this."

"On the contrary, I actually hold all the cards here." I leaned back in my chair and put my feet up on her desk. "Someone with a more curious mind, madam, might have wondered a bit about that video and how it was shot. Do you honestly believe that Jay and I are both so fucking stupid we would have sex in the steam room with someone else in there recording us?" I gestured to the door at the back of her office. "Where does that door lead?"

"The storeroom. Kindly remove your feet from my desk."

"There is obviously a peephole in the wall the storeroom and steam room share." I left my feet on her desk. "I'm sure the rest of the membership of Body Quest would be fascinated to find out about that."

All the color drained out of her face.

"And I am relatively certain only employees have access to the storeroom," I went on. "I am certain the members would find that even more fascinating—and so would a judge." I winked at her. "I mean, how does anyone know that's the only tape in existence? Maybe other members have been taped in the steam room. Granted, they might not be doing anything untoward, the way Jay and I were, but I think you'll find that most people will take a very dim view of being photographed or videotaped in the nude without their knowledge." I removed my feet from her desk and leaned forward. "Judges take a very dim view of that as well."

Her mouth opened and closed. No sound came out.

"In fact, I forwarded the video to my attorney this morning." I folded my arms. "He was quite fascinated, especially when I explained it could have only been shot by one of your employees and that neither Jay nor I gave our consent to being taped, and there are no signs posted in the men's locker room that there are surveillance cameras." I leaned forward. "So not only is there a civil suit looming—my attorney seems to think we can sue for, oh, I don't know, at least a couple of million—there are also some criminal liabilities involved as well."

"Oh, my God." She barely whispered the words.

"But I hate the whole notion of civil and criminal trials," I went on. "So, I had my attorney contact the owners of this business and inform them of what exactly was going on around here. They weren't very happy. But we offered them a way out." I stood up and walked over to the storeroom door. "Apparently, Body Quest is struggling financially. Some months you wind up in the black, sometimes you're in the red—which doesn't really speak very well to your management style or abilities." I turned the knob. The door was locked, but it didn't matter. "So, I had my attorney make the owners an offer, which they accepted. Once the paperwork is finished, Rosemary, I will be the new owner of this business." I walked over to the desk and put my hands down. "We anticipate the closing will take place on Monday."

"I—I—"

"When I walked into this office, Rosemary, I hadn't really made up my mind what to do about you." I smiled. "But once you started in with your condescending, superior attitude, with absolutely no interest whatsoever in the egregious criminal invasion of my and Jay's privacy—at the hands of one of your employees, in your place of business—

you made up my mind for me. Once the sale is closed on Monday morning, you're fucking fired." I waved my hand around the office. "I suggest you start packing up your personal property. If you have not removed it all from this office by one on Monday afternoon, it will be thrown into the trash. You will be escorted off the premises by the police." I walked over to the door, and paused. "Wow, that felt really good. Thank you, Rosemary. I really enjoyed this. Have a nice day, you miserable bitch."

She stared at me, her mouth open, as I shut the door to her office.

It did feel good.

Money is power.

I walked up to the front desk. Robby was smirking at me, one eyebrow raised. "Hello, Robby." I smiled at him. "I bet you didn't know that whenever you use your phone to videotape or take a picture, there's a digital marker on the images that is particular to that phone. It's kind of like fingerprints."

His smirk vanished.

"So, I hope fucking Chad—or whatever little reward he gave you—was worth it." I winked at him. "I have someone tracing that video of me and Jay back to the phone that originally recorded it even as we speak. I hope for your sake it wasn't yours—because we are going to press criminal charges." I clicked my tongue. "I bet you didn't know it was illegal to record people without their permission, especially when it's done maliciously, to embarrass or humiliate the people being recorded. Did you know that?"

"I—"

"And by the way, I certainly hope you have other irons in the fire." My smile grew. "You see, I bought the gym today. Monday I take possession. And you're fired." I turned and started walking away, then stopped and turned back. "And I really feel I have a responsibility to any future potential employers of yours to let them know about your criminal tendencies." I tilted my head to one side. "I think I saw a Help Wanted sign when I drove past the McDonald's on Shaw on my way here. That's about the only job you're going to get for the rest of your life. Give my best to Chad, will you?"

God, it felt great.

I started whistling "Paparazzi" as I walked back to the car.

I sat behind the wheel of my car and laughed.

Then I started the car and drove home, where I took care of a few more things. Everything was lining up exactly the way I wanted.

Money, indeed, is power.

Chapter 13

I hesitated, my hand poised to knock on Chris's door. It was just before six, and the pledges weren't due to arrive until eight o'clock. The Great Room was already set up for Big Brother Night, and the more I thought about it, the more nervous I was getting. I'd been so wrapped up in all the Chad drama I hadn't given Big Brother Night a second thought. I'd stopped at a liquor store and picked up the family beer, but I still felt incredibly unprepared. *Maybe taking a little brother is a mistake,* I thought as I stood there. I knew who Galen Donovan was—I remembered him from Rush and I'd talked to him a little bit at some of the parties, but I didn't know much else about him. For that matter, I didn't know a whole lot about any of the pledges.

Chris was right—I was failing as a brother.

But whatever it was he wanted to talk to me about, I was almost positive it wasn't about Big Brother Night.

Some of the brothers were out playing basketball when I'd pulled into the parking lot. When they saw my car, the game had stopped, and they'd gathered under the hoop, talking to each other. When I parked, I waved. Only one of them had waved back.

My heart sank a little. That wasn't a good sign.

Of course they've all seen the video, I told myself as I walked toward the house. *But why this cold-shoulder treatment? We're SUPPOSED to all be brothers, bonded by the fraternity. So much for brotherhood and the ideals I was taught as a pledge.*

I wasn't as confident as I'd been when I'd talked to Jeff earlier. Underneath it all, I'd been a true believer in Beta Kappa. Sure, I'd been a shitty brother this semester—blowing off meetings, not coming to parties, and not coming around as much as I probably should have. I'd been so wrapped up in my own life—*revenge on Chad,* a nasty little voice whispered in my head—I'd not given the brotherhood as much attention as I should have, as they'd expected me to when they'd offered me a bid last semester.

But this rejection really stung.

There were other brothers in the backyard, sitting around the picnic tables. I waved—and again, a couple waved back but the others pointedly ignored me.

And as I walked into the house, my heart sank with each step I took toward Chris's office. *This is about Big Brother Night, that's all it is,* I kept repeating to myself. Taking a little brother was nerve-racking enough, given everything else that was going on.

But I'd be a good big brother to Galen. I would. I would help and guide him through his pledge semester, and would make sure he'd make a better brother than I'd been so far.

I took a deep breath, and knocked.

When Chris opened the door, he looked unhappy. "Come in." He waved me into the office and shut the door behind me. He walked around the desk and plopped down hard into his chair. He really looked miserable.

I took a seat in the chair across from him. "What's this about, Chris?" I asked, trying to control my rapidly beating heart. *Stay calm, don't get emotional—remember, logic is the key.*

"God, this sucks." He moaned. "You have no idea how much I regret running for president."

"It's got to be a rough job," I commiserated. *Stay calm, stay calm and focused. Chris is a good guy and he likes you.* "This isn't about Big Brother Night, is it?"

"In a way it is." He looked like he was ready to cry. "Jordy, this is really hard for me—I hope you know that, but I don't have a choice." He cleared his throat. "You're not getting a little brother tonight. I'm so sorry." He couldn't look me in the eyes. "Roger's agreed to take Galen—he was his second choice."

"And why?" I asked. I was sure I knew. I felt bad for Chris, who was obviously not enjoying this, but I was damned if I would make it easy on him. "What have I done?"

"I'm sure you're aware of the video e-mailed to the brothers?" He looked up at me finally. His eyes looked bloodshot.

I nodded. "Oh, yes, I'm aware of it. It was sent to me, too." I shrugged. "I'm sure people were shocked; I certainly was, and I'm sorry about that. But I wasn't the one who shot it, and I wasn't the one who circulated it."

"Unfortunately, some brothers came to the Executive Council." He shook his head. "I'm sorry, Jordy, I tried to head this off. But there are brothers insisting you have to appear in front of the entire brotherhood on Monday." He sighed. "So, tomorrow afternoon at one, I have to ask you to meet with the Executive Council to discuss this. After you tell us the circumstances, we'll deliberate and decide whether or not a hearing is called for." He sighed. "I'm so sorry, Jordy."

"A hearing?" I shook my head. "I don't understand."

"The bylaws of the national chapter state that if a brother conducts himself in a way that embarrasses the brotherhood, the brotherhood can hold a hearing to determine whether or not to expel him." Chris rubbed his eyes. "And unfortunately, since it is possible you might be expelled from the brotherhood on Monday night, we can't let you take a little brother." He moaned. "This is *such* shitty timing. I'm sorry, Jordy. But at least you can explain things to the Executive Council tomorrow and maybe we can head off actually holding a hearing."

"Couldn't we do this today? This seems a bit unfair to me," I replied, starting to get a little angry. I took a deep breath. *Stay calm*, I reassured myself. *Don't lose your temper, don't get angry.* "I'm the victim in all of this, Chris. Someone taped me having sex without my consent and spread the video around in a deliberate attempt to publicly humiliate me. That's who should be subjected to a hearing. That's who conducted himself in a way embarrassing to the brotherhood." I took another breath. "Chris, I'm not saying that what I did was right—it certainly wasn't. That was the steam room at my gym, and it never should have happened. But the person behind all of this *also sent it to the management at my gym*. The guy in the video was my trainer. He's been fired. This little attempt to embarrass *me* ruined someone else's life—and this had nothing to do with him. Nothing. Is that the kind of person we want in Beta Kappa?" Granted, I'd already fixed that mess, but Chris didn't need to know that.

"Jordy, if it were up to me, this wouldn't be happening," Chris replied sadly. "Unfortunately, the house is a democracy. I tried to convince the complaining brothers to drop it, but they wouldn't." He buried his face in his hands. "I like you, Jordy. I've always liked you, from the moment we met. I think you're a definite asset to this house—even if you haven't been as active as you should be this semester—and you definitely have more to offer Beta Kappa than a lot of the deadweight we have around here. I'm not going to vote against you."

"I appreciate that, Chris." I managed to keep my voice level, but inside I was boiling. "Can I at least know who the complaining brothers were? I have a right to face my accusers." *It didn't come from Chad, of course. He's too smart for that. But he's pulling the strings off stage.*

"I can't tell you that." He cleared his throat again. "I warned them this was the kind of thing that could tear the house apart—people being forced to take sides—and no matter what the outcome of your hearing, there's going to be hard feelings. This happened once before—"

"To Jeff Morgan." I nodded. "He told me about it this afternoon."

"Jeff's hearing cost us some brothers." Chris shook his head. "There were brothers who didn't want us to let gay guys in the house. There were some who hated the idea so much they left the brotherhood because of it. Others didn't want gay guys in the house but were willing to put up with it rather than leave. As you know, we have a diversity policy—but there are guys who will vote to get rid of you just because you're gay. It's homophobia, of course, but they'll say your conduct was embarrassing to the house and disguise it that way."

"It's the same thing all over again, isn't it?" I gave him a rueful smile. The anger drained out of me, and logic was taking over again. "And after me, it'll happen again to some other gay brother. All it takes is one person with a cell phone that shoots video, Chris."

"I talked to Eric, and he's agreed to be your rep at the hearing, if it comes to that." Chris sighed. "I'm hoping we can resolve this at the Exec meeting tomorrow, and bury it. I'll make all these points when we're in session after you tell us your side of this. I'm on your side, Jordy, for what that's worth."

"I appreciate it, Chris." I stood up and offered him my hand.

He gave me the fraternity handshake. "I'm really, really sorry."

I put my hand on the doorknob. "Seriously, Chris, I understand, and I don't hold you responsible for any of this." I started to turn the knob. "Will you answer a question for me, though?"

He nodded.

"Was I given a bid because the brothers wanted me or because my parents are wealthy?"

"Honestly? It was a little of both."

I nodded. "Thank you for being honest—that makes all of this a little easier." I started to open the door, and stopped. "One other thing I want you to think about—and all the brothers should be thinking about this, too."

"Uh-huh?" His eyebrows went up.

"Why would I want to be a part of a group that would treat me like this?"

He didn't answer. When the silence got awkward, I walked out of his office.

When I shut the door, I stood there for a moment as emotion overwhelmed me. Even though I'd been expecting it, there had been a part of me that refused to accept possible expulsion. I tried to get my heart rate and breathing under control.

It was too good to be true, that hateful voice whispered in my head again. *You don't belong here any more than you did at St. Bernard. People are the same everywhere, Jordy. They didn't like you here; they only wanted you because you're rich. All those noble ideals they drilled into your head as a pledge are worthless.*

The motto—"the helping hand"—is a fucking joke. Everything this place supposedly stands for is a joke. You wanted to believe in it all so bad it blinded you to the truth. Beta Kappa is just like everything else—a bunch of bullshit, a bunch of mean-spirited assholes wrapped in a pretty package of nobility and working for a better world. And you fell for it all, hook, line, and sinker.

As much I hated that voice, I knew this time it was right.

I heard someone coming down the stairs and I started walking down the hall. I didn't want to talk to anyone. I just wanted to get as far from the house as I could. Fuck the meeting tomorrow. I was never going to set foot in the house again.

"Jordy?"

I stopped walking. I knew that voice. I wiped the tears out of my eyes before I turned around. "Hello, Bobby." I forced a smile on my face. "How are you?"

He had a smile on his face I wanted to wipe off. As he walked up to me, I hated him with every fiber of my being. I wanted to punch him, and keep punching until there was nothing left but a bloody pulp. I felt my hands curling into fists. "Good." His smile broadened. "It's a beautiful day, isn't it?"

"I need to thank you," I heard myself saying.

His smile faltered. "For what?"

"Sending that video to everyone in the house." It was weird. It was like I'd left my body and had floated up to the ceiling, looking down and watching, with no power over what was said and done. "I always knew you were a bottom-feeding, backstabbing asshole, but now it's pretty clear to everyone."

He flinched and took a step back. "Fuck you, Jordy," he said, but it was halfhearted.

And then I returned to my body, and everything was

clear. "No, Bobby, you actually fucked yourself." I crossed my arms, my smile never faltering, my voice remaining calm. *Yes, that's it, stay calm. Logic over emotion, Jordy, that's the way you win.* "I suppose you're proud of yourself."

His eyes narrowed. "Actually, I am," he hissed at me. "I never liked you. I never thought you should have been allowed to join. So, yeah, when I saw that video, I was happy to send it around to everyone."

"What did I ever do to you?" I asked. I was curious; I wanted to know *why* he'd never liked me. I'd never given it much of a thought before, had rarely interacted with him.

"You think you're better than everyone else," he snapped. "And it's about time you were brought down a peg or two."

"You've been listening to Chad." I shook my head sadly. "But I do want to thank you for doing it. I've learned a valuable lesson, and I always appreciate learning." I started to turn away, but I couldn't resist one last shot. "By the way— I hope none of your term papers are due soon."

He looked puzzled. "I have one due on Tuesday. Why?"

I started laughing. "Good luck finding them. I have this weird feeling you're going to have to start over from scratch."

All the blood drained out of his face. "What?"

"You really should shut your computer down when you aren't working on it." I winked at him. "Did you know that when you're connected to a wireless network, anyone with the right software could hack into your hard drive? And delete things? Important things?" I shrugged. "I sure hope nothing like that happened to you."

His mouth worked for a few moments, but nothing came out. His face reddened, and he spluttered, "You son of a bitch! I can't wait to vote to expel you Monday!"

"There's not going to be a hearing, Bobby, I hate to tell you." I smiled. "All that effort, all that energy, to get me expelled from Beta Kappa, all for nothing."

He turned and ran back to the stairs. "Have a nice life, Bobby!" I called after him. I heard his heavy footsteps as he ran up the stairs. I imagined the look on his porcine face as he tried to find his files and realized all his work was gone for good, would have to be re-created from scratch.

What a pity.

I started walking down the hall to the back door. *This is the last time I'll ever be inside this house,* I thought as I walked. *I was so happy here. For the first time in my life, I was happy. Even with all the Chad shit, I felt like I belonged here—I belonged somewhere. But it was all a charade. Beta Kappa wasn't what I thought it was, so all that happiness, that feeling of belonging, was predicated on a falsehood, was based on something that never really existed outside of my own imagination. I'll just walk out the door and be done with all of this. It's just as well. I can just drop the whole thing and be free. I got Jay his job back, so that wrong was righted. As for Dante, oh, well. It could have been something, but I was going to leave for Harvard after next year, anyway. So it would have ended by then. So, I'll just go there next semester. Let them expel me from the brotherhood. I don't really care anymore. It's not something I want to be a part of anymore, anyway. It's spoiled, ruined for me. Even if I were to go to the hearing and survive it, things around here would never be the same for me.*

I reached Roger's door and stopped.

I shook my head. *I can at least make peace with him, apologize and say good-bye.* I only hesitated a second, and then knocked.

He opened the door and smiled. "Jordy—this is a pleasant surprise."

I gave him a hesitant smile. "Really?" I noticed that his complexion had cleared up. "May I come in? I need—I need to talk to you."

"Sure." He stood aside and let me walk in. His room was

clean, everything in order, and there was even a laundry basket filled with dirty clothes.

I whistled. "Your room looks nice."

He shrugged. "I got tired of being a slob. Have a seat. I was just about to roll a joint." He sat down on the edge of his bed and picked up a plate with a pile of weed on it. "You want some?"

"Sure." I sat down on his desk chair. The desk was neat, everything organized. "I can't get over the way your room looks."

He started rolling the joint and grinned at me. "Well, I kind of owe it all to you." He filled a paper with some weed and started putting it together. "After the semester started and I saw what you had done with yourself, it kind of inspired me." He licked and lit it. He took a deep inhale and passed it to me. He blew the smoke out. "I started thinking about it, really. I was like, you know, all you do is sit around and feel sorry for yourself. Instead of that, why don't you make some changes?"

"Cool." I inhaled. I coughed out a cloud of smoke and took a swig from my water bottle.

He took the joint back. "So, I decided to sign up for a weight-lifting class." He flexed his right arm. "And look— some muscles! I started eating better, and my skin cleared up. I decided it was past time I started taking some responsibility for myself and, you know, take better care of myself, and it didn't really hurt me to keep my room in order, stay organized and all." He waved the joint around. "So, thank you."

"You don't need to thank me," I replied, feeling like an even bigger louse than I had before. "You did all this yourself. I had nothing to do with it."

"I also want to apologize to you." He offered me the

joint, and when I waved my hand he stubbed it out in an ashtray.

"For what?" I laughed. "Actually, the reason I came by was to apologize to *you*." And say good-bye.

"You don't need to apologize to me, Jordy." He took a deep breath. "I was a shitty big brother to you, Jordy—"

"No." I interrupted him. "I won't let you say that, Roger. No." I shook my head. "It was me, all me. I blew you off all the time to go hang out with Chad and his friends. You have nothing to apologize for."

"I have a lot to apologize for," Roger said. "You see, I didn't feed you during Hell Week on purpose. I was trying to punish you, get even because you liked Chad and his friends better than you did me. I'm so sorry—but in my own defense, I thought for sure they would feed you."

I felt like I was getting smaller by the moment. Every word out of his mouth was making my soul shrink even further. "Jeff told me about you and Chad when you were pledges," I said haltingly. "Roger, I'm so sorry. If I'd known—"

"I didn't want to tell you about it because I was *ashamed*." He hung his head. "I was so in love with him, Jordy, I really was." He wiped at his eyes. "All through high school, you know, I was picked on. Well, it really started in junior high school. The first time someone called me a *fairy* I didn't know what he meant. I thought they were calling me a *ferry*, you know, like a boat that carries cars?" He laughed. It sounded horrible. "I didn't know what they were talking about. And it just kept on and on, and the whole time, year after year, once I knew I was really *gay*, and somehow they all knew it . . . well, I just hated myself. I really did. I wanted to kill myself."

"That's how I was at St. Bernard," I said in a very low voice.

"It wasn't until I got out of high school, out of that horrible little Podunk town, and came here—" He shook his head. "I decided to join a fraternity—well, actually it was my dad's idea, because he thought it would make a man out of me." He shrugged. "And then I came to Beta Kappa, and the minute I walked in, I knew I belonged here. They had openly gay brothers, and no one cared. For the first time I could be *myself*."

I nodded, biting my lower lip.

"And then Chad . . . oh, God, Chad. I was so in love with him. And then I got Jeff as my big brother, and they were both so great, you know? They taught me, they showed me it was okay to be gay, to be myself." He sighed. "Jeff was such a great big brother to me. . . ."

"Jeff thinks he failed you," I replied.

"Seriously?" He stared at me. He shook his head again. "But—I guess I'll have to talk to him." He stood up and started pacing. "I let what Chad did to me make me bitter, Jordy. I don't know why he hates me so much. It's not like I ever did anything to him, you know—but I kind of figured the reason he co-opted you was because you were *my* little brother." He barked out a laugh. "Talk about self-absorbed, right? Of course, it's all about me. And I didn't even try, you know, to make an effort with you after that, because I didn't think I could compete with Chad. And then when I finally had the chance to be a big brother to you, on Hell Night . . . what did I do?" He wiped at his eyes. "I took advantage of you. You were upset, you were drunk, and . . ."

I felt like I was about the right size to fit into a thimble. "Forget about it, Roger, *please*." I shook my head. "Seriously, just stop, okay?"

"But—"

"No more." I took a deep breath. "Let's just forget the past and start over again, okay?" *This isn't right,* I told myself. *You shouldn't let him think he's to blame. You're being a coward and this isn't the way to start over.*

But even as the words flashed through my mind, I said nothing. I remained a coward.

And another voice sneered inside my head, *Well, he DID take advantage of you. You never in a million years would have had sex with him if you hadn't been drunk and so upset and felt so ugly and worthless—*

I used him to make myself feel better.

What kind of person am I?

I forced a smile on my face, pushing the voices out of my head. "There's nothing to forgive, Roger," I tried again. "I—I actually came by to say good-bye."

He stared at me. "Good-bye?"

"You saw the video, didn't you?"

He nodded. "Yeah, I got Bobby's shitty e-mail." He laughed. "You should read my response. He's such a shithead."

"Some of the brothers went to the Executive Council." I shrugged. "They want to have a hearing at Monday night's meeting. I'm supposed to tell the Exec Council my side of the story tomorrow, and they'll decide if there's going to be a hearing. But from the way people have been acting around me since I got here, I think it's a foregone conclusion I'm going to be expelled from the brotherhood on Monday." I took a deep breath. "And you need to forget about Hell Night, Roger. You didn't take advantage of me. If anything, I used you to make myself feel better. I should apologize to you."

"But—"

"If you think you failed me as a big brother, you can make it up to me by being the best big brother ever to Galen, okay?" I reached out and patted his hand. "I hope we can still be friends, Roger. I'd like that very much."

"What are you talking about?"

"I'm not going to fight this," I replied. "I'm not allowed in the house until I talk to the Exec Council tomorrow. I'm banned from Big Brother Night—and I'm not going to fight it." I took a deep breath. "When I get home I'm going to e-mail Chris my resignation from the brotherhood."

"What?" He blinked at me. "Are you fucking kidding me?" His voice rose. "You're just going to quit?"

"I didn't sign up for this." I grabbed his hands. "Roger, when Chris was talking to me just now, I realized that I don't belong here. Everything I loved about Beta Kappa wasn't real." My voice sounded hollow. "I don't want to be a part of a house that would put me through this without even listening to my side of things first. I don't want to be a part of a house where everyone automatically assumes the worst about me and doesn't even give me the benefit of the doubt."

"You're going to quit." He lit the joint again. "You're not who I thought you were."

"I guess not."

"When I met you at Rush," he exhaled, "the reason I was drawn to you—the reason I liked you so much—was that I could see what a good person you were. I could see, even though you couldn't see it yourself yet, that you were strong and had a lot to offer, and I knew you would never, ever quit. I was wrong." He laughed. "You are a quitter. You're going to let Chad York railroad you right out of this house without putting up a fight. Chad York, who made you feel like dirt. Chad York, who belittled you and mocked you and made fun of you behind your back while pretending to be your friend. You're going to let him get away with it." He shook his head again. "I'm so disappointed in you, Jordy. I don't think we can be friends after all. I don't want to be friends with someone like you."

I sat there for a moment, stunned.

He was right.

I was giving up and letting Chad win.

Once again, I was letting emotion control my actions and make my decisions for me.

Remember, you have an ace in the hole and you haven't played it yet.

"You're right." I stood up and gave him a hug. I kissed his cheek. "Don't ever believe you aren't a good big brother, Roger. You're the best."

He smiled at me. "You're going to fight?"

"Oh, yes." I opened his door. "And I'm going to win."

I stepped out into the hall and shut the door behind me.

I felt like I could conquer the world and slay giants.

And there was one giant in particular who really needed to be slain.

I took the stairs two at a time. Chad's door was open. He was lying on his bed wearing only a pair of shorts, reading an economics textbook. "Hey, Chad, do you have a minute?"

His eyes narrowed, but he smiled. "Always for you, Jordy."

I shut the door behind me. "I'm just curious, Chad. I want to know why."

"I don't know what you're talking about." He gave a little shrug.

"Give me a break, Chad. I'm not Brandon or Rees. I have a brain," I replied, folding my arms. "You put your little buddy Robby up to making that tape. You got Bobby to circulate it to the brothers. You got Jay fired from his job." I clicked my tongue. "You really have no conscience, do you?"

"I didn't have sex in my gym." His eyes glittered. "You

both knew the risk you were taking. Why should I feel bad about it?"

It was like I was seeing him for the first time. I no longer wanted him or felt any attraction to him. All I could see was his interior ugliness, disguised for so long underneath some pretty packaging. The ugliness radiated out through his eyes. I made excuses for his meanness, his pettiness, because sometimes he was kind, sometimes he was vulnerable, and I'd cared for him so damned much I let that outweigh everything I knew was true about him but had denied.

I'd been so fucking stupid.

I'd allowed my heart to trump my brain. Emotion, not logic. Fantasy, not truth.

"All I really want to know, Chad, is what did I ever do to you?" I shrugged. "I was never anything but nice to you—even though you were so hateful to me."

"Please." He waved his hand. "You didn't want to be my friend. You wanted to fuck me."

"So?" A few months earlier—hell, a few *days* earlier—I would have been horrified to realize he'd known how I felt. I no longer cared.

"It was so pathetic." He kept smiling. "Really, you have no idea how pathetic you were. You know, I felt sorry for you. That's why I took an interest in you. I thought I could help you." He gestured at me. "And I did help you. Look at you now. You'd still be that pathetic, chubby schlub if not for me."

"I'll give you that," I replied evenly. "Maybe that was how it all started, but now I do it for myself."

"And how do you thank me? By going after my ex?" he hissed. "You don't do that kind of shit, Jordy. And you just turned yourself into a shameless whore. It's really disgusting. And I thought Dante had a right to know what he was getting himself into." He laughed. "I'm not somebody you want to fuck with, Jordy—as I think you're finding out."

I crossed my arms. "I knew you were behind it all, Chad. It didn't take a genius to figure that out."

"So, you and Dante are over. He'll never want to see you again, you know." Chad mocked me. "And your gym—you're done there. And Monday you're going to get drummed out of the brotherhood. Are you happy? Was sleeping with Dante worth it?"

"This has nothing to do with Dante," I replied. "I didn't sleep with him until Thursday night. You had your little buddy at the gym tape Jay and me on Wednesday. How long had he been waiting for a chance to tape me doing something?"

He shrugged.

"You were out to get me from the minute I walked into this house," I went on. "You were so hateful to me that first night of Rush, and then of course once you found out I was rich—well, that was really what it was all about, wasn't it. You made me fall in love with you, didn't you? You were playing a game with me. You showered me with attention, acted like we were friends—all so you could pull the rug out from under me."

"Money isn't everything—and you needed to learn that lesson."

"The great irony of it all, Chad, is I would have spent every cent in my trust fund to make you happy." I leaned back against the door. "But you had to be superior, right? Put me in my place?" I shrugged. "Money isn't everything? I know that, Chad. But coming from your sad, working-class background, you have no idea what it's like to have money."

His jaw tightened. "Spare me the poor little rich kid story, okay?"

I laughed. "Oh, Chad, if anyone is pathetic, it's you. You

so missed the boat on everything, you know that?" I walked over to his bed. "When you have money, Chad, you learn very early on that there are some people who will suck up to you because of it. You learn there are people who will hate you for it. And you learn how to protect yourself." I patted his leg. "Poor, poor Chad. Even now you have no idea, do you."

His eyes were slits. "What are you talking about?"

"Poor people should never fuck with the rich." I gave him an extremely pleasant smile. "It was bad enough that you played games with me, and deliberately hurt me. But you know, I could overlook that. I could even understand it, on some level. But when you start hurting other people to get at me, that I can't overlook, Chad. I can't let that slide. I need to teach you a lesson."

"Fuck you," he seethed. "There's nothing I can learn from *you*."

I walked back to the door and opened it. "When I am finished with you, Chad, all that's going to be left is a smoking crater. And then"—I stepped out into the hallway—"I am going to sow the ground with salt so nothing ever grows there again."

"Bring it, bitch." He sneered at me.

I laughed. "Oh, Chad, poor, silly, stupid Chad. Even now you don't get it." I winked at him. "It's already brought."

I slammed the door behind me.

Chapter 14

I felt incredible as I walked out to my car.

I happily waved at the brothers playing basketball, a big grin on my face. The ones who didn't return my wave just stared at me. I felt like I could read their minds. *Why is he so happy? Doesn't he know he faces expulsion from the brotherhood on Monday?* That just made me laugh out loud as I started up my car.

Poor, stupid fools. Did they really think they could beat me?

I drove out of the parking lot, but rather than driving home I turned left on Shaw Avenue and headed out to Avignon. Dante was the only loose thread left, and since he wouldn't take my calls or answer my texts, he left me no alternative but to go over and hash it all out in person.

He was out in the driveway washing his car when I pulled up. He looked amazing, as always. He was wearing a pair of white cotton workout shorts that were damp with sweat in the back, and beads of water glistened in the late evening sun on his amazing torso. Stubbled hair made his chest look like it had been tinted bluish. In spite of myself, I could feel myself getting aroused.

Don't get distracted. Remain on point and stay focused.

He frowned as I got out of my car and turned the nozzle on the hose off before tossing it into the grass. "I don't want to talk to you, Jordy."

"You've made that clear," I replied as I walked up the driveway. "But you left me no choice. You could have had the decency to answer my texts or call me back."

He turned his back to me and picked up a sponge out of the bucket of soapy water. He started wiping at the front hood of the car, lathering it up. When he leaned forward, the shorts rode down a little bit, exposing the top of his butt crack and some white cheek. He really did have a phenomenal ass. "You're a fine one to talk about decency."

I picked up another sopping sponge and walked around to the other side of the car. I slopped some suds onto the hood and started scrubbing. "So, Chad did send you the video," I said. "And that was all it took?"

"You had sex in a public place with someone," he replied, not looking at me. "I thought I meant something to you."

"That video was taken *before* our date—the day before, in fact." I rolled my eyes. "When I was with Jay I had no idea you were even going to ask me out. I didn't realize you were looking for a virgin—especially since you'd already dated Chad." I laughed. "Unless of course you thought Chad was a virgin—but surely you're not that naive."

He stopped what he was doing and looked at me. "It was before?"

"I swear to you, Dante, it was on Wednesday afternoon." I held up my right hand toward the sky. "I swear on my mother's life."

"Oh." He looked confused. "But Chad said . . ." He threw his sponge down into the bucket. "I'm an idiot. Chad was trying to cause trouble." He walked around the car and pulled me into a sloppy wet hug. "I'm sorry."

"You're getting me wet." I laughed, pushing against his chest. "But there's something else we need to talk about. Well, a lot we need to talk about."

"Okay—just let me hose the car down and we can go to the sanctuary." He kissed my cheek and walked back to the hose. Before I knew what he was doing, he'd turned it on and aimed it at me.

"HEY!" I ducked down behind the car. I was completely soaked. "Damn it, Dante!"

I heard him laughing, and I moved away from the car as he started rinsing the suds off, but I didn't stand up again until he'd turned the hose off. When I stood up, he winked at me. "You look good wet."

"You always look good, wet or dry," I replied, following him into the house and then heading out to the backyard. He came out with two towels slung over his shoulders, a bottle of wine in one hand, and two glasses in the other. He put the wine and glasses down and tossed me one of the towels.

"Get out of those wet clothes," he said, wiping his own chest and arms down with his own towel.

I kicked off my wet shoes, pulled off the socks, and undressed until I was standing there in just my underwear, which was damp. I laid my clothes out in the sun and wiped myself down with the towel before wrapping it around my waist and sitting down. I took the glass of wine he held out to me and took a sip. "Good wine," I said, setting it down on the table. "I love that it's so peaceful back here."

"I guess I owe you an apology," Dante replied. He reached across the table and grabbed my hands. "You know, the other night when you were here, I felt like we connected, like it was something special. Even with my long-term boyfriend, Cade, the sex wasn't like that. That was, I don't know, that was more than sex to me. I thought you felt it, too."

"I'm not a saint, Dante," I said. "I've been with other guys, but you're right. It was never like that before. Every other time, it was—don't get me wrong, it was always fun—but it wasn't, I don't know, I didn't feel connected to the other person. It was just sex. The other night, I felt like we made love." I cringed inwardly. I'd always thought that phrase was stupid, and it still sounded stupid to me, but it was the only thing I could think of to describe how I'd felt. "It was like we connected."

"That's why I was so hurt when I saw that video." He shook his head. "And Chad said it was shot Friday afternoon. It was like being punched in the face, Jordy. It was a horrible feeling. I just wanted to hide out here and avoid the world."

"I'm not going to lie to you," I went on. "I did have sex with someone else on Friday night."

"Okay." He looked at me, and I winced when I saw the hurt in his eyes. "How could you do that, after Thursday night?"

"I'm not a saint, Dante, like I said, and if that's what you're looking for, then I'm not the guy for you." I took a deep breath. "I like you, I like you a lot. I think I could fall in love with you—and not just because you have one of the most flawless bodies I've ever seen." He grinned at this. "You're a nice guy." I gestured around the backyard. "I mean, this tells me so much about you. Only someone truly special would create this much magic in one space. All day today, all I could think about was how badly I wanted to escape over here and hide. It's so peaceful and serene, and that's what I need in my life. But we barely know each other. I'm not opposed to getting to know you better."

"I'd like that, too," he said softly.

"But if we're going to do this, we have to do it right." I took another drink of the wine. "We have to be honest with each other. And I don't ever want to have to lie to you. I want to know that I can tell you the truth without you deciding to give up."

He nodded. "As long as we're honest with each other, I can deal with it." He touched my hand. "That was the problem with my ex. He cheated on me." He shrugged, his eyes getting wet. "After it was all over, I realized it wasn't so much the cheating that bothered me, it was the lying. He never told me—I had to find out from someone else." He sighed. "I guess that's why I reacted the way I did to the video. It was like I was going through the same thing all over again, and it was a horrible feeling, one I don't ever want to go through again."

"I'll never lie to you, Dante." I closed my eyes. "And please don't ever lie to me. I think I can deal with anything else, but I can't deal with lying. Lying breaks trust, and it's hard to trust again when someone has broken that trust."

"I agree." He lifted my hand to his lips and kissed it.

"I slept with Brandon Friday night," I said softly. "He came over because I was supposed to help him with his term paper, remember? But he didn't want my help, really—he wanted me to give him a paper on the same subject I'd written in high school. And I guess he decided if he seduced me I'd give it to him." I shook my head. "And I fell for it, of course. I'm not used to having hot guys want me. He used me to get my paper."

"And you wanted to come over here and be with me after?"

"Being with Brandon made me understand how special what we have is, Dante," I insisted. "When I was with him, I realized what was missing from all of my sexual experiences. It was just sex—like it was with everyone else. And I don't want just sex. It's not enough for me anymore."

"Well." He sighed, and my heart skipped a beat. "I know what you mean, Jordy. When you texted me about coming over, I was on my way to Fusions. I'd seen the video, and I was hurt and angry . . . but the later it got, the angrier I got. I decided to go to Fusions, and I met someone and went home with him. And it wasn't the same. It was—unsatisfying. And when I came back home, I cried." He laughed. "I actually cried. Because I thought what we had was lost, and I didn't want it to be over. But I couldn't . . . couldn't forget what Cade had done to me, and I couldn't go through it again."

He touched my hand again. "Jordy, if we're going to try to make this work, I don't want either of us to see anyone else. Not if we're going to make a go of this. I know that's a lot to ask, but do you think you can do it?"

I nodded. "Yes, I think I can. I can't promise I won't fuck up, but I promise I'll try. And if I do fuck up, I promise to tell you about it. You won't ever have to hear about it from someone else. And you have to promise me if you fuck up, you'll tell me."

"I can do that." Once again he lifted my hand to his mouth and kissed it. "You want to go sit in the hot tub?"

"I don't have a suit."

"You don't need one." He winked at me, standing up.

I took my glass and followed him over to where the hot tub was bubbling. Strands of steam rose from the water as the sun began setting in the west behind the mountains. I put my glass down and slid my underwear off before stepping into the hot water. I gasped at first, and then slowly settled down onto the ledge. I looked up to see Dante smiling at me. The sun was behind him, and he looked like a muscular giant blocking it out. He slid his shorts and underwear off and slipped into the water, sliding along the ledge next to me until our legs were touching. He refilled my wineglass and set the bottle down. He slid his arm around me, and I nestled my head down on his muscular shoulder.

"I also need to tell you what's going on," I said. His arm felt wonderful around me. I felt safe there, and I never wanted that feeling to end. "Chad sent that video to everyone at the house. The guy in the steam room with me was my personal trainer, and that was the steam room at my gym. My trainer was fired."

"Holy shit!" he exclaimed. "What a shitty thing to do!"

"Oh, it's all okay." I laughed. "I had my financial adviser buy the gym today. I went in and fired the bitch manager, and I'm actually going to hire Jay to run the place. Jay's my trainer."

"You *bought* the gym?"

"Yeah. I mean, it was the least I could do," I explained. "It was my fault. Chad was trying to get to me, and poor Jay got caught in the crossfire."

He kissed the top of my head. "That was really sweet of you, and I get why you did it, but that's not what I was asking. Where did you get the money to buy a gym?"

I pushed away from him and stared into his eyes. "You honestly don't know? Chad didn't tell you?" I started laughing. *He didn't know.* He liked me for *me.* I felt my eyes filling with tears. My breath caught in a sob.

"Hey, hey, I'm sorry!" He grabbed me and pulled me into a hug. "I'm sorry, what did I say? Don't cry, baby." He kissed the tears falling down my cheek.

"I'm crying because I'm *happy.*" I started laughing, and almost choked. "Seriously, you don't know?"

"Don't know what?" He smiled at me. "What's the big secret?"

I put my head down on his chest. "I'm rich, Dante—filthy, stinking rich." I wiped at my eyes. "I'm so used to being judged for it . . . people either like me for it or hate me for it. I have a trust fund worth, oh, I don't know, a hundred or so million dollars. My parents are worth close to seven hundred million dollars, give or take."

"Wow." He grinned at me. "You mean I've landed an heiress?"

"Yeah, you've landed an heiress." I grinned back.

"Well, I don't care about the money." He kissed my forehead. "All I care about is you."

I struggled to keep from crying again.

This was what I'd been missing my entire life. Sure, my parents loved me. Maybe their staff did, too. But never had someone else, outside of my family and the people on their payroll, cared about me and loved me. I could feel my heart swelling until it felt like it was ready to burst. I threw my arms around him and kissed him.

"Hey now, hey now!" Dante whispered. "Shhh, baby."

I wiped at my eyes again and smiled at him. "Anyway, some of the brothers filed a complaint about my 'conduct' with the Executive Council and demanded a hearing on whether or not I should be expelled from the brotherhood."

"Seriously?" He shook his head. "That's nuts."

"I think that was what Chad was after all along." I shrugged. "He pretended to be my friend, but he's always hated me. I don't know why—"

"He's jealous," Dante replied. "Trust me. There's something broken inside of him. Everyone likes you, Jordy—

from the minute they meet you. You just have such a good spirit and such positive energy, you attract people to you. And you've got such an adorable face"—he kissed the tip of my nose—"and the way you smile, your whole face just lights up, so it makes people want to make you smile. You're funny and smart, and apparently richer than God. Of course he's jealous."

"I never thought of it that way."

"You're so damned hard on yourself." He smiled at me. "Like all that stuff about how ugly and fat you used to be. You were neither, do you know that? You just convinced yourself that you were."

"Oh, please." I grinned at him. "Like you would have looked at me twice back then."

"Not everyone is as shallow as Chad." He got up out of the water and wrapped a towel around himself. "I'll be right back."

I watched him as he walked into the house, then looked up at the sky. The sun was down now, and the sky was clear and full of stars. "Thank you, universe," I said to the sky. "I don't think I've ever been this happy in my life." I took a sip of wine and slid down until I was completely submerged in the hot water except for my head. The bubbling water felt amazing. It was like all the tension in my body was gone, and I never wanted to get out of the hot tub. For that matter, I just wanted to stay in Dante's backyard forever. While I was back there, it was like the rest of the world didn't exist.

This must have been what it felt like in the Garden of Eden, I thought as the sliding glass door to Dante's bedroom opened and closed again.

"Take a look at this." Dante knelt down beside the hot tub, a framed photograph in his hand.

I slid up and took the picture, and did a double take. "Is—is this Cade?" I gulped.

The photograph was of Dante and another guy. Both were wearing jeans, with their shirts off, with their arms around each other, smiling into the camera. Dante looked gorgeous, as always. But the other guy—well, he had a great smile. But his torso was covered in hair, and his stomach hung over his pants. He had no muscle tone at all, and his arms were skinny. And yes, there was that great smile, but his face was nothing to write home about.

He took the picture from me and stared at it. "Yes, that's me and Cade at Gay Pride in San Francisco two years ago— right before we broke up." He put the picture down and slid back into the water. "When I first met Cade, I was blown away by what a great smile he had. He had this amazing energy; he was just so nice to be around. I just felt better whenever he was around, you know?" He shrugged. "My friends couldn't believe it when I started dating him. He was a good person."

"But he cheated on you." I couldn't wrap my mind around it. "I can't believe he cheated on you. But then I can't believe *anyone* would."

"Looks don't matter to me—they never really have," he answered.

"Thanks," I joked.

He laughed. "Well, looks matter when you want to find someone to fuck, sure. But for a relationship—who the person is matters more. I mean, a really nice guy who's out of shape can always get into shape, but an asshole is always an asshole." He leaned over and kissed me. "I was attracted to you the moment I met you the first time—at that party at the fraternity Chad brought me to. I could sense your energy—and that smile! Oh, that gorgeous smile." He placed his hand on my leg under the water. "That night I asked you out for coffee, I really didn't care if Chad was going to break up with me or not. I'd already decided I wasn't interested in him. I just wanted to get to know you a little better, see if I was right about you. That night when I showed up at Fusions—I was looking for you."

"Wait a minute," I interrupted. "I thought Chad broke up with you."

"No." He made a face. "I broke up with him the day after we went out for coffee."

And the last piece fell into place.

That was why Chad turned on me so viciously. He'd always been mean—to me and about me—but he must have really cared about Dante. Somehow, he sensed Dante was interested in me.

He blamed me. Because, of course, it couldn't have been Chad's fault Dante lost interest in him. It had to be *my* fault. I tried to break them up. I must have said something to Dante at coffee that made Dante dump him.

Well, I thought, *understanding why he acted the way he did doesn't justify why he did what he did.*

If he couldn't have Dante, he wasn't about to let me have him. It was funny—I'd thought about it, wanted to do something to break them up, but not because I wanted Dante. But I hadn't done anything except be myself, and Dante liked that better than Chad.

Scratch that—it wasn't funny. It was actually kind of sad.

"So, all that stuff about him breaking up with you at Starbucks, that was all just a ploy?"

"Guilty as charged." His hand moved up my leg.

"*Tsk, tsk.* I feel so, I don't know, *used.*" I started laughing, but stopped when his hand snaked over into my crotch. "Don't be starting something you aren't going to finish."

"Oh, I intend on finishing."

I closed my eyes as his hand closed around my stiffening cock. It felt good.

"So what are you going to do about the fraternity?" he asked me, startling me out of my reverie.

"I haven't really made up my mind," I replied. "I mean, they're not going to throw me out. I'm not about to let that happen. If I leave Beta Kappa, it'll be my choice, not Chad and his friends'." I grinned. "The Exec Council has a big surprise in store for them when we have our little meeting tomorrow. Chad's failed—there will be no hearing. But whether or not I stay in the house—I haven't really decided yet."

He let go of my cock. "What are you going to tell them?"

"You sure you want to know?"

He nodded, and I told him. When I finished, he whistled. "Damn. Boy, you play hardball."

"Do you still think I'm a good person?" I tilted my head.

"Yeah." He pulled me in close and kissed me again. "I do. What they're doing is bullshit, and I think it's great you're not only standing up to them but giving it back to them, too. Fuck them." He winked. "And fuck them *hard*. Metaphorically, of course."

"Thanks." I touched his face. "I think I'm falling in love with you, Dante."

"I sure hope so." He kissed the tip of my nose. "Because I sure am falling in love with you."

"Do you mind if we get out now?" I held up my hand. "I'm starting to prune." I sighed and looked back up at the stars. "It's such a beautiful night."

Dante got out of the water and held his hand out to me. I took it and climbed out of the water. "Any night with you is a beautiful night," he whispered, pulling me into him. He put his arms around me and squeezed me tight, lifting me off the ground and spinning me around. "Jordy, I'm so happy. You make me so happy."

He took my towel and started rubbing my head, moving down to towel off my entire body. His hands were gentle, and it felt so good I didn't want him to stop. He picked up his own towel and wiped himself down. He poured the rest of the wine into our glasses and tossed the empty bottle into a recycling bin. "Come on inside," he whispered, beckoning me to follow him as he slid open the glass door to his bedroom. I grinned and followed him into the bedroom. "Get into the bed," he whispered.

I obeyed, still watching him. I slid into the bed and pulled the covers over me. The sheets felt incredibly soft and silky against my skin. "Lie back and look up at the ceiling," he instructed.

"Okay, but I'd rather watch you," I replied. I put my head back on the pillow and looked up at the ceiling. He flipped a switch and the ceiling panels began to move. As I watched, they folded back, exposing a ceiling made of glass, and the stars spread out above me. "Oh, wow."

He slid into the bed next to me, slipping his left arm under my head and resting his hand on my left shoulder. "What do you think?" he whispered.

"Wow," I said again. "That's amazing."

"I always loved the night sky, and I thought it would be cool to make love under the stars." He rested his head against mine. "I haven't opened it up since Cade left."

"You never opened it for Chad?" I teased.

"I never had sex with Chad in here." He shrugged. "We fucked in the living room. I only let special people into my bed."

"But—" I started to say, *you had sex with me in here the first night,* but realized what that meant and couldn't finish. I felt tears coming to my eyes again. I muffled a sob.

"Shhh, baby, don't cry." He kissed the top of my head. "I told you, I knew when I first saw you. That's the one, I thought, and it was just a matter of time till it happened, you know? I knew someday you'd live here with me, and every night we'd go to sleep under the stars, in each other's arms."

What?

"Um, Dante—"

"Shhh." He laughed, kissing the top of my head again. "I know it's too soon to talk about you moving in here, but someday, I hope you will. Just being around you, Jordy, makes me happy. I feel—this is going to sound cheesy, so don't you dare laugh at me—but I feel somehow whole when I'm with you, in a way I haven't since Cade left."

I could feel the tears rising again. "Dante—" I rolled away from him, my back to him, and stared at the wall. I started to cry softly into my pillow.

He rolled over to me. "Baby, what's wrong?"

"I'm not going to be here!" I burst out. "I'm only going to be here for two years. I'm going to Harvard after the next school year."

He started kissing my neck. "Jordy, shhh. That's okay, it's okay, baby, don't cry, please, I hate seeing you cry."

I turned back over, wiping at my tears. "I . . ."

"We'll worry about that when the time comes." He nuzzled my neck. "In the meantime, all it means is we have to enjoy every moment we have together, okay?" His warm hand drifted down to my crotch, and he put it on my cock, which was already stiffening.

In that moment, I was ready to say, to hell with Harvard, to hell with everything, I want to spend the rest of my life with you, being with you in this incredible bed under the stars. But he was kissing my neck and I was getting aroused, turned on, as his hand worked my cock while his tongue traced circles on my neck.

Oh, my God, it felt so good.

He moved down to my chest, toying with and teasing my nipples with his tongue. My back arched, and I started moaning. I couldn't help it—it felt so amazing. His body was right there, so I started stroking his back, his broad hard muscular back, and his mouth moved down my torso, his tongue snaking in and out of my navel.

"Oh, God, oh, God," I moaned, as his other hand slid under me and one of his fingers started flicking my asshole.

"I know you prefer to top," he whispered, "but I really want to be inside of you."

I swallowed, my breath coming almost too rapidly for me to speak. "I've never done that before," I whispered back, "but you can if you want to."

There was nothing I'd refuse him.

He moved until he was on top of me, all of his weight on me, but I didn't care, he didn't feel heavy, he felt wonderful, and his cock was grinding against mine, and I wrapped my legs around him. Our mouths came together, and he bit my lower lip gently, and I was ready to scream, it all felt so good, it all felt so right—and he was squirting lube into his hand, and then one of his fingers entered me—and there was a sharp pain that made me stiffen, but he whispered, "Relax, baby," and his finger slid into me, and maneuvered, and I bit my lip not to scream but not because it hurt but because it felt amazing, it felt like he was opening me, and then his thick cock was pressing against me, and I opened, relaxing, and he slid in, ever so slowly, and I could barely breathe, it hurt but it felt good at the same time, and he went in a little more, and I arched up into him, and he kept whispering, *I love you I love you I love you,* over and over again, and then I needed him inside of me, I needed to feel him all the way inside, and he went in all the way, and it was all I could do not to scream, it was amazing, I'd never ever felt anything like it before, and I was loving it, I loved it, I loved him, and I wanted him and I loved him and he was moving faster and faster against me, and his eyes were closing, and I could feel my cum starting to rise, but I didn't want to come, I wanted him to fuck me and fuck me and never stop, I wanted him inside of me always—

—and I screamed as I came, my entire body convulsing, I couldn't stop and I couldn't catch my breath, and my cum was raining down on me, and I could see the stars above me—

—and then he was rigid, moaning and shaking as he came.

He leaned down and kissed me softly on my lips, and I moaned a bit as he pulled out.

He pulled off the condom and tossed it in the trash, and started wiping me down with one of the towels we had outside, and he was wiping himself off, and he fell down onto the bed next to me.

"I love you, Dante," I whispered, because that was all the noise I had strength enough to make.

"I love you, Jordy." He kissed my cheek and wrapped his arms around me again.

I turned my back to him, cuddling back up against him.

And fell asleep, safe in his arms, where I wanted to be forever.

Chapter 15

I awoke under a blue sky, with puffs of white cloud drifting lazily across it.

I wiped sleep out of my eyes and sat up, realizing I was alone.

I looked at the clock on the nightstand table. It was almost eleven. "Shit," I said, jumping out of the bed. I had to be at the house for my meeting in two hours. I started looking for my clothes, and remembered I'd left them outside. I dashed over to the sliding glass door, opened it, and smiled at Dante. He was sitting at the picnic table, drinking coffee and reading the paper. "Morning, sleepyhead," he called.

"Why didn't you wake me?" I picked up my shirt. It was still damp, and so were my shorts. I sat down at the picnic table. "Christ, I'm going to run home and get clothes."

"Relax and have some coffee." Dante picked up a carafe and poured another cup. "You've got plenty of time. Just go take a shower and drink some coffee."

"I don't have anything to wear," I moaned, taking a sip of coffee. "Hey, this is good."

"Only the best for my baby." He smiled. "Now, jump in the shower. You can borrow some of my clothes."

"Your clothes won't fit me," I replied. "And I have to run home, anyway—the stuff I need for the meeting is there."

He got up and picked up my clothes. "I'll put these in the dryer while you shower, and you can change when you get home." He winked. "I put out a toothbrush for you in the bathroom. Now, go. You don't want to be late."

I took the coffee with me into the bathroom and turned on the shower. I quickly lathered up and washed my hair. As I let the heavy spray pound my body, I felt like I could conquer the world. *This is it*, I thought, rinsing the lather out of my hair. *What are you going to do, Jordy? Are you going to fight to stay in the house or are you going to drop your bombs on them and walk out with your head held high?*

I got out of the shower and dried off. I brushed my teeth. When I walked back into the bedroom, my clothes were lying on the bed. I slipped on my underwear and got dressed. According to the clock, it was now eleven-thirty. I sighed and headed back outside. Dante was back at the picnic table. I sat down and refilled my coffee cup. It really was good coffee. "Okay, I'm going to drink this cup and head home," I said as Dante folded the newspaper and put it aside.

"It's going to be okay, don't be nervous," Dante said. "You want to come over when you're finished?"

"Yeah." I looked around the sanctuary. "I think I'll need some peace and serenity when I'm done." I finished my cup of coffee and smiled at him. "I'll pack a bag when I'm at my place. Unless you don't want me to stay over?"

"I want you to move in." Dante raised an eyebrow. "Whenever you're ready, just pack your things and you've got a home here."

"I don't think I'm ready for that yet, but I know I'm going to be spending a lot of time here," I replied. I stood, stretching and yawning. I leaned down and kissed him. "Last night was incredible, Dante. I love you."

"I love you, too," he answered. "My thoughts will be with you this afternoon." He winked. "Kick their ass."

I laughed and then walked out to my car. There was no question about *that*, but I still didn't know what I wanted to do about being a brother. It really depended, I supposed, on how the meeting went. As I drove back to my apartment, I kept going back and forth. But ultimately I felt incredibly betrayed by the brotherhood. But it wasn't the *entire* brotherhood, either—only a select few.

I didn't know what I was going to do. As I walked into my apartment, I finally decided it would depend on how things went at the meeting. The one thing I knew for sure was, after the meeting was over, I was going to *decimate* Chad. I gathered the documents I needed, shoved them into different file folders, and labeled each one with a Sharpie. I put them in the order I would most likely need them and placed them inside my backpack. I glanced at the clock. It was just after twelve. I'd started a pot of coffee when I'd first gotten home, so I got a cup and sat out on my balcony. I had about fifteen minutes before I had to head over there, and as I sat sipping my coffee, I went over all the arguments I was going to make. I looked over at the pool, and sure enough, Jeff was out there, lying on his stomach on a deck chair. I smiled. I really loved both Jeff and Blair. Maybe things would have been different if they both hadn't been so busy these last two semesters—but then maybe it wouldn't have made a bit of difference. They were great guys and had a great relationship I envied.

There's no reason you and Dante can't have what they have, I told myself. I smiled. *Chad and I would have never had what I have with Dante—I can't believe I was ever so crazy as to think I was in love with him.*

It was partly my own fault. I had to take responsibility for my own actions, for my own behavior, or I was no better than Chad. I didn't hate him—okay, I did hate him, but not for what he'd done to me. I couldn't ever allow myself, no matter how forgiving I might want to be, to forget what he'd done to Jay—and what he'd done to Dante. He'd *hurt* them both in his drive to get at me, which was cowardly, malicious, and unforgivable.

But how is what he did any different than what you're about to do?

"The difference," I said out loud, "is that Jay and Dante were innocents. The people I'm bringing down today aren't."

And that was the bottom line.

My phone chirped, and I picked it up. The text was from Chris: *The meeting will be in the Chapter Room at 1, and you WILL be able to face your accusers.*

"Perfect." I smiled, finishing my coffee. I texted back: *I look forward to it. Thanks, Chris.*

At a quarter till one I pulled into the Beta Kappa parking lot. No one was out playing basketball, and no one was sitting at the picnic tables in the backyard. I got out of the car and took a deep breath. *Judgment Day,* I thought, slinging my backpack over my shoulder. I thought about saying hello to Roger, seeing how things went with his new little brother, but decided against it. There'd be time for that after, and I needed to stay focused. As I walked up the sidewalk toward the back door to the foyer, I glanced up and saw Chad sitting in his window. He smirked at me and gave me a sarcastic wave. I smiled back and flipped him the bird. *Just about an hour or so, and you're getting yours, you fucking bitch,* I thought as I kept walking. The back door was open. The pledges, looking the worse for wear, were mopping up the Great Room. I flinched from the smell of sour beer. I waved them off—I didn't want to shake their hands and have them all ask me how my day was going. I did smile, though, at their obvious discomfort. *I was one of you not that long ago*, I thought, *and I hope this whole experience turns out better for you than it has for me. I hope you never get disillusioned the way I've been.*

The door to the Chapter Room was open. Three brothers were already sitting in there when I walked in, and all three avoided looking at me. Bobby Dunlap wasn't a surprise—I'd expected him to be one of the complaining brothers. Even Rees wasn't a shock to me. Of course Chad had put him up to it—but Brandon? That was like being slapped in the face. He wouldn't look at me, and at least had the decency to turn red, shifting uncomfortably in his seat. The irony was, I'd felt bad including him in my file. Obviously those feelings had been wasted.

It wasn't a surprise that Chad was pulling the strings from backstage, either, while keeping his own hands clean.

That's what you think, Chad.

"How's that paper coming, Bobby?" I asked as I sat down.

"Fuck you," he spat back at me. "You're getting exactly what you deserve, asshole."

Brandon looked up, a puzzled look on his face. "What are you talking about?" He looked from Bobby back to me.

"He fucking hacked into my computer and deleted all my files," Bobby hissed. "I ought to kick your ass."

"You're welcome to try," I shot back. "Nothing would give me greater pleasure than beating your sorry ass to a bloody pulp." I folded my arms. "I've trained in mixed martial arts, Bobby. I'll break every fucking bone in your miserable body. Bring it on, bitch."

He blanched, and I smiled. I hadn't trained in MMA. But one thing my dad always said, nine times out of ten, intimidation worked—especially with cowards.

Brandon met my glance and bit his lower lip. He mouthed

sorry to me, but I wasn't having any of it. *No, Brandon, I'm the one who's sorry—sorry for you. Sorry you're such a spineless piece of garbage that all Chad has to do is snap his fingers and you'll do his dirty work for him. You're pathetic, and I'm sorry I ever thought we were friends.*

At precisely one o'clock, the Executive Council filed in, shutting the door behind them: president Chris Moore, looking grim; vice president Craig Yamamoto, slender and scowling; treasurer Dave Morton, who'd always been nice to me and looked like he wanted to be somewhere, *anywhere*, else; secretary Tim Haas, carrying the big ledger where he recorded all meetings for posterity; pledge marshal Eric Matthews, who gave me an encouraging look; and house manager Jason Spielman. They sat down in the chairs lined up at one end of the room behind two tables from the Great Room, and Chris had his presidential gavel.

Chris picked up the gavel and banged it. He cleared his throat. "We are here to hold a preliminary hearing to determine whether or not a full hearing before the brotherhood is necessary. Let the record show that the accused brother, Jordan Valentine, is present, as well as his accusers, brothers Robert Dunlap, Brandon Benson, and Rees Davidson. The charges against Brother Valentine are, first, conduct unbecoming to a brother of Beta Kappa; second, conduct reflecting negatively on the brotherhood of Beta Kappa; and third, violating the honor code of Beta Kappa. Should Brother Valentine be found guilty of any one of these charges before the entire brotherhood, the brotherhood will vote on whether he should be expelled from our fraternity. This is a very grave and serious matter, and I will not have these proceedings taken lightly." He looked at my accusers. "Do you wish your accusations to stand as they are, or modify them in any way? This is your final opportunity to end this." His voice had a note of pleading in it, and I loved him for it. Chris was uncomfortable with all of this, obviously, and wanted it over.

Bobby rose. "I would like to add another accusation." His voice quivered with outrage. "He hacked into my computer and deleted all of my term papers, all of my class notes, everything. I don't know how I'm going to pass this semester without that stuff!"

I stood. "I don't have the slightest idea what he's talking about."

"You admitted it to me!" Bobby snapped.

"I never said I hacked into your computer," I replied evenly. "As I recall, Bobby, I simply gave you some friendly advice about not leaving your computer on when you weren't using it, if you were connected to a wireless network. Advice, I might add, all of you would be wise to take."

"My files are gone!" Bobby spluttered. "You—you—"

"Do you have any evidence to back up your accusation, Brother Dunlap?" Chris asked.

"Well, no." Bobby's face reddened. "But—"

"Then the accusation will not be added to the current charges," Chris cut him off.

"Brother Morton, I would like the record to show that Brother Dunlap slandered me maliciously." I bowed my head. "And that is the cornerstone of my defense—that all of this is a malicious and mean-spirited attempt by certain brothers to drum me out of the brotherhood. I have evidence I will present to the Executive Council of this conspiracy, and will prove to you that the mastermind behind all of this doesn't even have the courage to accuse me himself, but rather is such a coward that he got these three brothers"—I waved my hand at them—"to do his dirty work for him, and that his motivation is not a concern for the brotherhood and its reputation, but rather a personal—and I might add, incredibly spiteful—vendetta against me. I would also add that this is most definitely conduct unbecoming in a brother of Beta Kappa and reflects very poorly on the brotherhood as a whole."

A smile played at the corner of Chris's mouth. "Go on, Brother Valentine."

"Thank you." I smiled back at him. "This entire hearing has come about because of a video that was circulated electronically to all the brothers. I do not deny that I am in the video. I do not deny that the video is of me having sexual relations with another man, in the steam room of my gym, Body Quest Fitness Center. And I will further stipulate that perhaps such conduct is contrary to the code of honor all Beta Kappas are held to. However, this video was shot without my knowledge and circulated in an attempt to get me expelled from Beta Kappa." I cleared my throat. "What happened in that steam room was an error of judgment on my part—I freely admit that. But what one of us has not made an error of judgment? Who hasn't done something that possibly was a violation of our fraternity standards? The difference is that *mine* was recorded without my knowledge and then circulated. If these charges are allowed to stand, and I am expelled, this sets a dangerous precedent for our chapter. Any brother with a grudge against another can simply record the first brother doing something, file charges against him, and get him expelled from the brotherhood, starting an incredibly vicious cycle, pitting brother against brother. Is this what any of us want? Is this what we want Beta Kappa to become?" I unzipped my backpack and removed the first folder. I handed each member of the Executive Council a piece of paper. "I would like to enter this document into the record. It's a copy of the blueprint of the floor plan of Body Quest Fitness Center. I have highlighted the location of a peephole in the wall between the storage room and the steam room. This is how the video was recorded, and an employee of Body Quest, named Robby Mackey, did it. I was able to trace the electronic signature on the video back to Mackey's cell phone. Mackey, if necessary, is willing to stand up in a court of law and state that he made the video at the instigation of Chad York." I got out another file and passed out another piece of paper. "This is a copy of an e-mail from Brother Chad York to Brother Bobby Dunlap. It was Brother York, who has been sexually intimate with Robby Mackey, who convinced him to record me any time I was in the steam room, hoping I might do something indiscreet. Once Brother York had the video, he immediately e-mailed it to Brother Dunlap. Please note the text of the e-mail—where Brother York instructs Brother Dunlap to circulate the video to the entire brotherhood and states, *'For obvious reasons, I can't do it myself.'* " I turned and looked at Bobby, who'd gone white. "As we all know, it *was* Brother Dunlap who sent the video to everyone. I would add that the video was also sent to the manager at Body Quest. The other person on the video is my trainer, Jay Collins. As a result, Jay's employment was terminated, and the gym attempted to terminate my membership as well."

"You said *attempted*," Craig Yamamoto pointed out. "What happened?"

"As Jay Collins was an innocent victim of this vicious vendetta against me, I purchased the gym and fired the employee who shot the video, and the manager." I shrugged. "I have also reinstated Jay's employment. I could not, in good conscience, allow him to have his life destroyed by the machinations of Brother Chad York."

"You *bought* the gym?" Rees whistled from behind me.

"Yes. I bought the gym," I answered him. "As the brother-hood is well aware, my parents are very wealthy. What the brotherhood does not know is I have a trust fund of my own, worth approximately one hundred million dollars, and that money is mine to do with as I please. And I was very pleased to spend several hundred thousand dollars to right this wrong. I would like the record to show that correcting this injustice done to Jay Collins by Chad York was very ex-pensive for me to do." I folded my arms. "And yet I am the one who stands accused before the brotherhood of conduct unbecoming to a brother, as Chad York intended all along."

Chris cleared his throat. "I think we've heard enough," he said, "and now the Executive Council will—"

"I'm not finished." I cut him off. I took another file folder out of my bag and passed out another printout. I closed my eyes. "Let the record show this document is a list of several brothers of Beta Kappa, the title of a term paper, the class it was for, and the instructor."

"What is this?" Tim Haas asked.

I smiled. "As you will note, Brother Haas's name is on the list. Also on the list are two of my accusers, Brothers Benson and Davidson. This, as Brothers Haas, Benson, and David-son are very well aware, is a list of term papers turned in by the brothers named as their own work, when the truth is the papers were written by me." I turned and looked at Rees and Brandon, who were squirming in their seats. "Just like video recordings, Microsoft Word documents have an elec-tronic signature. Someone who knows what to look for would be able to determine the computer those papers were originally written on, which can easily be proven to be mine. The university takes a very dim view of cheating—as does the national chapter of Beta Kappa. The students on that list will be expelled, and no other university would allow them admittance. I also believe the National Chapter would demand they be expelled from the brotherhood— and might even launch an investigation into this chapter, as would the university. It is entirely possible the scandal would result in our charter being pulled and the house shut down."

"You wouldn't dare," Rees blustered. "You'd be expelled, too."

God, this was so easy. It was all I could do not to laugh. I'd hoped someone would bring that up. "Do you think I care?" I turned and looked at him. He was slouched down in his chair and wouldn't look at me. "I have a trust fund worth nine figures. My parents are worth over half a billion dollars. I don't need a college degree. I don't need to work a day in my life. Sure, at first my parents would be disappointed in me, but once they found out the whole story, why I exposed this to the world, they would be *proud*." I reached into my backpack and retrieved the last file. I passed out the final photocopies. "Let the record show I have passed out one final document."

"What is this?" Chris looked like he was going to throw up at any moment.

"When I pledged this fraternity, I had my financial adviser investigate the finances of the house," I replied, smiling. "It's called *due diligence*. I wanted to know what I was getting into—and stupidly, I thought if the house had financial trouble, if I made it through and was initiated, I could help out." I shook my head. "This house has been very poorly run from a financial standpoint for quite some time. I was shocked to discover that not only is the house years behind in dues payments to the National Chapter but also years behind in making payments on the mortgage held by the National Chapter. The National Chapter, apparently, has been in a quandary for years about what to do about this chapter—which on the surface is flourishing but doesn't understand the concept of fiscal responsibility. They were more than happy to sell the back debt to me, as well as the mortgage. They were delighted that a brother from this chapter cared so much about this house he would actually take over the financial burden from *them*." I exhaled. "What you are holding is the agreement between me and the National Chapter. I own the mortgage on this house. I own the back debt of this chapter. And I am well within my legal rights to demand repayment of the back debt, as well as the outstanding mortgage payments, or take possession of the house. And evict Beta Kappa once and for all."

I picked up my backpack and slid it over my shoulder. "Decide what you want about the hearing." I walked to the door. "I really don't give a rat's ass anymore. I joined this house because I wanted to be a part of it. I believed all the bullshit you drilled into my head as a pledge, about brotherhood and honor. I believed everything this house supposedly stood for. What an enormous disappointment to find out it was all just a bunch of bullshit. Fuck you all."

"What are you going to do?" Chris asked hoarsely.

"When this nonsense first came up, I couldn't believe how stupid all of you were, thinking I would come in here and cower, beg, and plead not to be thrown out. I thought I'd blackmail you, since I hold *all* the cards. I thought, well, I can force them to kick out my accusers, I could make them kick out Chad, and maybe we could purify this house and make it what it was intended to be from the beginning. And you people had the nerve to question my character?" I laughed. "But the more I thought about it, the less I cared. Do I want to be a part of a house where this kind of bullshit masquerades as brotherhood? Do I want to be a part of a brotherhood that simply pays lip service to the ideals it supposedly upholds? And the more I thought about it, the less I wanted to." I opened the door and smiled. "So, you can all just stew for a while and wonder what I'm going to do. And by the way, fuck all of you."

I slammed the door behind me.

I took a deep breath.

That felt *good*.

And now, there was just one last piece of business to attend to.

The house was silent as I climbed the staircase and walked down the upstairs hall to Chad's room. His door was open, and I stood in the doorway. He was still sitting in the window, looking out. I cleared my throat, and he turned his head. He gave me a nasty smile. "So, is the hearing scheduled for tomorrow night? I can't wait."

I shook my head. "No, Chad, there's not going to be a hearing. I'm sorry to disappoint you." I smiled. "In fact, I would imagine the Executive Council is pretty much shitting themselves right now, terrified about what I'm going to do next. I'd say it's pretty safe to say I put the fear of God into them—and I'm God."

His smile faded.

"You've lost, Chad." I stepped into his room. "Not only this battle, but you lost the entire war."

"I don't know what you're talking about," he replied. "And get out of my room."

"Dante and I are back together, so you failed there, too," I went on. "He loves me and wants me to move in with him. I know someone as twisted and soulless as you can't comprehend love, but he does love me. And he hates you for what you tried to do to us. But I'm pretty positive that doesn't really bother you much—you're used to being hated, I'm sure."

"Go to hell."

"Good comeback," I mocked. "Congratulations, though. I'm sure when you launched your little scheme to get me thrown out of the brotherhood, it never once occurred to you it might blow up in your face. I bet it never occurred to you—because you've undoubtedly pulled this kind of bull-shit before—that wimpy little Jordy Valentine was not only a worthy opponent but more than willing to fight even dirt-ier than you were, was capable of going for the throat and being even nastier than you are." I laughed. "It's actually sad how *pathetic* your little games really are. I warned you yesterday that going up against someone with a lot of money at his disposal was a huge mistake. I gave you a chance to call this whole thing off, to get your little puppets to withdraw their stupid charges against me, but not you! Not the great Chad York! You would never back down and admit defeat. Not to nerdy Jordy." I shook my head. "I not only beat you, Chad, but I can bring this whole house down."

"What are you talking about?" He stared at me. "You're not making sense."

"I won't bore you with the details of my enormous tri-umph." I folded my arms. "You'll hear all about it soon enough. But there are a few things you need to know."

"You're already boring me, so go away." He waved his hand and looked back out the window.

"I always thought it was interesting how contemptuous you were of your family." I ignored him. *Time to go for the jugular.* "I remembered how you said your dad acted like you thought you were better than everyone else because you wanted to go to college. So, I did some checking—or rather, I had some of my people do some checking. You see, I wondered how on earth you were paying for college with-out working, if your family was as working class as you claimed. How were you paying for everything? Imagine how shocked I was to find out your father, the one you trashed whenever you talked about him, had *actually taken out a second mortgage on your home to send you to college.* That your siblings, whom you hold in such contempt, were all contributing and helping out to send you to college, so you could get a degree and make something of yourself. Do you have any idea, do you even care, how hard they are struggling to pay those monthly mortgage payments so you can be here and talk shit about them?"

"That's none of your damned business." His face had drained of color, and his voice was shaking.

"Your mother works in a diner," I went on. "On her feet all day, waiting tables, so you can be here. Your father takes extra shifts at the garage so he can put food on the table and try to stay ahead of the huge financial burden he's taken on, so you can be here. And you don't even appreciate it. Not. One. Bit." I shrugged. "I don't know why that surprises me. You are probably the most self-absorbed, arrogant piece of shit I've ever met in my entire life."

"You don't know a thing about me."

"Maybe. Maybe not. Who's to say?" I took another step forward. "But here's what I do know. Tomorrow morning, my financial adviser is buying the garage where your father works—and the diner where your mother works. By tomorrow afternoon, they will be closed down and your parents will be unemployed." I stroked my chin. "Now, I wonder how they're going to be able to keep up with those mortgages? How are they going to be able to keep you in school?"

"You wouldn't dare!"

"I wouldn't?" I smiled at him.

"Why would you punish them?" he yelled. "They haven't done anything to you!"

"Kind of like how my trainer did nothing to you? But you

were willing to ruin his life." I took another step closer to him. "And what did Dante ever do to you? Oh, yeah, he dumped your ass because he saw what a shallow, worthless piece of garbage was wrapped up inside such a pretty package." I barked out another laugh. "Oh, yes, did I forget to mention that my financial adviser is also buying up the paper your parents' bank holds on their home? We're offering twice what they're worth—no bank will be able to turn down such a profit."

"You sick motherfucker!"

"And how long do you think they'll be able to keep up those payments without jobs, Chad?" I started laughing. "And as soon as they are late, we're going to foreclose. Your family is going to be unemployed and homeless, Chad, and they have *you* to thank for it."

He was trembling. "Don't do this, Jordy, please, I'm begging you. They haven't done anything to you—"

I cut him off. "They raised *you*, didn't they? You're a product of their parenting. Did they not love you enough, Chad? What did they do to make you such a monster?" I shrugged. "It really doesn't matter, I suppose. I don't care. All I know is you have to be stopped, and taught a lesson. What was it you said to me yesterday? There's nothing I could possibly teach you? Do you *still* think that's true, Chad?" I reached into my backpack and pulled out the classified ads from the paper. I tossed it on the bed. "You'd better start looking for a job, Chad. I took the liberty of circling a few that look right up your alley—McDonald's is hiring, and so is T.G.I. Friday's."

He moved, to get out of the window, but lost his balance.

For a brief second, I saw his eyes widen in terror as he tried to get his balance back.

And then he was gone.

Now

"That's a hell of a story," Joe said.

"Isn't it, though?" Jordy replied. He was standing at the window, staring at the pool through the blinds. "So, I guess you could say it *is* my fault he fell, but I didn't push him." He reached up and pulled the cord for the blinds, so they rose until the entire window was exposed. "You can also see why Bobby Dunlap was so quick to blame me. I suppose the other brothers who said I did it were Rees Davidson and Brandon Benson?"

"Yes," Joe said. He switched his recorder off. "And given your story, if it's true, I can see why all three of them would be so quick to try to get you arrested."

"It's actually kind of stupid, if you think about it," Jordy went on. "Like having me arrested is going to change the facts?" He turned and faced Joe. "I can still get Rees and Brandon expelled, regardless of what happens to me. And Bobby?" He shrugged. "I might not be able to get him expelled, but I can file a civil suit against him. I guess it all depends on what Chad says when he regains consciousness. If he says I pushed him." He barked out a bitter laugh. "Granted, his brains might be a little scrambled, but if he's able to think about it, he might figure out if he claims I pushed him, I won't ruin his parents."

"Are you really going to do that?" Joe asked. He crossed his legs and looked at Jordy. *Who knew there were such depths behind that pretty face?* "Don't you think that's a bit extreme?"

Jordy shrugged. "I never really planned to in the first place. I just wanted him to know that I could if I chose to."

"And your fraternity? Are you really going to shut it down?"

"Do you think I should?"

"It's not my decision to make," Joe replied. *What would I do in his place? Revenge always seems like a good idea, but most people never really follow through on it. I wanted to get even with Sean when he left me, but I finally just let it all go and moved on. And sometimes that's the best thing to do—let it all go and move on.* "But it seems to me you'd be punishing a lot of people for the behavior of a few. You said a couple of times you really liked the majority of the brothers, and it was the first place you ever felt you belonged. Are you willing to destroy all of that?"

"Is it part of your job to play therapist, Detective?" A slight smile tugged at the corners of Jordy's mouth.

"No," Joe admitted. "It isn't. But in my job, I see a lot of shit, Jordy. A lot. And most of it could have been prevented if someone had just said *enough* and put a stop to it. You have that power—the power to put a stop to it all. And you said yourself, several times, that a person shouldn't make decisions based on emotional reactions but should instead analyze the situation and use logic. Is it logical to punish the entire house and destroy something you once believed in because it's emotionally satisfying?"

"It's a very good point, Detective," Jordy replied. "And

one I'll take into consideration." He scratched his elbow. "It's interesting, though. I figured Chris Moore would have called by now with their decision—but then, I don't really see they have much of a choice." He raised his eyebrows. "Maybe they're all too busy dealing with Chad falling to think about me." He sat back down in his chair. "So, are you going to arrest me?"

"Not at this time," Joe replied. *Arrest you for what? Until Chad wakes up and tells his side of the story, I can't arrest you for anything.* "You did admit to hacking into computers—that's a crime. And using a fake ID, also a crime, and of course the pot smoking, but I don't see any point in pursuing any of that." Joe stood up. "I guess that's everything. Don't leave town."

Jordy smiled. "Well, thanks for listening."

"It was very interesting." Joe walked to the door. "I'll be in touch."

The door shut behind him. Joe shook his head as he started down the stairs. *It was,* he thought, *truly one hell of a story. I wonder if all of it is true.* His phone rang when he was halfway down the stairs. "Hey, Grace."

"Joe, I'm leaving the hospital," she said, "and I'm calling it a day. The kid said he wasn't pushed. He just lost his balance and fell. He's got a concussion, some broken ribs, and a broken arm, but he'll live. So this whole thing was a colossal waste of our time. I'm heading home and having a beer."

"Thanks, Grace. See you tomorrow." He closed the phone and walked to his car. Before he unlocked the door, he glanced up at Jordy's window. The blinds were still open, and Jordy was standing there. *He really is beautiful, and rich, too. But the poor boy has been so damned unhappy. I hope everything works out for him.* Joe got into his car and started the engine, and drove out of the parking lot.

All the way home, he couldn't get the kid out of his mind.
He parked in his driveway and walked into his empty
house. *Another night alone,* he thought, getting a beer out of
his refrigerator and cracking it open. *I wonder how his story
will end,* he thought as he kicked off his shoes and sat down
on his sofa. The house was so quiet—it was almost unnerving. He turned the television on and flipped through the
channels until he found a marathon of *America's Next Top
Model.* He drank three beers while he watched the empty-
headed models argue and bitch and fight. Finally, around
ten, he turned the television off and went to bed, alone.

The next few days passed with the usual routine. Get up,
go to work, follow leads, close cases, interview suspects,
and make some arrests. Punch out for the day, head to the
gym, do his workout, and come back home to the empty
house. Order in, watch television, drink some beers, and go
to bed. It was mind numbing, this routine he'd fallen into.

But he couldn't stop thinking about Jordy Valentine.

He kept waiting to read in the newspaper or see on the
news a breaking scandal about cheating at the university, a
fraternity scandal, but there was never anything. *I guess he
decided to let them off the hook, which is probably the best thing.
Revenge is best forgotten, left in the past, and you should always
just move on.*

Move on.

Like you've moved on, he thought to himself on Wednesday as he went through his workout at the gym. *You've never
moved on from Sean—you've never even tried. That's why the kid
affected you so much. For the first time since Sean left, you actually
noticed another man that way—a young man you can never have.*

And when he left the gym, he made up his mind. He had
the next two days off—and he hadn't been out in months.
Why not go to Fusions, see who was there? The more he

thought about it, the more he liked the idea. It *would* be nice to be around gay men, to listen to music and have a few cheap drinks. Maybe even dance a little bit. *Who knows? You might even meet someone.*

And maybe Jordy will be there, a little voice whispered inside of his head.

He pushed that thought aside. That was a stupid thought, not worthy of him. Jordy was too young, for one thing. And for another, the kid was in love with—what was his name? Danny? *Dante.* That was it. Nah. It was unlikely they'd be there—and besides, even if he was off-duty, he knew the kid was underage and he should do something about it. *Stop thinking like a cop,* he told himself as he showered. *Sure, you are attracted to the kid—who wouldn't be? But you just want to know how it all ended.*

He put on a white tank top and a pair of tight jeans, examining himself in the mirror. *I don't look bad,* he reassured himself, smiling at the mirror. *My body might not be as tight as it was when I was in my twenties, but I'm still a good-looking guy and my body looks pretty good.*

All the way to Fusions he debated whether it was smart to go in or not. Several times he was tempted to turn around and go home, forget the whole thing, watch some porn on the Web, and go to bed. But he was tired of masturbating while watching two hot guys have nasty sex. He wanted to have nasty sex, and there was bound to be someone at Fusions who'd want him, someone young and hot and horny, someone to fill up the emptiness and loneliness of the house that was too big for just one person.

Maybe I should sell it, get a condo or an apartment somewhere, he thought as he turned onto the street where Fusions was. *The house is part of my problem. It's a lot of work, for one thing, and it is too big for me, makes me feel lonely.*

You don't have any friends.

He wondered about that for a moment as he parked the car in the lot across the street from Fusions. Before Sean, he'd had a lot of friends, but they'd all dropped away. Sean hadn't much liked his friends, and the feeling was mutual. After Sean left, he'd thought about calling them but held off. *I blew them off for Sean, and now that he's gone I can hardly try to patch things up with them*, he'd reasoned. It would be a shitty thing to do, and he was tired of being a shitty person.

I need to make new friends, kick-start my life into gear again. And tonight—maybe tonight will be the first night of the new Joe Palladino.

He paid the cover charge and walked into the bar. It was already crowded, and the music was loud. He thought it was Beyoncé but wasn't sure. He walked through the crowd, checking out some of the hot guys, and was pleased to notice some of them were checking him out as well. That made him feel better. He headed to the bar to get a drink. The bartender was hot, muscular, and wearing a white singlet that left very little to the imagination. "As I live and breathe, Joe Palladino." The bartender grinned as he walked up to where Joe was standing. "What can I get you, babe?"

Joe tried to remember the bartender's name and couldn't believe he was still slinging cocktails at Fusions after all this time. The name was gone, lost in the mists of memory, so he ordered a gin and tonic with lime. He watched the bartender mix the drink and noticed he had a heavy hand with the gin. He smiled to himself, remembering what that meant—the bartender liked him. The bartender grinned as he put the drink down on a cardboard coaster with a flourish. "Fifty cents, Detective."

Joe put a dollar bill down and took a sip. It was strong, as he'd suspected it would be. He winked at the bartender and ignored the two quarters he put down on the bar. He turned and looked at the dance floor. The song had changed, and he had no idea what he was listening to now. He just stood there and watched people, cruising and being cruised, wondering if he should approach someone—deciding finally to see if someone approached him. He was out of practice. Why make an ass out of himself when hopefully someone would come up?

And then he saw him.

Jordy was on the dance floor, underneath one of the flashing red lights, dancing like he didn't have a care in the world. His shirt was off, tucked into the back of his loose-fitting jeans. The top of his underwear was showing, and his eyes were closed as he danced. *He is a good dancer,* Joe thought, deciding then and there he wasn't going to do a damned thing about the fake ID. He was off duty, damn it, and that was all there was to it. As he watched, a guy with an unbelievably muscular body came up behind Jordy, slipping his arms around him and kissing his neck. He had dark hair, was wearing really tight jeans, and his shirt was off. *Dante,* Joe guessed, and smiled. Jordy had been right— Dante was a muscle god. They looked beautiful out there together on the dance floor, and in spite of himself Joe wondered what it would be like to watch them fucking. *It'd be hotter than most porn I've seen,* he mused, shaking his head and laughing at himself. *But at least I know the two of them are still together and are trying to make it work. Good for you, Jordy. You deserve it.*

A lean, muscled young man pushed his way through the crowd and stood next to him at the bar. Joe looked at him and smiled. He was really cute. He was lean, with a nose that was just a hair too long for his face, but whoever he was, he was in a really good mood. The young man was wearing jeans like Jordy's—baggy and hanging low off his waist, and he was wearing a red tank top with the letters BK on the front.

Beta Kappa.

"Hi there," Joe said. The guy was waiting for the bartender, who was busy with a couple of drag queens.

"Hi," the young man said, giving him a radiant smile.

"Beta Kappa?" Joe gestured at the shirt with his drink.

"Very good," the young man replied. "I'm Roger."

"Joe."

"Nice to meet you, Joe." Roger stuck his hand out, and they shook, smiling at each other.

He heard Jordy quoting Chad in his head, *"Fusions isn't really Roger's kind of place."* "Your last name wouldn't happen to be Devlin, would it?"

Roger's jaw dropped. "You *are* good." He grinned. "Should I be impressed with you or freaked out because you're some kind of weird stalker?"

"I'm not a stalker," Joe replied. *This kid is much cuter than Jordy made him sound.* "I guess I'll have to tell you the truth. I'm a cop."

Roger did a double take. "Okay, now I am freaking out a little. Why would a cop know my name?" His grin got wider. "Should I be looking for the nearest exit so I can slip out after I distract you, Officer?"

"I hope not." Joe winked. "I was hoping this was the start of a beautiful relationship."

"Maybe it is," Roger flirted, reaching out to touch Joe's arm. "Nice and solid. I like that. But seriously, how did you know my name?"

"Because he's the cop who interviewed me after Chad fell," Jordy said from behind them. Joe turned. "Hello, Detective."

"Just call me Joe, Jordy."

"You know, I wondered if I'd ever see you again." Jordy smiled. "Dante, this is Joe Palladino, one of Polk's finest."

Dante stuck out his hand, and Joe took it. "I want to thank you, Detective—I mean *Joe*—for believing Jordy." He kissed Jordy's cheek. "It sure would have sucked to have the love of my life locked up."

"Well." Joe shrugged. "Had no reason to arrest him—especially after Chad came to and said he'd lost his balance and fallen. The whole thing was a waste of time." *Not really. I enjoyed listening to Jordy's story. And otherwise I wouldn't be here.* "How are you, Jordy?"

"I'm good, Joe." Jordy smiled. "Do you guys mind if I talk to Joe alone for a second?"

"As long as you bring him back." Roger's hand brushed against Joe's butt. Joe started a bit and grinned back at Roger.

"Jesus, Roger." Jordy rolled his eyes. "He's really become out of control, Joe—I should warn you." He gestured with his hand. "Follow me."

Joe followed Jordy through the crowded bar to a hallway to the back bar, where the music wasn't quite as loud. A drag queen was working behind the bar, and there were a few guys standing around talking. Jordy sat down on a bar stool beside a tall table. Joe hopped on one on the other side. "I wanted to thank you," Jordy said.

"For not arresting you?" Joe waved his hand. "Like I said, there was no reason."

"No, not for that." Jordy smiled a little sadly. He took a deep breath and exhaled. "Talking to you—telling you my story—it gave me a chance to go over it all again, and it made me think about things, put them in the proper perspective." He hugged himself. "I didn't foreclose on the house or carry through on any of my threats."

Joe sipped his drink. "Why not?"

"It's *negative*," Jordy replied. "You were right. You asked me if it was right to punish everyone in the house for the bad actions of a few. And it wasn't. So, the next morning I went by the house. I retired the debt, and the mortgage. I turned it all back over to the house. The brothers now own the house free and clear." He sighed. "And I didn't ruin Chad's family." His eyes twinkled. "But I put the fear of God into Chad. He's a completely different person now— you wouldn't believe the change in him." He shrugged. "Whether it's going to last or not, who knows? But for now, he's trying to be a better person."

"And Brandon, Rees, and Bobby?"

"The brothers bounced Bobby, and Brandon and Rees were put on probation." He held up a hand. "Before you say anything, I had nothing to do with any of that. At the meeting on Monday night, Chris told everyone what had happened—and it was their decision." He shook his head. "I kind of feel bad for Bobby, but it wasn't me. And I've made peace with Brandon and Rees, too. Whether they change is anyone's guess—but they both apologized to me, and I think they're going to be okay from now on."

"And what about you, Jordy? Are you still a brother?"

"I wanted to belong somewhere," he said, playing with the straw in his drink. "But I don't belong at Beta Kappa anymore. I went ahead and resigned from the brother-hood—after everything that happened, I just thought it was for the best. Besides, it would be weird being there after paying off the house debt, you know? Everyone would feel, I don't know, obligated to be nice to me. And I don't want to be around that."

"Are you still looking for somewhere to belong?" Joe asked, genuinely curious. He felt an overwhelming affection for Jordy, but it wasn't attraction. He *was* a good kid, and it sounded like he was coming into his own at last. He could see it in the way Jordy carried himself, confident but not arrogant, at peace with himself and the world.

"Oh, I found where I belong." Jordy flashed his amazing smile, and his entire face lit up. It was like klieg lights had turned on behind his eyes. "With Dante. That's where I belong. The guys from the house are still my friends—I'm not abandoning them entirely. Actually"—he laughed—"after I resigned on Monday morning, the brothers voted that night and made an exception. They granted me alumni status. It was very sweet—and I was touched." His eyes glistened. "They really are a great bunch of guys. I kind of lost sight of that for a while. And you saw Roger—he really is out of control."

"I'm happy for you, Jordy." Joe touched his hand. "Really, I am. It wasn't my place to say anything—being a cop and all, and being there on business—but I was hoping you'd do the right thing. Revenge is a dark place to go, and I don't think it would have made you happy in the long run."

"You're a very nice man, Detective Palladino." Jordy raised his glass. "I hope we can be friends."

Joe clinked his own glass against Jordy's. "I think I would like that very much, Jordy."

Jordy hopped down from his bar stool. "And besides, it *never* hurts to have a friend on the police force." He threw back his head and laughed. "Come on, let's join the others."

Joe followed him back into the other bar, laughing. *It feels good to laugh*, he thought. *How long has it been since I've laughed?*

Too long—it had been far, far too long.

"There you are." Roger handed him another gin and tonic. "I was beginning to think I was going to have to find someone else to flirt with."

He really is adorable, Joe thought, and laughed. "Don't be starting something you don't plan on finishing, *boy*."

"Boy?" Roger's face registered delight. "Oh, I like the sound of that. Do you dance, tall, dark, and handsome?"

"I would love to."

"Well, come on, then! What are you waiting for?" Roger grabbed his hand and dragged him out onto the dance floor.

Joe looked around the dance floor as Roger started dancing. Jordy and Dante were dancing, their arms around each other and their foreheads touching. The song changed to Lady Gaga's "Bad Romance," and Joe started to dance.

He looked at Roger, who smiled and threw his arms around him. "Wanna have a bad romance, Officer?" Roger asked, an impish grin on his face.

Joe started laughing. "I think I can handle that, boy."

"I'm a lot to handle, Officer."

"I have no doubt," Joe said, throwing his head back and laughing.

And they danced on.

Together.